The Lady and the Lion

BARBARA RUSSELL

OLIVERHEBERBOOKS

one

London, 1866

From now on, Vivienne would do as she pleased and always express her opinions without caring about what other people thought of her; she hoped Mother was all right with that.

As a good start to her new resolution, she'd convinced her mother to let her see the show of Cade's Circus of Curiosities, the event of the moment. Everyone in London talked about the famous travelling circus with no animals, acrobats, or magicians; the attractions were extraordinary people with unique skills.

In the carriage with Mother and their maid, Dobkins, Vivienne couldn't sit still. It was so rare that Mother allowed her to go out, for an event that wasn't a tea party or a ball, that London seemed like a foreign city with its cobbled streets and imposing red brick buildings.

"Human curiosities," Mother said in a disapproving tone. Her mourning black gown added an aura of gloominess to everything she said. "They will attract hundreds of people from all over the city."

"Exactly." Vivienne nodded. "Isn't that exciting?"

"Not in the least." Mother stroked absentmindedly the small silver case where a lock of dear late Adele's hair lay.

Vivienne had loved her elder sister, who died too soon from scarlet fever a few years ago, but she didn't feel the need to clutch Adele's hair constantly.

She winced inwardly as guilt gnawed at her. Years after the tragedy, Mother was still mourning. Her pain deserved respect.

"Where there are large gatherings," Mother said, "there are also infections and diseases."

Dobkins exchanged a glance with Vivienne. Adele had contracted scarlet fever without attending any major gatherings; she'd taken a walk in the park and fallen sick two days after and died in less than a week. But pointing that out would start an argument Vivienne didn't want to deal with.

"What are the main attractions?" Mother slid the silver case into her purse.

"Just to name a few, the strongest man in the world, my lady," Dobkins said. "The most flexible woman in the world, and a young man who has been raised by lions."

"Raised by lions?" Vivienne scrunched up her face. "It sounds impossible."

Mother put a hand on her forehead. "Imagine what kind of germs that man is carrying. Heavens, lions! Vivienne, you aren't going to get close to him. Let's go back home."

"No, please." She took Mother's hand. "I really want to see this show." Most of all, she craved something different from the extremely controlled days she spent with Mother between piano lessons and visits to old matrons.

"I'll have a hot, soapy bath drawn for Lady Vivienne when we're back, my lady," Dobkins said.

Mother pondered that before nodding. "Add kerosene to the water."

A protest died a quick death on Vivienne's lips. Kerosene. She would smell like a stove for a week. But if she expressed her opinion, Mother would be upset, order the coachman to return home, and Vivienne would spend the day cooped up at home...as it had happened dozens of times.

Compromises. She accepted her fate without enthusiasm, and London's cloudy sky seemed to mirror her feelings.

She pretended to listen to Mother's long list of things she wasn't supposed to touch to avoid catching any infection.

After hearing Mother complain many times about how recklessly people behaved regarding hygiene and illness prevention, she'd developed the ability to retreat into herself and block the chatter and noises around her. She wouldn't hear anything, only her thoughts. Sometimes, she played a song in her head to calm the frantic beat of her heart. Perhaps this skill would grant her a place in Cade's Circus.

The red-and-white striped circus tent was visible from a distance, rising in the middle of the field of London's main racecourse. People crowded the path leading to the tent. The carriage rolled to a stop, and Vivienne jumped outside without waiting for the footman and ignoring Mother's warning to mind the step, lest she break her ankle.

She joined the queue of excited and chatting ladies and gentlemen, waiting to enter the tent.

Mother wrapped an arm around her shoulders and pulled her closer. "Don't stand so close to other people. Look at these people. Mixing with anyone and everyone. There should be a separate line for us. It's disgusting."

A lot of things were disgusting, according to Mother.

Vivienne loved dancing and making new friends; she loved new gowns and fancy food, and she wouldn't mind starting her own family, which was the purpose of having a Season. But Mother's gloomy behaviour and fears disheartened her. Why couldn't she enjoy the parties without having to worry about getting sick? Besides, catching a contagious disease wasn't as easy as Mother feared. She'd gone to tea parties and to the theatre and never got sick.

An attendant in a black-and-yellow uniform stood at the entrance of the circus. "Welcome to Cade's Circus, the best, most entertaining experience of your life."

With a quiet warning to be careful not to touch the man, Mother dropped the coins for the tickets into Dobkins' hand. A quarter-pound each. The most entertaining experience of their lives wasn't cheap.

They fell in line with the other spectators about to enter the dark tent when Mother stiffened, taking Vivienne's arm. "Goodness, what is *he* doing here?"

"Who?" Vivienne gazed around and didn't need an answer.

The disgraced Captain Jackson stood next to the canvas wall, smoking a cheroot. Smoky clouds puffed out of his lips as he surveyed the queue with keen interest. His black beard needed to be trimmed, and his red-rimmed black eyes seemed to beg for a good night's sleep.

Vivienne averted her gaze before the captain noticed her scrutiny. "He's a free man, Mother. Even drunk army surgeons have the right to attend a show."

Mother considered the captain responsible for Adele's untimely death. Vivienne didn't know anything about medicine or medical drugs, but she remembered Adele's gaunt and sweaty face as the disease had consumed her from the inside out. No one could have saved her sister.

Mother scowled. "Don't be clever with me. I don't want him to see us. If he tries to talk to us, I don't want anyone to think we're associated with that creature."

A little too late. The whole of London knew how close the captain and Father, Earl of Huntington, had been until Mother's accusations had made him *persona non grata* in every London circle.

"That quack should be imprisoned," Mother hissed, clenching her purse.

"Please. He did his best and was deeply distraught by...what happened," she whispered the last words.

"You listen to your father's excuses and not to me." Mother pressed her lips in a flat line. "As usual."

Dobkins gave Vivienne the slightest shake of her head. Better not to discuss that further. An argument would be a waste of breath. Disparaging and destroying the captain's life after Adele's death was Mother's only reason to carry on living.

Vivienne chanced another glance at him. Her heart was torn in two. Captain Jackson had shown great compassion and sorrow for Adele, but her mother had fallen into desperation and melancholia from the day they'd buried Adele. She understood Mother's anger towards the captain, but she didn't think the captain was entirely to blame.

The captain was staring at them, a dark eyebrow arching. A puff of smoke came out of his mouth.

"Bother. He noticed us. Come quickly." Mother grabbed her hand and pulled her forwards. "Despicable man. I heard he's become a thief, so desperate he is for his liquor. The police almost caught him after he broke into Garrad's."

"How do they know it was him if they didn't catch the thief?" She walked along a passageway in the dimly lit circus.

Mother shrugged. "Rumours."

Ah, so therefore it had to be true.

She got distracted once inside the circus. Except it wasn't a normal circus with rows of seats around the central ring, but it was a wide hallway closed by canvas walls swaying slowly at the passage of the audience. The red canvas colour and the dim light from the lanterns gave the illusion of entering the maws of a monster.

The cloth had to be thick because Vivienne didn't hear the chatter from the people queuing outside.

"Welcome, ladies and gentlemen." An imposing man with a top hat bowed at the entrance of a curved corridor so long she didn't see the end. Everyone fell silent. "I'm Cade, your host. Behind me lies a series of stages to show you the prowess of my human curiosities."

A low murmur spread.

Cade smirked and paused for a long moment. "We found and selected extraordinary people from all over the world, a unique collection of talents and wonders. Be warned, some of the curiosities aren't for the faint of heart. You may experience great distress. Proceed at your own risk." He waved and beckoned them to follow him. "Enjoy the marvel of Cade's curiosities."

"Perhaps we should leave." Mother wrung her hands.

Vivienne started to walk on. "I'm sure there's nothing too frightening. It's just a way to create the right atmosphere."

The passageway was lined with open stages on one side. Bright lights lit the platforms, and she had to squint after the semidarkness of the hallway. The place looked more like an art gallery than a circus with the human curiosity on display as if they were paintings.

"You can choose to stop at a stage or to walk on," Cade said, leading the group. "But I'm sure you'll find all the curiosities fascinating."

The first curiosity was a young woman who could bend her body at angles Vivienne wouldn't have believed possible. Dressed in a pair of loose trousers and a tight shirt, she curved her back and arched her legs so that her toes would reach her lips from over her head. The move seemed easy and effortless, but Vivienne winced at the thought her back would break.

Loud applause soared at the woman's ability to wrap her legs around her neck or stand upside down, balancing her weight on her thumb. Vivienne had to admit it was impressive.

"It can't be normal," Dobkins said.

Mother didn't look amused.

The next curiosity was Hercules, the strongest man in the world, as a plaque at the base of the stage read. Tall and muscular, he towered over the crowd a good foot and a half.

"Don't get too close." Mother pulled her back. "I don't like the smell."

She sighed and craned her neck to see what was happening on the stage.

Cade beat his baton on the floor. "I need a volunteer to make sure that the anvil on the stage is real."

"I'll go." A man from the crowd stepped forward and tried to lift the anvil. His face reddened, but he didn't lift the heavy-looking block an inch. "Very much real, folks."

Cade nodded at Hercules to start.

Hercules lifted the anvil with a single hand and raised it over his head without any change in breathing. Shocked shouts came from the audience. He lifted a bench where six women were sitting without a drop of sweat.

Next came the woman with what was claimed to be the high-est-pitched voice in the world, capable of breaking glass with one high note.

"Remove your glasses," Cade said. "Stash them into your pockets."

"Heavens. This is dangerous. We might get hurt." Mother pulled Vivienne back, weaving through the crowd.

"I won't see anything from here." Vivienne shrugged herself free.

"Vivienne."

"Mother, please."

The woman on stage cleared her throat before letting out an acute note that she held for almost thirty seconds. Vivienne covered her ears as the water glasses in front of the singer shattered into sharp pieces.

She clapped her hands with everyone else after the performance. That had been incredible.

"Move to the next one," Cade said.

What would be next? She sped up to get a good spot before someone tall blocked her view.

"Vivienne, don't run," Mother said from behind her.

She slowed her pace, huffing.

Mother rubbed her forehead, closing her eyes for a moment. "I need a breath of fresh air. Let's go outside."

"You go. I want to see the next one."

Tension tightened Mother's features.

"I'll be right here. Go. I'll see you in a moment," she said.

Dobkins nodded. "My lady, come. Let's go outside. Lady Vivienne will wait for us here. It'll take us a minute."

Vivienne was already walking towards the next stage. Before Mother could protest, she sprinted off.

Her smile vanished when she caught a glimpse of a cage. Not a stage, but a proper, solid cage with thick iron bars and rushes on the floor.

"I must ask you not to scream," Cade said in a low tone. "Screams upset him. Ladies and gentlemen, the Lion Boy!"

Vivienne couldn't see anything when a few people shoved her out of the way and took her spot.

"Excuse me!" She was ignored.

Loud thuds erupted from the cage with the metallic shackling of chains, and the people in front of her gasped, stepping away and bumping into her. More people rushed towards the stage.

She was pushed back as excited spectators shoved her right and left. What was the fuss about? Aside from thuds, she didn't hear anything.

Mutters spread. A woman seemed about to faint. A child gripped her mother's legs.

Vivienne squeezed herself through the crowd and finally saw the inside of the cage.

A half-naked young man covered in dirt was crouched in a corner of the cage among rags and worn blankets. A leather cloth covered his crotch, but aside from that, his well-defined muscles were exposed.

But that wasn't what petrified her.

two

Vivienne couldn't take her gaze off Lion Boy.

His leonine mane of dark-blond hair and bushy beard hid his face, except for his amber-coloured eyes. He bared his teeth and threw himself against the bars with uncanny speed. She gasped and stepped away, hitting someone with her back.

"Careful." The smoky voice behind her belonged to Captain Jackson. The smell of tobacco and whisky gave him away as well. He gently steadied her, giving her space.

Should she thank him? Mother would be furious.

Vivienne searched the frenzied crowd, but her mother had to be still outside.

"Why isn't the lion roaring?" a man asked. "Where's his roar?" He stepped closer to the cage. "I bet he isn't even dangerous."

Lion Boy reached through the bars of the cage and grabbed the man by the jacket, dragging him towards him. Shouts erupted. Vivienne was again shoved right and left. The man in the clutches of Lion Boy cried out, and the sounds of his head hitting the bars horrified her.

"Enough!" Cade reached through the bars and hit Lion Boy

repeatedly with his baton until he let the man go and withdrew to a corner.

A vicious, cat-like hiss came out of him.

Someone pushed her back, and Captain Jackson steadied her again. She was too shocked to tell him not to touch her.

"Goodness." She clamped a hand over her mouth. "The young man is truly a lion."

Captain Jackson huffed. "Lion Boy my arse."

She turned towards him at his crass word. "Excuse me, what do you know about him?"

"If he was raised by lions, then I was raised by the bloody fairies." He puffed out a cloud of smoke. "My guess is that he can't talk, and I could bet my left bollock he's drugged."

"Drugged?"

"Cocaine to make him violent to start with. Hashish to make him strong. Hercules reeked of hashish. Mark my words. See Lion Boy's eyes? The pupils are fully dilated. His skin is wrinkly, a sign of dehydration. He looks thirsty and sweaty. Likely, he's so confused he doesn't understand what's happening. I wouldn't be surprised if Cade starved him before the show as well."

Cade kept hitting the young man with the tip of his baton. "Lion Boy would kill everyone in this tent if he were out of the cage."

"Not likely," Captain Jackson muttered. "In a few minutes, Lion Boy will run out of energy and collapse. Then Cade will give him another shot of cocaine before he performs again."

Vivienne believed he knew what he was talking about, despite what her mother thought of him, and her chest tightened with sympathy for the poor young man. Her gaze locked with his, and she saw his fear and desperation.

She'd seen that desperate gaze in some of the injured animals she'd rescued before Mother forbade her to touch any wild creature.

The spectators laughed and mocked Lion Boy, calling him names.

He cowered and hugged his bent knees, shivering so hard his teeth chattered.

"See how he shivers? That's the cocaine wearing off," the captain said.

"But if he's drugged and speechless, he shouldn't be here, treated like a strange creature for people's entertainment. That's incredibly cruel."

He blew out more smoke. "I shouldn't be treated like a strange creature either, yet it happens."

He walked away, but she followed him, her stomach churning at the pitiful noises coming from the cage and the people still mocking Lion Boy.

"Shouldn't we do something to help him?" She tugged at the sleeve of the captain's jacket.

He gave her a glance charged with disgust. "The rich, lucky lady, who knows nothing of the world, wants to help an unfortunate, poor chap. How touching." He resumed his walk.

"But seriously. We must talk to the police and tell them the man needs help. Obviously, the circus owner exploits him. Lion Boy can't have a normal life in that cage."

"Save your breath to cool your tea." He moved on to the next stage, but Vivienne wasn't interested in seeing any more curiosities.

She was rather sick with them now.

He shoved his hands in his pockets. "If the police cared, Cade would be out of a job. I've seen at least three police officers in the crowd."

"He's a frightened young man," she insisted.

"Exactly." He scowled. "He isn't one of those street dogs you saved from starvation. His situation is more complicated than you can imagine, and what makes you think he isn't happy to do this?"

"Captain, he can't be happy. He's suffering, and you're a doctor—"

"Leave me alone, Lady Vivienne."

She meant to follow him, but she spotted Mother's velvet hat coming through the crowd and heading towards her.

She hid behind a flap between two canvas walls and waited for the spectators to walk away. Footsteps thudded. She held her breath and kept an eye on the passageway through a narrow opening as Mother walked past without spotting her.

"Vivienne?" Mother called, craning her neck right and left. "Can you see her?"

"She must be in front of us," Dobkins said. "Maybe she's at the other end."

More people walked past.

When there was a moment of calm before the next wave of people arrived, she came out of her hiding place and checked that no one was close before approaching the cage.

Her legs trembled, and her palms became clammy, but she wouldn't do anything too dangerous. She only wanted to understand if Lion Boy wanted to be there.

Lion Boy sat with his head hanging over his chest, his shoulders shaking lightly. Tears streamed down his cheeks, leaving strips of clean skin under the dirt. Bruises covered his arms and legs. He looked exhausted.

"Can you understand me?" she said.

He raised his head, and once again, she was struck by his deep amber eyes. Eyes that showed too much pain. The pupils weren't as dilated as before. Guessing his age was difficult, but if she looked past the dirt and the beard, she would say he was a couple of years older than she was, nineteen maybe.

"Do you understand me?"

He launched himself at the bars, grabbing them with both hands. She cried out, jumping back out of reach. She stared at him, her heart beating in her throat. He stared back through the curtains of his long, dirty hair. He stretched out an arm, inch by inch, towards her. His lips moved, but no sound came out.

"Do you understand me?" she asked again.

He nodded, withdrawing his arm.

She licked her dry lips and searched the passageway. No one was in sight for now. "Were you raised by lions?"

He shook his head.

"Can you talk?"

Another no.

Captain Jackson was right.

"Do you want to leave this place?" She stepped closer.

He nodded.

"You don't want to be here."

No.

"They beat you and starve you."

Yes.

"Do they give you drugs?"

Yes.

The promise to help him burned on the tip of her tongue. But the captain was right again. Taking home a stray dog was one thing. Helping a young man escape a circus was another. Still, how could she leave him without giving him a ray of hope?

"I'll do everything I can—"

"Vivienne!" Mother grabbed her arm and dragged her away from the cage. "What were you thinking? Getting close to this beast."

Dobkins gasped, her eyes widening.

"He isn't dangerous." Vivienne actually wasn't sure about that. "We must help him. He can't talk and doesn't want to be in a cage. And he's drugged."

Mother touched Vivienne's face as if searching for injuries. "He can't talk because he wasn't raised by humans. And he's filthy. You'll catch a disease."

"No, really. We must call the police. He's frightened and needs our help."

Dobkins shifted her gaze from her to Lion Boy.

"I'm telling the truth," Vivienne said. "He can understand me. I asked him questions, and he's in pain."

"It's not your responsibility."

"I want to help him."

"We've been here for too long." Mother took her hand and dragged her away.

She glanced back at Lion Boy one last time before Mother turned a corner and the cage disappeared from view.

THE BOY's desperate face kept flashing across Vivienne's mind as she sat in front of her vanity that night. Her skin smelt of kerosene, no matter how much rose cream she applied. She hadn't protested about the smelly bath, not to enrage Mother further, and she was too worried to care anyway.

Dobkins brushed her hair, gently untangling the long dark tresses. "You're quiet, my lady."

"I can't stop thinking about that poor young man, locked up in a cage, beaten, and drugged. And for what? So that Cade can show him to the world and make money. It makes me ill."

"How do you know he's drugged?"

"Captain Jackson said—"

"Did you talk to him?" Dobkins walked around the stool to stare at her.

"I didn't mean to. I bumped into him when we were in front of Lion Boy, and he told me the young man had been drugged and likely couldn't talk. I want to help Lion Boy."

"I understand, but let's say Captain Jackson is correct. How do you think you're going to help Lion Boy? There's nothing you can do for him, and I'm sure it's all a show. When the circus is closed, the young man will have a laugh and leave the cage. He's probably making a lot of money as well."

"It didn't seem like that. You should have seen his eyes. He was crying. He was frightened and couldn't voice his protest. It's awful." A sob shook her. "No one cares."

"You care too much." Dobkins finished braiding Vivienne's hair.

"I want to go back to the circus when it's closed and see for myself if I'm right."

"Absolutely not! You aren't going anywhere. It's dangerous. And not because of the germs."

"I need to see him again before the circus moves out of London. I need to make sure he's all right. Will you come with me?" She squeezed Dobkins's hand. "Please."

"When you brought that injured fox home in the country, I supported you. Then there was the kingfisher, the frog, and countless dogs and cats, and I've always been by your side, even when your mother started to worry about what sort of diseases those wild animals might carry. I understand you always want to help the unfortunate ones, but this is different."

"Exactly! He's a young man. We can't leave him alone. He needs help. No one understands how much he's suffering. No one actually sees him."

Dobkins shook her head and prepared the bed. "To bed. It's late."

"I'll go with or without you."

"I'll tell your father."

"Please. I only need to see him for a moment and talk to him. If he's happy as you say, I'll leave."

Dobkins shook her head. "Madness."

"I'll be quick, and I don't care if Father punishes me. Will you come?"

Dobkins exhaled. "Only if you promise to stop talking about rescuing Lion Boy afterwards."

three

Lion Boy slumped on the floor of the cage at the end of the day's last performance.

Another exhausting day had ended, leaving him sore, thirsty, and spent. He had only a moment of peace before voices and footsteps came from behind him. He didn't even stir. He would recognise Cade's booming tone and Murdock's uneven steps everywhere.

Cade unlocked the cage, smirking. "Grabbing that man was a great idea. You'll do it again tomorrow. The crowd went crazy."

What man? He barely remembered anything about each performance aside from the pain, the anger, and the laughing faces.

No, that was a lie.

He remembered a young woman with hair the colour of a raven's feathers and the eyes like a quiet lake. She'd been the first person ever to talk to him as if he were a human being. Although he wasn't. He didn't even have a name.

Or perhaps she was the product of his hallucinations. He had no idea. Maybe he'd only dreamt of a beautiful lady feeling compassion for him. Yet he remembered her asking him questions.

"Quickly." Murdock staggered closer. "You need your drugs, and I don't have all evening."

The lights from the oil lamps glinted off his bald head. Short and with a bad leg, he shouldn't be difficult to beat in a fight. Lion Boy towered over him a good foot and a half. But the sheer terror Murdock triggered in him paralysed him.

Cade was a violent, greedy man but stupid. Murdock—the circus's physician—had both the brains and the coldness to be dangerous. Oftentimes, Lion Boy wondered who the real ring-master was. Cade might be just another Murdock's slave, the face of the organisation, while Murdock was the puppeteer working in the darkness.

"Crawl out." Murdock waved him closer, showing him a glass bottle.

Lion Boy's senses heightened as he rushed to grab the magic potion that would take the pain away.

Cade winced. "Disgusting."

Murdock hid the bottle behind his back. "Cade is right. Manners, you cur."

Lion Boy wanted to tell him he was too tired to play games, but only a pathetic whimper came out of him.

"Beg."

He slammed a hand on the rough wooden planks of the cage in protest.

Murdock's slap hit him across the cheek. When the effects of the drugs wore off, his skin was left extremely sensitive and tender. Lion Boy's face burned with pain.

Tears welled in his eyes. He joined his hands and hung his head, begging his tormentor to torment him.

Cade shook his head. "You don't have a spine."

"Good boy." Murdock tossed him the bottle, and Lion Boy barely snatched it before it hit the ground, his reflexes sloppy.

He drank the content with one sip, already anticipating the relief washing over him.

It took time before the pain vanished. He waited for relief. His muscles loosened, and his head cleared right before he dropped asleep on the floor.

He woke up with a start as one of the other circus workers shook him. Maybe it was dawn, or maybe it was still night. He didn't care. Time didn't have a meaning.

"Lion, come on. You have work to do."

Lion Boy shuffled out of the cage to the corner of the tent where there was a water basin. The chain locked around his ankle rattled with his steps. A few attempts at escaping in the past had earned him the inseparable iron companion. Murdock removed the shackle before a performance and put it back afterwards.

He quickly washed, ignoring the bite of the icy cold water, and put on a fresh shirt long enough to cover him to his knees. The shackle prevented him from wearing trousers.

In the part of the main tent that was designated as the circus workers' kitchen and canteen, he wolfed down two cups of tea, a few slices of bread, and bacon. The others filed out, saying good night to each other and ignoring him.

He was a circus freak inside a circus of freaks.

The chain was several feet long to allow him to do his chores, but it got stuck every two minutes, forcing him to retrace his steps.

As he scrubbed the dirty plates and mugs left by the others, his mind conjured up the clear blue eyes of the young woman. Her name was…no, he didn't remember. Or she hadn't told him.

Hell, she wasn't real. His mind wasn't trustworthy. With all the weird potions Murdock gave him, his brain had to be like gelatine.

Murdock's laughter echoed from the other side of the canvas wall. Of course, the swine was happy. He must have earned heaps of pounds today.

The chatter and laughter of the workers came as they headed to their caravans to rest before another performance.

He looked forward to leaving London. The days spent travelling from one city to the next were more bearable than the performances. At least he didn't have to see the faces of those people who laughed at him or stared at him in horror.

The chain clinked when he went to scrub the benches. He gnashed his teeth as his muscles burned. Complaining or asking for a potion to numb the pain would only grant him another beating from Cade. Besides, Murdock had to be in his caravan by now, ready to go to bed. If Lion Boy disturbed him, he would starve him again.

When he finished with the dishes, he knelt to sweep the floor from the mess of leftover food.

A noise like a rustle came from the other side of the canvas wall closest to him. He paused and listened. Nothing.

Sometimes thieves crept inside, searching for money. Good luck. There was nothing Murdock protected more fiercely than money. He was also a crack shot, and Cade was a fierce fighter.

A thief wouldn't realise what had hit him. Not to mention Murdock's knowledge of drugs, potions, and medicinal herbs. He knew how to poison someone.

Another noise made Lion Boy stop again. It could be a rat trying to sneak inside the tent. Except the noise grew in intensity. Whatever was crawling towards him was bigger than a rat. A whiff of kerosene hit his nose.

He walked towards the source of the noise. Soft voices reached his ears. He lifted the flap and froze.

A woman's face appeared. Not just any woman, but the raven-haired young beauty he'd seen during the last performance. The smell of kerosene wafted from her.

She was half-crouched, her head tilted back to stare up at him. He hadn't hallucinated. She was real, blue eyes and all. He wasn't sure how he felt about that. Relieved, confused, with his foggy memory, worried perhaps. If he'd done something to her, hurt her, he would never forgive himself.

Her large sapphire eyes widened. For a moment, they only stared at each other with equal shock and surprise.

Then she straightened, brushing dirt from her coat. "It's me. Vivienne," she whispered. A hood partially hid her features but didn't hide her princess-like looks. Judging by her fine clothes and perfect speech, she had to be wealthy.

"I promised I would help." She looked down and covered her gasp with a hand when she noticed the chain. "He chained you!"

He nodded, failing to understand her shock. Perhaps the drugs numbed his feelings as well.

"What?" An older woman with flaming red hair stuck her head inside. She gave him a quick, assessing glance. Her mouth hung open. "Good Lord."

"I told you he needed help, Dobkins."

Dobkins was breathing hard. "Why are you chained?"

"He doesn't talk. He can't answer." Vivienne faced him. "Can you write down your name?"

Writing? He shook his head. Besides, the whole situation was so bizarre he wouldn't be able to write anything, even if he'd known how.

"You can't write?" Dobkins seemed more shocked by that piece of information than by the chain or his wild looks.

"Bother." Vivienne put her hands on her hips. "How can we communicate? We must think of something."

"You must be joking. We don't have time." Dobkins tugged at Vivienne's hand. "We should leave."

Vivienne didn't budge. "They force you to stay here, don't they?"

He nodded.

"You aren't happy."

It took him a moment to answer. Not because he didn't know the answer, but because it was the first time someone had asked him about how he felt and if he was happy.

He swallowed past the lump in his throat. No one cared about him. He was nothing more than a tool for Murdock to make money.

The realisation wasn't anything new, but Vivienne's compassion and worry made him see himself through her eyes. And the sight wasn't pretty.

Once, one of the workers had got a nasty cut during a performance but hadn't realised until someone had pointed out the blood. That was how he, Lion Boy, felt.

"You are terribly unhappy." Vivienne stared into his eyes...her expression of pain echoed his pain.

He'd never met someone who understood his suffering.

"This is awful," Dobkins said.

He nodded and mouthed slowly, "Hate it."

Vivienne's eyebrows drew together. "You hate it here."

He nodded and returned her stare to make her understand better the depths of his pain.

When a clear tear slid down her cheek, he was sure he would drown in it.

"We'll take you out of here." Her voice cracked.

"Lady Vivienne," Dobkins whispered.

Vivienne faced her, her fists clenched. "We must."

Lady? She was indeed an aristocrat.

"You can't promise him anything," Dobkins said. "You can't give him false hope. That's cruel."

"No." Vivienne wiped her tears quickly. "No false hope. I'll find a way to help him." She grabbed his rough, ruined hand, leaving him breathless.

Her soft skin was like petals against his calloused palm. His heart pounded faster. His eyesight sharpened. Too many things that had never happened to him were happening at the same time.

"I promise. You'll leave this awful place and be free." Determination shone in her gaze.

Her solemn tone filled him with hope.

For one wonderful second.

Then reality hit him. She would never be able to free him. He'd tried to escape and failed. Murdock was too cunning and ruthless. Cade was too strong. Deceiving Murdock, or worse, stealing from him, was impossible. His friends were thugs as ruthless as he was.

He was Lion Boy. He slid his hand out of hers and waved them away.

"I'll find a way," Vivienne whispered.

They were kind to worry about him, but he had to be honest with himself. They would never help him. There was nothing they could do for him.

He waved them away again, raising his eyebrows.

"We must leave," Dobkins said.

Vivienne hesitated. She reached out, and her gentle touch on his wrist sent a powerful jolt of emotion through him. "I promise."

Right then, at that moment, he believed her.

four

Vivienne had never disobeyed her mother, not even that time when she'd ordered her to stay home during a particularly freezing winter so she would not catch a cold, or when she'd ordered her to stop taking walks into the woods because woods were full of germs, or when she'd forbidden her to eat street food because it wasn't hygienic.

She couldn't think of a single episode when she'd blatantly opposed her mother or father. Especially after Adele's death. Her parents had been so distraught, she hadn't dared cause them any pain.

Maybe that was the reason why her legs shook so hard and her mouth tasted bitter as she strode along the pavement the day after meeting Lion Boy. Her pulse was galloping as well because she was about to do something her mother didn't simply disapprove of but utterly despised.

Lion Boy's sadness had been so intense as to be contagious. His pain had screamed injustice. His eyes had begged for help. She wouldn't be able to look at her reflection in the mirror if she didn't do something to help him. Any decent human being would want to help him. Almost any... She hoped Captain Jackson was one of those decent people. Or, if he wasn't, that he would be tempted by a good offer.

Dobkins hurried to match her strides, sidestepping people in a hurry. "This is madness. There must be another way to help that young man."

"You were right. Freeing Lion Boy is complicated."

But Captain Jackson could be the solution. And that was pretty much her whole plan. What would happen if the captain agreed—or disagreed—was anyone's guess.

"This area isn't safe," Dobkins said, gazing around. "Granted the captain still lives here."

"You sound like Mother."

She prayed he still lived here. And Dobkins was right. The captain's flat was close to one of the poorest areas of London.

There were open cracks on the front doors and walls of the buildings. Some windows were broken, and bangs boomed from the blast furnaces. But the cobbled streets were nice and smooth without potholes, and the pavements weren't crowded with foot-pads. Still, she wasn't in Mayfair anymore.

She paused before knocking on the captain's door and made sure that the hood of her cloak covered her face. If someone recognised the Earl of Huntington's daughter seeking the man her mother had spent the past years smearing the reputation of, a scandal would spread like fire. Gossip didn't bother her. Her mother's wrath was more concerning. But the worst thing would be that she wouldn't be able to help Lion Boy.

Dobkins searched the street. "The captain will never agree to help Lion Boy. He cares only about himself."

"Maybe, but I don't need him to care. I need him to accept my money."

"What money?"

Vivienne didn't have time to answer as the door swung inwards and the captain swept into view. His jet-black hair was dishevelled, and his black eyes were bloodshot. Not promising.

He scowled. "What the bloody hell do you want?"

"Have some respect." Dobkins jabbed a finger at him.

"What the hell do you want?" He scowled harder.

Vivienne swallowed. "I need your help about a delicate matter."

He laughed, a croaky, deep laugh that turned into a coughing fit. "Go away." He started to shut the door, but she blocked it, slipping her foot inside.

She grimaced when the door slammed against her toes. "I'll pay you."

"My lady," Dobkins whispered. "Remember what I told you about making promises we couldn't keep?"

She ignored her. "I'm serious."

"How much?" He folded his arms over his chest.

"A lot. I'll explain the details if you let me talk."

"Talk."

"Inside."

"Of course." He scratched his beard. "Where are my manners?"

"You've never had them," Dobkins said.

He gave her a mocking bow. "You don't want anyone to see you here."

"I don't make the rules." Vivienne held his stare.

"Saucy wench." He held the door open and waited for them to brush past him before shutting the door with a kick.

Flakes of paint dropped off the door it rattled so hard.

The room would have been cosy if not for the heaps of crumpled clothes scattered everywhere, the dirty glasses, and the ashtray filled to the rim with cheroots' butts. There had to be no oxygen in the room, because the smell of tobacco saturated the air to the point of enveloping everything in a yellow mist.

"Welcome." He spread his arms.

Dobkins tiptoed inside. "We're going to catch cholera here. Mark my words."

A deep crease appeared between his eyebrows. "Apologies, but my personal suite in Buckingham Palace is being renovated." He pointed at the door. "You're free to leave whenever you want."

"No, please." Vivienne held up a hand. "I really need your help."

"Why me?" His voice didn't sound sharp.

"Because..." How could she say, '*Rumour has it you're a thief,*' nicely? "You have experience with this sort of thing."

"What sort of thing?" He propped an elbow on the mantelpiece overloaded with empty bottles, bringing attention to the fact he wasn't wearing a jacket and his shirtsleeves were rolled up.

"Lion Boy."

"For hell's sake." He threw a hand up.

"I have no idea how to help him. He's either locked up in his cage or shackled to a chain."

"They chain him?" A hint of shock crept into his voice.

"We saw him. He has a shackle around his ankle and a long chain. They treat him like a prisoner. He doesn't want to be there. Dobkins, I'm right, am I not?"

Dobkins nodded. "The young man is desperate and afraid."

"Right." Captain Jackson scratched his chin. "And how does a former army surgeon fit into this situation?"

"You know how to pick a lock, don't you?" Vivienne asked.

He narrowed his eyes. "Why would I know how to pick a lock?"

"There are rumours about you having broken into Garrard's." Vivienne didn't move when Dobkins tried to pull her towards the door.

"Are there now?" He chuckled bitterly. "Ridiculous."

"I know my mother wasn't fair to you, and even my father wouldn't be happy to know I'm here. But I'm only interested in helping that young man. He doesn't deserve to be treated like an animal. No one does. And he's so desperate and hopeless...I must help him."

He rubbed his eyes, making them redder. "Let's say I get him out, hypothetically speaking, what then? Where do you plan to hide him? You're aware the police will search for him, aren't you? Cade won't let him go easily. The boy raised by lions is the main attraction of the circus. Cade will hunt him down. Lion Boy needs a place to stay hidden, and I'm not even considering the challenge of taking care of someone who's been locked up for the best part of his life. If he gets caught again, he'll be broken. Dead."

Vivienne wrung her hands. She hadn't thought about all the details, but the captain was right. Taking Lion Boy to her house was out of the question. She couldn't think of anyone she trusted to keep him hidden. She had to find a way to keep him safe. Why hadn't she thought about that?

"He could stay here with you," she said in a low tone.

Captain Jackson put his hands on his hips. "Are you barking mad?"

"Do not speak to her that way!" Dobkins said. "You will show respect when you talk with Lady Vivienne. I don't care how long you've known her—"

"Since she was a child in cloth diapers, and who later got herself into trouble for wanting to save wild animals," he said none too gently. "Not much has changed."

"She's a lady, and you'll treat her as such." Dobkins jutted out her chin.

He muttered something Vivienne didn't catch. "So everything is on my shoulders," he said. "I have to take him out and hide him *here*, taking all the risks. And for what?"

"I'll give you my diamond bracelet," Vivienne said.

Dobkins gasped.

"It's worth thousands of pounds. And I'll help you take care of him. I'll come here every day and do everything I can to help you." She would need another plan for that, but he didn't need to know. "You're a physician. You care about people. I know you do." She didn't mention Adele. That would be a low blow. "You wouldn't let that poor young man suffer at the hands of a cruel man, and you'll know what to do to make him feel better."

He lit a cheroot. She nearly gagged at the smell.

"Why are you so desperate to help him?" he asked.

"Because I saw his pain, his desperation, and his hopelessness. I'm sure he doesn't believe anyone will ever help him. Please, Captain. We'll keep him hidden until the police stop searching for him. The circus should leave London soon, anyway, and if we cut his hair, give him a bath, and decent clothes, no one will recognise him."

That was a stretch, but in new clothes and well groomed, he wouldn't attract attention.

He opened the window and blew out a puff of smoke. She breathed deeply as fresh air rushed inside. He stood there smoking for a few long moments without looking at her. The only movement was that of his fingers dropping the ashes.

She slumped her shoulders. If he didn't want to help her, then she would do it herself. Somehow, she would.

"We're wasting time, my lady. The captain doesn't care about anyone but himself and his liquor." Dobkins took her arm. "Let's go."

"I'll do it," he said, curling up his upper lip in derision, either because he agreed to help or because she was here asking a favour.

She exhaled in relief. "Thank you, Captain. Thank you."

He thankfully put out the cheroot. "But you're going to help me once he's here, as you said. And if he's trouble, I'll kick him out, and you'll find him somewhere else to stay, and at the first sign of trouble with the police, I leave with or without him."

"What a lionheart," Dobkins said.

Vivienne offered him her hand. "I promise."

He shook her hand. "And I want the damn bracelet."

"Of course." She turned towards the door, but he called her.

"It wasn't Garrard's but Harvey & Gore's." He had the audacity to smirk.

five

Hours couldn't pass fast enough for Vivienne.

The captain wanted to go to the circus late that night—after he would receive his payment. She'd agreed although she refused to wait for him in his house as he'd demanded. So she paced her bedroom.

Not fully trusting him, she wanted to go with him to the circus. Besides, Lion Boy was her responsibility. It was only fair she was present when he left his cage, in case he didn't trust the captain, either.

A quivering fear knotted her stomach. Without any particular criminal skills or rebellious traits, the chance she made a mistake was bigger than Big Ben. A mistake meant Lion Boy would stay in that cursed circus forever.

Only an oil lamp lit her bedroom as she moved in front of the window, waiting for the signal to leave. London seemed to have drowned in black ink, so dark it was. Or maybe she saw darkness everywhere since she'd met Lion Boy. He'd opened her eyes to a world made of abuse and suffering, of people enslaved for greed. A shiver slithered down her spine, even though she was wearing heavy clothes.

If she was going to be honest, she felt a kinship with Lion Boy. Not that she wanted to compare her safe, uneventful life with his, but she lived in a cage as well. A cage made of fears, prohibitions, and lack of choices.

She jumped, startled when a soft knock came.

Dobkins entered the bedroom, carrying a black velvet bundle and a satchel. "I found an old pair of trousers and a shirt that should fit Lion Boy, and I took the bracelet from the strong room." She opened the bundle.

The dim light sparkled on the bracelet, casting shiny glitters around the room. But when Vivienne touched the cold, hard diamonds, she was reminded that the world was as cold and hard as the gems.

"Your mother is going to notice its absence." Dobkins slid the bundle into her pocket.

"I'll tell her I wore it for my morning riding in the park and lost it. She'll be upset and I'll get scolded, but it's worth it."

Dobkins shook her head. "To give this fine piece of jewelry to that disgrace of a man."

"Why do you hate the captain so much?"

"I don't hate anyone." Dobkins recoiled. "I don't like how he behaved after..."

"Adele's death," she whispered.

Dobkins nodded. "I don't think Lady Adele's death was his fault, but after her death, the accusations, his reaction was to selfishly drink himself into a stupor, and he hasn't stopped since then. He has also become spiteful and angry with everyone. Not to mention he turned to crime. I can forgive a moment of discomfort, but a moment that lasts years while he keeps destroying himself is too much. He wallows in pity."

"Mother's discomfort has been going on for years, too."

Mother was still wearing mourning gowns, but mostly, her mind was stuck in the past.

Dobkins gave a little shrug. "The countess lost a daughter. Her pain is justified."

Yes, but Vivienne wanted a normal life, as much as she'd loved her sister. "The diamond is not for the captain but for an innocent young man who deserves a better life." She fastened a long dark cloak around her shoulders and walked out of the bedroom with Dobkins.

The tick-tock sound of the grandfather clock in the hall itched along her skin. The stairs had never been so long. Her breath thundered in the quiet, no matter how softly she inhaled.

Thank goodness Mother took a sleeping potion every night; she wouldn't hear a thunderstorm.

Vivienne stopped shaking once they stole out of the rear entrance and reached the high street. Dobkins hailed a cab, waving her arms frantically.

In the cab, Vivienne wiped her clammy hands over her skirt. Sweat dampened the back of her neck, and her heart beat in a frenzy as if wanting to crawl out of her chest.

Dobkins didn't look calm, either. She peeked out of the window every other second and breathed quickly.

Vivienne swallowed as her mouth grew suddenly dry. "You can return home once I'm with the captain. You don't need to risk anything."

"And leave you alone with a potentially dangerous wild young man and a certainly dangerous man like the captain? Over my dead body. I agreed to come with you, and I won't change my mind. Besides, as you said, it's for a good cause."

The ride to the captain's flat was both too long and too short. Vivienne wanted the whole affair to be done quickly, but also wanted not to start it. Her legs trembled when she got out of the cab and walked to the captain's door.

She knocked a few times, her breath turning into mist in the night.

The door opened. For once, the captain looked sober. His

black eyes were sharp, and his dark clothes were clean. The smell of tobacco hadn't changed.

"I told you to use the back entrance," he hissed, ushering her inside quickly.

"I forgot. Sorry."

He shut the door quietly. "You forgot? Do you understand what we're risking?"

"It's done. You don't have to shout at her." Dobkins showed him the bundle. "No one saw us. We have the bracelet. We'll give it to you once Lion Boy is here."

He examined the jewel under the light of a lamp, raising his eyebrows. "Fine piece indeed. Well, ladies, make yourself at home. I'll see you later." He donned a black coat and put a hand on the knob.

"We're coming with you," Vivienne said.

He barked a raspy laugh. "Absolutely not."

"For once, I agree with him," Dobkins said.

Vivienne insisted. "We're involved in this plan, and we need to know if something happens to you. We must go together."

He scoffed, hands on his hips. "I don't want a clumsy, inexperienced pair at my heels. We'll get caught in a moment."

"We'll wait for you outside of the circus," she said. "We won't interfere with your work. Besides, I've already been there, and I can tell you where the cage is. It'll save you time. And I'll hail a cab while you free him, so when you come out with Lion Boy, we'll be ready to go. I also have a bag with some clothes for him. He'll need them."

Captain Jackson paused, stroking his chin. "We'll discuss the details on our way there." Scoffing, he beckoned them to follow him.

Dobkins rolled her eyes.

Vivienne should have been excited, happy even, to help Lion Boy, but she couldn't ignore the fact that she might get arrested.

six

A soft but insistent scraping noise awakened Lion Boy.

He propped himself up, blinking in the dark. Sometimes rats would slip inside the tent, and he always put aside some stale bread to give them. Rats were good company, contrary to what people said. But then again, for those who had friends and pets, rats weren't company at all.

For a quick, foolish moment, he thought Vivienne had kept her promise and come to rescue him. Hope was a bitter poison.

Murdock allowed him to sleep out of the cage since he was chained, but there was little to no difference between the hard ground of the common hall in the main tent and the cage. At least he had more space to stretch out.

When the lower hem of the canvas wall in front of him lifted too much to accommodate a rat's body, he tensed. The other night, he'd been lucky when, instead of thieves, it'd been Vivienne. But he couldn't be lucky twice in a row.

Besides, the chain didn't allow him to reach the caravans and warn one of the workers, and he couldn't shout for help. The only good thing was that he was used to feeling pain and could throw a punch to defend himself if he needed it.

The last, silly glimmer of hope that the person approaching might be Vivienne was snuffed out when the large silhouette of a man came into view. Lion Boy breathed harder when the man slipped inside. Closing his fists, he prepared to gather the chain and use it as a weapon.

"No need to worry, lad," the man said in a low voice, remaining hunched on the floor. "I'm here to take you out."

What?

He searched the darkness. Only the light coming from an oil lamp lit the hall. The man unfolded the scarf to reveal an unfamiliar face.

"Drop that thing." The man eyed the chain. "As I said, I'm here to help you. Do you remember me?"

He shook his head.

"I'm with Lady Vivienne. You should remember her."

His heart jumped to his throat. She did it. She came for him.

"I'm Captain Jackson." The man stole across the tent on silent feet, carrying the smell of tobacco and whisky. "Is that chain the only thing holding you?"

He nodded.

It was a dream. It had to be. But if it were a dream, his brain would conjure up Vivienne rather than a stranger.

"Don't do anything stupid, lad, all right?" Captain Jackson crouched to examine the lock. "I bet Cade is a stingy old fart. Stay still. It won't take long to open this cheap thing."

His head became light. The tent tilted. He didn't allow himself to feel any joy. That was a sentiment for when he was free.

Captain Jackson slid a pair of long, shiny tools into the lock and twisted them. A moment later came the wonderful, scary click of freedom. Then the captain gently opened the shackle and put it aside, freeing his ankle.

"Follow me and be careful where you put your feet." He held the flap up for him, but Lion Boy couldn't move.

He stared at his free ankle in disbelief. He was free. The

meaning of those simple three words was incomprehensible to him.

"Quick," the captain half-hissed, half-whispered.

The urgency in the captain's voice shocked Lion Boy. He slipped under the flap, expecting Murdock to jump on him at any moment. His ankle throbbed without the cold grip of the shackle.

Perhaps it was a dream, and tomorrow he would wake up in his dirty cage.

The captain held up a hand, stopping him. One of the workers was walking past on the other side of the canvas wall, humming a tune. Only a layer of fabric separated them.

When the sound of the footfall and the humming died down, Lion Boy followed the captain through a series of turns until the wonderful scent of freedom hit his senses—the smell of coal lingering in the air, of wet soil, and of the Thames. He filled his lungs with every single smell, because every scent made him feel alive.

"Quickly." Captain Jackson waved at him. "We must be quick now."

He winced as his bare feet hit the uneven path that led to the edge of the field. No moon shone in the night, but the distant lights of the city were a beacon of hope.

"Put these on." Jackson handed him his jacket, hat, and scarf. "Hide your face as much as you can. We can't do anything about shoes for now."

The fabric smelled of tobacco but was warm and soft, definitely the finest garment he'd ever worn. He ignored the stings in his bare soles as they sped up across the field. They climbed over the low fence enclosing the racecourse, and he paused to glance back at the circus. The tent loomed over the ground, like a giant hand stretching out towards him.

He hated that place intimately. Escaping had been so easy as to be almost ridiculous.

All it'd taken had been a pair of thin tools.

The captain tapping his shoulder interrupted his flowing hatred.

"Lad," Captain Jackson urged him on. "We're nearly there. Come on."

The circus disappeared from view when they turned a corner. The more distance he put between Murdock and himself, the more his head became dizzy. He doubted it was only happiness. There was something else lurking. Something he couldn't name.

His pulse sped up when he saw Vivienne wrapped in a dark cloak. She rushed towards them, coming out of a quiet spot.

"You made it." She sounded breathless.

He wanted to take her hand and kneel in front of her in gratitude but thought better of it. He was dirty, and they shouldn't linger.

"The cab?" Captain Jackson asked.

"Waiting with Dobkins. We'll have to walk for a few minutes. I didn't want the driver to see you two coming out of the racecourse."

"Good thinking." The captain patted his shoulder, encouraging him to go on.

"For you." Vivienne handed him a pair of trousers and a shirt. "I didn't think about the shoes. Sorry."

Sorry? She was saving his life.

He slid on the trousers and the shirt. He'd never been so finely dressed in all his life.

Captain Jackson helped him. "Come on, lad. Almost done."

It had to be a dream. It had.

He followed Captain Jackson in a trance, wishing he could thank his rescuers for giving him a life again.

The walk might have been a long or a short one; he couldn't tell, but they left the racecourse well behind to follow meandering cobbled streets.

If the area was a rookery or a place fit for a king, he couldn't tell. In the semidarkness, the brick walls, the smooth pavement, and the diamond windows looked spectacular, new, and beautiful. The lamp posts lit the city, hiding the ugly side of it, and he needed that for now. He only wanted to focus on beauty.

Vivienne tossed a few smiles at him, and his heart stuttered. Next to her radiant beauty and fine clothes, he became painfully aware of his wild looks. Dirty long hair, untidy beard, and bare feet. He had to look like the wild man Murdock wanted everyone to believe he was. Yet her smile was sincere.

"The cab is over there," she said.

They stopped in front of a public house where a cab was waiting. A bright yellow glow came from the window, along with happy voices. For once, he was happy, too. Almost.

"Can we go now?" the driver asked from the box.

"Yes, go." Vivienne handed him a few coins.

Lion Boy sat on the seat next to Captain Jackson while Vivienne and Dobkins sat in front of him.

He was sitting, but his body was still running, fleeing. He touched the carriage wall and the leather seat, needing to make sure everything was real.

"You're free." Vivienne's shining eyes replaced the moonlight. "You don't have to see Cade ever again. You have a whole new life ahead of you."

"Let's keep the optimism to a minimum," Captain Jackson said, glancing out of the window. "We've barely left the circus. The hardest part starts now."

The wave of relief and joy Lion Boy expected didn't come, no matter how many times he repeated to himself he was free.

Instead, sheer, undiluted fear overwhelmed him. His muscles trembled against his will. The world spun. His vision darkened, and a choking sensation gripped his throat. Breathing brought fire to his lungs. The walls closed in on him. London was so big...the streets would swallow him. He couldn't do this.

He tried to open the cab door although he wouldn't know

why. But he had to leave. To run away so he would not get caught again.

"What are you doing?" She shut the door with a snap. "You'll get hurt."

His breath came out in quick pants. He thumped the seat and the walls.

"What is going on there?" the driver asked, slowing down the horses.

"Nothing," Dobkins said. "An argument. Please do go on."

Lion Boy reached out for the knob again, but the captain yanked his arm back.

"Please stop it. You'll get us caught." Vivienne's face filled his field of vision.

He hissed, desperate to shout his fear. His throat hurt with the effort as he thrashed about on the seat.

"Lad, calm down." Captain Jackson trapped him into a steely hug. "Take deep breaths, close your eyes, and stop moving. You'll get all of us into big trouble unless you stay calm."

He struggled to get free, but the captain didn't loosen his grip.

"Please." Vivienne searched his eyes. "We're all in danger."

"Breathe." Captain Jackson held him tightly. "Close your eyes and breathe."

He did as told, but try as he might, breathing didn't help. The captain gripped him like vines, crushing him. He fought against the captain as panic overwhelmed him again.

"Sorry, lad, but if you leave now, you're going to get hurt, or worse, caught."

"You're safe with us," Vivienne said. "We don't want to exploit you as Cade did. You aren't going to pass from one master to another. We really want to help you. We care about you."

She'd misunderstood his emotions, and to be honest, he hadn't even thought about the possibility they wanted to use him. He wasn't even sure where the panic came from. But her voice calmed his erratic pulse a little.

Dobkins sat horrified in a corner. "What have we done? We're making his situation worse."

"He's frightened. That's all," Vivienne said.

"Calm down." The captain blocked Lion Boy's arms. "I don't want to knock you out, but I will if you don't give me a choice."

"Tonight, you aren't going to sleep in a cage or with a shackle on your ankle," Vivienne said.

As Captain Jackson kept holding him and Vivienne talked to him, he could breathe a little better.

"Keep talking to him," the captain said. "I think it helps."

Vivienne inched closer to him. "You're going to stay with the captain for a while. He's an army surgeon with a lot of experience, and he'll keep you safe until the police stop looking for you. But you must stay hidden in the captain's flat. I'll visit you. You won't be alone. Just a bit more patience. The captain's flat will be a nice change from your cage. The circus will have to leave London sooner or later."

He regarded her from under the rim of the hat, fascinated by how confident she sounded. The way she'd explained the situation made everything seem so simple and easy.

"We'll cut your hair and beard and give you new clothes," she said. "After the circus leaves London, you'll be able to go out. I know I'm not giving you a lovely future for the next few weeks, but this sacrifice will be worth it. I'll keep you company as much as I can. We'll work together, and you'll be safe and free forever."

He stopped shivering, and his breathing evened.

"I'll be there with you along the way." She sounded serious.

The captain slowly released him. "Breathe, all right? We're nearly there."

A hand on his heaving chest, he sagged onto the seat, wondering why he wasn't crying. But then again, he wouldn't believe he was truly free until the circus left London. Until some time passed.

"Don't be afraid." Vivienne touched his hand, and he was startled hard enough to jump on his seat and hit the wall with his knee.

"Again?" the driver called. "Enough, or I'll kick you out."

Dobkins grabbed Vivienne and pulled her back. "Don't touch him."

The captain gazed from Dobkins to him. "Everything is fine, lad. Vivienne, don't touch him for now."

When she nodded, Lion Boy's heart sank. He hadn't meant to scare her, but her touch felt so good it was painful. He longed for someone to hold his hand or hug him although he knew he was too repulsive for that.

"I'm sorry," she whispered, withdrawing from him.

He shook his head, wishing to let her know she'd done nothing wrong. Freedom had been granted to him, and instead of showing gratitude, he was scaring his rescuers. Not a great start.

They stopped in a dark alleyway, and aside from red brick walls and wet cobblestones, he couldn't see much. His legs shook so badly he needed the captain's help to climb out of the cab.

A cold gust blew against his face, clearing his mind. He looked up. The stars twinkled against the black velvet of the sky, and he wondered when the last time he'd seen a starry night had been.

Perhaps months ago in summer when Murdock had let him sleep in his cage outside the tent.

When he looked away, he found Vivienne staring at him with concern. She stretched out her hand as if to touch him, but then she moved back from him. That hurt, but not being able to speak to her hurt more.

He had heard both Dobkins and the captain warn her away from touching him. He watched as she folded her hands in front of her.

"This way." Captain Jackson led him to a narrow door barely visible in the darkness. He pushed it open and paused on the threshold. "You'd better go home now."

"But he might need me," Vivienne said.

"Not now. I'll take care of him." Captain Jackson waved him in. "Don't challenge our luck, Lady Vivienne. Someone might have realised you're missing."

"He's right. Let's go." Dobkins tugged at her hand. "And it's almost dawn. The household will wake up soon."

Vivienne hesitated. "I'll see you tomorrow."

Lion Boy could only nod.

"Get inside, lad," the captain said.

He did as told, wishing he could stay outside and watch the sky.

As he stood in the middle of an untidy room, he glanced over his shoulder. Dobkins handed a bundle to the captain. A few whispered words were exchanged before Vivienne raised a hand in farewell. Then she disappeared into the night, and the captain shut the door.

Taken by another moment of panic, he moved to follow her—he needed her presence to keep the darkness at bay.

But the captain stopped him before he reached the door.

"Lad, you must trust me. If you follow her, you'll cause only problems for her and yourself. You'll see her tomorrow."

Tomorrow. There hadn't been a tomorrow in his life until now.

Each day had been the same.

Now he had a 'tomorrow.' And it was terrifying.

seven

L ion Boy sat on the edge of a chair inside Captain Jackson's flat. He gazed around, half expecting to see iron bars materialise around him. Empty bottles and crumpled clothes were scattered everywhere, and it smelt of smoke.

It was a hundred times better than a cage.

The word *freedom* echoed over and over in his mind, almost losing its meaning. He had no idea what freedom really meant.

The captain placed the bundle Dobkins had given him inside a drawer with a lock. It had to be a payment. He didn't care why he helped.

Captain Jackson put his palms on the table and hunched his shoulders as if he were exhausted. "Do you have a name?"

He shook his head.

"No? We should give you one." He sat in front of him on a rattling chair and studied him. "May I examine you? I need to understand if you have injuries or diseases."

He nodded.

"I'll have to touch you."

He stiffened but nodded. He was calm now, and the touch wouldn't catch him by surprise.

The captain checked his eyes and pressed his fingers to the sides of his neck. Then he examined his back and abdomen and paid particular attention to his fingernails and teeth.

"For how long have you been taking drugs?"

He shrugged, having no idea how to answer. For as long as he remembered. Murdock was an expert in potions; he'd always given him potions to drink.

The captain handed him a piece of paper and a pencil. "Write it down."

He shook his head. Shame burned the back of his throat. Perhaps his ignorance was more shameful than his dirty hair.

Captain Jackson's eyebrows flew high. "You can't write?"

Another no.

"Bloody hell." The captain rubbed the back of his neck in frustration. "No name, no voice, and no way to communicate. How can I help you?"

He fiddled with his hands, aware he'd disappointed the captain.

"We must think about something. Listen, lad." The captain dragged the chair closer, his black eyes becoming serious. "I want to be honest with you. Vivienne is as savvy as a fairy tale princess. She knows nothing about real life, while you know too much about it. She might be cheerful and optimistic about this, but the truth is bloody uglier than someone as sheltered as her realizes. You're facing some damn rough weeks, and when I say rough, I mean it. Drug withdrawal is excruciatingly painful. You'll wish at times you were dead."

He frowned.

"I thought they gave you only cocaine and hashish, but I think they gave you morphia and other drugs as well. I reckon they gave you cocaine and hashish only occasionally. The morphia was the regular drug. I can tell because you have hyperhidrosis."

He shrugged, not understanding the word.

"Excessive sweating. And you have marks left from scratches, and your eyes sometimes make rapid movements. Lad, you are a slave to powerful opiates."

Not that the information shocked him. Whatever the thing Murdock had given him was, it'd worked. He didn't feel pain or tired after he drank the potion to live.

Captain Jackson narrowed his eyes. "You aren't scared."

His life had been nothing but pain. He gave another shrug.

"I need you to understand what's happening to you. Your body is going to crave the drugs in a matter of hours. I'll give you some morphia but not as much as you're used to. Then I'll reduce the dose day by day until you are free of that poison. But it's going to be painful. Very painful. I have to tell you, some people don't survive the treatment. The shock of not having the combination of drugs in your blood might cause your heart to stop, on top of the physical pain you're going to experience. Your skin will be so sensitive a light brush will be as painful as the lash of a whip.

"But you must go through this if you want a chance at a normal life. Before you can learn to write or do anything else, you must rid your body of the drugs. Do you understand?"

He frowned and scrubbed the back of his neck as an itch bothered him.

"If you don't cleanse your blood of the drugs, you're going to die."

He was going to die? He raised his gaze to the captain.

"Drug cravings never end well. You'll want more, and more, and more until you'll have more morphia or cocaine in your veins than blood. Do you want me to help you get rid of your addiction?"

He knew what type of pain waited for him because every time the effect of the potion wore off, he experienced that pain. And yes, it felt like he was about to die, which was ironic. When he didn't crave the potion, he wished to die, but when the pain struck and he feared he was about to die, he wanted the potion.

Captain Jackson stared at him. "I need to know if *you* want to go through all this, and if you want to stay here. You're a free man now. It's your choice. As I said, I don't offer you an easy path, but once it's done, you'll be healthy again. You'll feel better. I promise. No more fatigue, confusion, or itchiness. But it is your choice."

Choice.

The word echoed in his head like a mockery. He might have a very limited knowledge of the world, but he'd seen enough people using morphia and cocaine to know what those drugs did to the body, although he had no idea drugs would lead to death.

The captain was telling him that to be completely free and decide what to do with his life, he had to get rid of the drugs. Pain was nothing new to him. Death didn't scare him.

He took Captain Jackson's arm and nodded, hoping he would understand.

The captain nodded back. "I'll do my best to help you recover quickly. But now, I'm going to tell you everything I'll need to do to you, and you won't like it."

eight

Sitting through the afternoon tea with her parents and their guest was sheer torture for Vivienne. Finding out how Lion Boy was faring was the only thing she could think of. She'd been lucky the night of the escape. No one had noticed her absence. But now she was eager to go. Two days had passed, and she hadn't seen Lion Boy. Dobkins hadn't received any message from the captain, either.

She couldn't get to the newspaper for any news of his escape. When Lady Chester had arrived, Father had folded his copy of *The Times* and set it next to him, hiding the front page.

The chatter about the usual gossip on some scandalous rake went on until Lady Chester asked Mother, "What about you? Any news?"

"We went to see a show, Cade's Circus," Mother said. "I wouldn't recommend it. Quite shocking. Not to mention it was full of dirty people."

"Cade's Circus, of course. That's where that wild creature escaped from!" Lady Chester said, catching her attention.

"Which wild creature?" Vivienne put down her cup of tea.

"Haven't you heard?" Lady Chester beamed, enjoying the

attention. "Cade's Circus of Curiosities had this creature raised by lions."

Vivienne frowned. "He's a normal human, actually."

Mother glanced at her. Even Father angled a look towards her.

Lady Chester continued, "It doesn't matter who he is because he's at large. He escaped from the cage he was locked in, and he's now somewhere in London. We're all in danger." She sounded too excited to be taken seriously. "I hope the police catch him or shoot him to keep us all safe."

Shoot him? "Do they want to kill him?"

"He's dangerous." Lady Chester bit into an oat biscuit. "I would think they will shoot him, so he doesn't attack someone. An article in the *Evening Standard* said Lion Boy was considered dangerous and shouldn't be approached."

Vivienne's stomach roiled. She folded her hands on her lap not to show how much they were trembling. He wasn't dangerous. He needed care and compassion and fewer stupid people talking about him.

"Enough of this grim story." Father patted her shoulder. "Play something for us, darling. An *allegro*."

Playing music would help distract her. She rose and sat down in front of the piano as a knot of worry tightened in her belly. Lion Boy's scared eyes flashed across her mind. He'd panicked in the cab. Not being able to talk had to be horrible for him. The police wanted to shoot him, and he couldn't even give his side of the story if he was caught.

She started playing Mozart *Piano Concerto 21 in C minor*, but her fingers turned clumsy all of a sudden. She made one mistake after another, playing the wrong tempo and keys. Even a non-expert would find her performance wretchedly poor.

"Well, that was an interesting performance." Lady Chester resumed drinking her tea. "What is wrong with you, Vivienne?"

Vivienne stood and muttered something about being tired before going back to her tea.

The conversation returned to the Season, and Vivienne focused on her tea.

"When are you going to have your Season, Vivienne?" Lady Chester asked. "All your elder sisters and brothers are married, are they not? It's your turn now."

Father cleared his throat. "Vivienne enjoys going to dinner parties and balls. This might be the year she has a proper Season."

She smiled at him. "I would love a Season."

"I don't think so." Mother straightened her napkin. "There's no hurry, and going out at night is deleterious to one's health."

"Every fledgling must leave the nest," Father said.

"When it's ready to fly," Mother rebuked.

Vivienne didn't comment. The conversation was nothing new, and while last year she'd wanted to have her Season, now, with the responsibility of Lion Boy, fewer social obligations and demands would be better.

Lady Chester followed the exchange with keen interest. "It's always difficult for a mother to let her child go into the world, especially after a tragedy."

Vivienne stiffened.

Mother clenched the silver box with Adele's hair. "What do you know about that? You didn't lose any of your sons." From her tone, it sounded as if she were wishing such pain on Lady Chester.

"Jane." Father shook his head.

Vivienne winced.

"Well." Lady Chester put her cup down. "It was lovely to see you. It's time for me to go."

Mother glared at Lady Chester, acting like the wronged one.

When Lady Chester left, Vivienne exhaled. Now she would be free to go.

"What happened?" Father touched her shoulder gently.

"Oh, the piano? I wasn't focused. My heart was not in playing, Father I'm sorry."

Mother put a hand on her forehead. "You're warm. Are you sick?"

"Just a bit tired."

"I'll send for our physician."

"It's not necessary." She forced a smile. A visit from the physician would mean she wouldn't be free to leave the house.

"You're pale, and I noticed you were a little jittery. That cursed visit to the circus has made you ill."

"This afternoon there's a poetry reading I would like to attend. Dobkins will come with me."

Mother shook her head. "I'm not sure—"

"Jane." Father stood and clasped his hands behind his back. "Let her go if she wants to. A young lady must cultivate different interests and spend time outside to make friends."

"Diseases don't care about a young lady's interests," Mother said. "I want Dr. Acton's opinion."

"Dr. Acton?" Father asked. "Who is he? What happened to Dr. Stewart?"

Mother huffed. "I dismissed him."

"I think Dr. Stewart was fine, but he didn't tell you what you wanted to hear." Father scowled.

Vivienne rubbed her forehead. Mother found a new family physician every other month, claiming the physicians were all incompetent.

"Well, I'm fine, and I would like to go." She forced a cheerful tone.

"I just want to take care of my family." Clenching the silver box, Mother left the sitting room in a flutter of black fabric before anyone else could speak.

Father touched the top of Vivienne head. "Go if you want, my girl. Don't stay home because of your mother's words. You must enjoy your life. Go now."

"Thank you, Father." She stood to leave, but he called her.

"She's hurting. You know that, don't you?"

"I know. She's hurting, as is everyone."

He released a long breath. "She's improved. Last year, she wouldn't have let you go."

In her opinion, Mother was far from improved. "I love you, Papa." She kissed his cheek before going upstairs to get ready.

WHEN FINALLY VIVIENNE left the house with Dobkins, the sun was hiding behind the clouds. Inside their cab, Dobkins looked outside and wrung her hands, gazing outside. "Police are everywhere."

Constables seemed to have multiplied overnight; they patrolled the streets in the centre of the city, stopping carts, coaches, and omnibuses.

Posters with a sketch of Lion Boy hung on the walls, framed with the words '*murderous*' and '*dangerous*.' They knew nothing about him. He wasn't the deranged creature people believed.

The officers became scarce as they drove farther.

"Do you think Cade believes Lion Boy escaped, or could he know someone helped him?" she asked Dobkins.

"They said escaped, not taken. I think the newspapers would have reported him taken."

"Lady Chester said the police will shoot him if they see him."

"Let's not worry about that."

Not worry? A thousand worries piled up in her mind. She paused, remembering what her father had said. Perhaps that was how Mother felt every day.

Despite the distance she put from the circus, the driver of the cab from last night still might have questioned the commotion inside, realised what was going on, and reported them. Maybe someone had seen them. Maybe Captain Jackson went to the public house to get drunk and left Lion Boy alone. So many things could go wrong.

She fidgeted until the cab stopped well away from their destination. They would need to walk a few minutes and around a corner to arrive at the captain's flat, but she was glad to put her nervous energy to use.

No constable was around in that part of the city. Either the superintendent didn't care about the people who lived there, or the area had already been searched.

She knocked on Captain Jackson's rear door with urgency, both because she wanted to get off the street and because she was eager to see Lion Boy.

The captain opened the door and beckoned them in. "Why are you here? I didn't send any message to Dobkins to ask you to come."

Vivienne ignored the heavy smell of tobacco. "I wanted to know how Lion Boy is faring."

He locked the door behind them. "There were bloody police everywhere this morning."

"Did they cause any problem?" Dobkins asked.

"No, but the last two days weren't the most enjoyable of my life." He poured himself a whisky. "A couple of times I thought they would knock on my door. I expected a search, but not of this magnitude." He raised the bottle towards them. "Any takers?"

"For Pete's sake." Dobkins pinched the bridge of her nose.

"How's Lion Boy?" Vivienne rose on her tiptoes to see past him, but the bedroom door was shut.

"You don't need to worry about him. Now you'd better leave." He finished off his whisky with one gulp and put a hand on the knob.

She didn't move. "No, I want to see him."

"Not now. In a few weeks maybe. For now, you must leave. And don't come back. Just wait for my message. You are putting him at risk by coming here"

"A few weeks? Let me see him. I want to make sure he's doing well."

"Doing well?" He put his hand on his hip. "Of course he's not *doing well*. He grew up in a bloody cage, beaten and drugged."

She winced at his tone. "I promised him I would visit him."

"Not now."

"Why?" Dobkins asked. "Did he escape?"

Vivienne gasped. "You got drunk, and he left!"

"Dammit!" He slammed the empty glass on the table. "He's here, and no, I'm not stupid enough to get unconscious while a drug-addicted young man prone to panic is under my care. A bit of trust would be appreciated."

She believed their doubts were justified. "You won't let me see him."

"And you trusted me enough to ask me to take him here." He pointed a finger at her.

She held his stare. The captain was right although she hadn't had any choice. "Fair enough. You're right. I jumped to conclusions."

"I wonder why," Dobkins said in a low voice.

Captain Jackson ran a hand through his messy hair. "He's resting. His blood must get rid of the morphia, cocaine, and all the other drugs Cade gave him before we can start discussing his future. Cleansing the blood from those poisons is a nasty affair. And it's a long one. Trust me, you don't want to see him while he's in that state."

A thud came from the bedroom.

"What's happening?" She sidestepped him.

He blocked her path. "You must leave." His tone was all harshness.

All the worry she'd accumulated that day burst out. Maybe the captain was trustworthy enough to keep Lion Boy at home, but what if the captain had hurt him?

She had to see Lion Boy even if for a moment. "Let me see him."

"No."

"I'm just going to say hello and then leave."

Before he could stop her, she darted past him to the bedroom, taking advantage of the captain's sluggish movements. Drinking heavily didn't work in his favour.

"Don't!" He tried to grab her arm.

She flung the door open.

Lion Boy was tied to the bed with thick ropes while he thrashed and writhed, kicking the bedsheets. His head moved from right to left. His mouth was open in a silent scream. Sweat glistened on his skin, and his pupils were so large the amber colour of the irises wasn't visible.

She gasped. "What are you doing to him?"

"You cruel man!" Dobkins rushed to the other side of the bed and pulled at the knots. "This poor young man has seen enough."

"He is in withdrawal, from the drugs. I have to tie him down. He could overpower me and run away. It's for his own good." The captain took Vivienne's shoulders and pulled her back from the bed. "I didn't want you to see this."

"You're torturing him!" She shrugged herself free.

"Good Lord." Dobkins put a hand on her chest, staring at Lion Boy with horror.

"Stop it, you two!" The captain stepped in front of Vivienne. "He would have hurt himself. His body makes involuntary movements. He isn't in control. He can get seriously hurt, and I warned him. He knew what was going to happen. I told him exactly what I needed to do to cleanse the drugs from his blood. I explained to him what would happen, and he said *yes*. He agreed. His body craves the morphia, and right now, he's in pain but barely conscious. I can't untie him. Trust me. I know what I'm doing."

Vivienne fought the burning tears as she closed her hand around Lion Boy's. "I'm so sorry."

The fact that only raspy noises came out of his mouth made the scene worse. He had to be in great pain. His clouded eyes fixed on her, or so it seemed.

"How long will it take for him to get better?" She stroked Lion Boy's knuckles.

"I can't say for certain. Two or three weeks, if he survives," the captain said.

"What?" She faced him, closing her hand around Lion Boy's.

Captain Jackson held up a hand. "I discussed that with him, too. He's aware of the risks, but unless he takes them, the drugs will kill him."

Lion Boy exhaled and stopped squirming, his chest rising and falling quickly. He turned his head towards her. His eyes cleared, and his lips parted, but she couldn't understand what he was trying to say.

"He needs water." Captain Jackson gently lifted Lion Boy's head and helped him sip from a glass. "Slowly. That's it."

Lion Boy sagged against the captain, his mouth still moving.

The kindness with which the captain was taking care of Lion Boy and his silent desperation to speak tore out a sob from her.

"Leave." Captain Jackson nodded towards the door. "He deserves to keep his dignity. You can see him when he's better."

Dobkins had stepped away. Vivienne cast a last glance at him, a long moment, before leaving the room with Dobkins on her heels. The captain shut the door behind them.

"What can I do for him?" Vivienne asked.

"Stay away. It's better for now. There are too many police around, which could go on for days, and a lady visiting this area might attract attention. I examined him. His vocal cords are badly damaged. An infection, most likely from a serious bout of influenza, is my guess. He was probably a child. He doesn't remember much."

"It's a miracle he survived," Dobkins said.

"Exactly, which makes me think his family didn't. Once Lion Boy became an orphan, Cade might have become his guardian, and the bastard saw an opportunity there."

Vivienne swallowed past the lump in her throat.

The captain's expression softened. "It would be good if you could try to find a way to teach him to read and write after this is over, so he can communicate with us. It's a nightmare to ask him only questions he can answer with yes or no."

"Do you know his name?" she asked.

"He doesn't have one."

A shock of stillness went through her.

"I thought to call him Samuel," he said in a low voice.

"Why Samuel?" Vivienne wiped her eyes.

Dobkins stared at Captain Jackson with something like respect. "Because it means 'He listens'."

"Lion Boy liked it." He lifted a shoulder. "The lad might be speechless, but I'm sure he can be heard by those who want to listen to him. Now, please leave. If something happens, I'll let you know."

Vivienne nodded. "Thank you, Captain. Please keep him alive."

nine

Two weeks had passed since the night they had helped Samuel leave the circus, twelve days since she had seen him tied to the captain's bed.

Captain Jackson had sent a message to her through Dobkins, saying Samuel was faring well, but seeing him wouldn't be a good idea, and after what Vivienne had witnessed, she didn't argue. The police were still looking for Lion Boy, and photographs of Samuel—dirty, with wild, long hair, and looking like a murderer—filled every newspaper and street poster.

And that was pretty much the only good news of the past weeks because going to the cemetery with her parents took a time already fraught with worry, and weighed her down further.

Dirt covered Adele's name on the tombstone. Father placed a large bouquet of white roses on the grave. Mother clenched the silver box against her chest, her face pale and looking frail.

Years had passed since her sister's death, but every time Vivienne visited Adele's grave, the pain hurt her as fresh as ever. When she was at home, taken by her daily routine, the pain remained dull. But there was no escaping from the truth in front of the cold gravestone.

Father swallowed hard but didn't say anything.

Mother caressed the tombstone. "Lady Grenville told me I should stop feeling pain for Adele's death. *You have four sons and four daughters*, she said, *Adele wasn't your only child*."

Father wrapped an arm around her shoulders. "People don't understand. Don't waste time on their words."

Vivienne stood next to her mother. While she found Lady Grenville's words indelicate and hurtful, there was some truth in them. Mother hadn't moved forwards. She'd stopped living. She'd stopped being a mother. She was a wraith fuelled by grief.

"I'll keep mourning my child for as long as I breathe," Mother said.

Vivienne held her hand. "We all miss Adele—"

"No, it's not true. I'm the only one who still thinks about her. Your brothers and sisters go to dinner parties and holidays abroad, and celebrate their children's birthdays. They aren't wearing black." She turned to Father then Vivienne. "Neither of you are."

"To keep living and enjoying my grandchildren doesn't mean I forgot my daughter," Father said. "Or that our sons and daughters forgot her. Exactly because they understand how fickle life is, they want to spend time with their own children. You can't blame them for that."

"So you agree with Lady Greenville." Mother slid her hand out of Vivienne's. "I should stop mourning."

"No." Father took her by the shoulders. "I want you to live your life again. You have us. You have grandchildren, who want to be with you. You have a family who loves you. *I* love you, Jane."

"And I should betray Adele? My own blood?"

Vivienne drew in a shaky breath. "Mother—"

"You were right. No one understands." Mother turned and hurried along the gravel path towards the main gate.

Father exhaled. "I didn't mean to upset her."

"It's not your fault. She lives in her world of pain, shutting us out. There's nothing we can say that would make her feel better. She doesn't want to feel better. She would feel guilty."

"I'm worried about you." Father took her arm, and together they walked towards the gate. "She suffocates you with rules and fears. She argues every time you want to leave the house, and you haven't had your Season. I confess I don't know what to do with her. I have tried to be patient. I have tried to talk to her. Nothing has worked."

"I just hope..."

"What?" He paused to stare at her.

"Am I a bad sister for wanting to be happy again? A bad daughter? I loved Adele. I'll always cherish her memory, but I want to smile and be happy."

"Darling." Father hugged her. "You aren't a bad sister, much less a bad daughter. Live your life and be happy. Adele would have wanted that." He kissed the top of her head.

She walked next to him, resting her head on his shoulder.

Yet she wondered if she was doing the right thing.

AFTER DAYS SPENT FEELING SICK, confused, and in pain, Samuel—he had a name now—felt human, maybe for the first time in his life.

The difference between before and after cleansing his blood was striking. His mind was clear, and his skin didn't itch. The downside was that there was nothing to shield his mind from the painful memories. His sleep was light and troubled, and since his feelings weren't numbed anymore, his shame increased tenfold.

As the morphia had painfully left his blood, food tasted better, and his appetite had grown proportionally. He felt guilty, considering he did nothing but empty the captain's pantry.

The room that functioned as a dining room, kitchen, and sitting room, even though untidy and chaotic was so much better than his cage. And if he was completely honest, he didn't look forward to leaving the flat to explore the outside world. Not yet.

What he saw of London from a small window was a jumble of loud people, noisy carts jerking along the street, donkeys braying and horses neighing, and the loud blasts from the nearby furnaces booming. He spent hours just watching that small corner of London. While he loved the colours and the activity, the world outside the flat scared him as well.

He hadn't seen Vivienne, or if she'd been there, he didn't remember her. He hoped she hadn't come when he was out of control from withdrawal. In the circus, his life had been on display for everyone to see and laugh at. The moment he'd been at his worst should be for him only. Having the captain as a witness was already hard enough to endure.

Not to mention the constant fear of expecting Murdock to barge into the house and drag him back in chains. The captain didn't know who Murdock was. He believed Cade was the ring-master. Murdock could easily deceive him. All because Samuel couldn't write and explain the true story.

He finished wolfing down a plate of bacon, eggs, and buttered scones while Captain Jackson filled a large tin container with hot water in the bedroom. Back and forth he went until the container was full.

"It's your moment, lad." He showed Samuel a pair of shiny scissors. "You need a proper bath, and we need to cut that..." He waved the scissors in a circle. "Thing. I tried to comb it and broke two combs."

Samuel rose from the chair, licking the grease from his fingers and palms. Hygiene had never been Murdock's first concern when it came to Samuel. He'd never had a proper bath, only cold showers with a sponge.

"Now, I'm not a stickler for manners," Captain Jackson said. "But it's better if you don't lick your fingers after a meal in front of a lady, or anyone. Wash them. There's a basin with soapy water over there. Then I'll cut your hair first."

Samuel did as he was told, wondering how many rules he had to learn to live among normal people. After he finished, he sat on a chair as Captain Jackson cut his hair without mercy.

Long, knotted dark brown strands fell to the floor, and somehow, he couldn't stop staring at them. He didn't remember having ever cut his hair. Those strands had been with him since his imprisonment had begun.

Another chain was broken.

Captain Jackson clicked his tongue. "I did my best, but you need to wash it before I continue." He pointed at the tub filled with steamy water. "In you go. The soap is there, and on that chair, you'll find some clothes, not elegant but decent. The harder you scrub, the better. And remember." He paused, brushing Samuel's hair. "When you look into the mirror, you're a man not an animal. Don't forget it."

Samuel had no idea what the captain meant but nodded. Alone in the bedroom, he removed his clothes and stepped into the tub. Steam fogged the air, and a pungent scent wafted from the soap when he picked it up.

The hot water was so far from the freezing baths he'd taken now and then. The sensation of the warm water on his skin cleaned even his thoughts.

He closed his eyes, relishing every moment of the wonderful hot bath.

Captain Jackson had taken care of him, washing him with a sponge when he'd been weak in the bed, but the feeling of scrubbing himself was more relaxing. He wanted to get rid of all the dirt from the circus. He wanted to wash away the pain and hopelessness.

He scrubbed himself until his skin was raw and red and the water was cold and dirty. The clean clothes chafed his skin, but the fresh scent of soap was intoxicating. The trousers were a bit too short, but between them and the shirt, he was properly dressed, like the people who had stared at him in horror.

When he came out of the bedroom, Captain Jackson eyed him with approval. "Excellent. Let's finish your hair."

As the captain worked on taming the wet hair and cutting the beard, Samuel wanted to ask a dozen questions. Why was the captain helping him? Where was Vivienne? What was he supposed to do now? What if Murdock found him again? The last thought sent a chill down his spine.

The minty scent of the shaving cream tickled his nose as the captain applied it to his face.

"I have a steady hand," the captain said, "but don't make abrupt moves. My hand could slip."

Samuel remained still as the captain ran a long, sharp razor over his cheeks and neck. A warm towel removed the last traces of shaving cream, and he touched his face. How odd it was not to feel the beard.

Then the captain attacked Samuel's hair again—it was a battle of scissors and combs.

"Done." Captain Jackson passed a comb through Samuel's hair before handing him a mirror. "I'm not an expert, but in the army, I cut the hair of many soldiers."

Samuel tilted his head right and left, watching his face in the mirror at different angles. His face. He didn't recognise himself.

His hair was cut very short. He ran a hand over the top of his head, ruffling the short strands sticking out in every direction. Without the grease and dirt, his dark blond hair shone with a golden hue he didn't know it had.

The beard was gone, and his skin didn't have any grime. He was surprised to find himself rather pale and with gaunt cheeks. His cheekbones protruded too much.

Captain Jackson stood back and looked at him. "Lion Boy is gone. You look nothing like him. That's a good thing. No one will recognise you."

Lion Boy was no more.

A man stared back at him from the mirror. Not a creature.

A sickening lump crept in his throat, and he swallowed hard. His eyes burned. If they were happy or sad tears, he wouldn't know. Maybe both.

The captain patted his shoulder. "You did well. You've been very brave."

He wiped his face quickly. There was a limit to what he was willing to show of himself.

The captain sat in front of him, his deep black eyes solemn. "We must find a way to communicate. You can't just nod or shake your head. While you were recovering, I did some research. There's a language made of signs done with the hands. It's called sign language, used by people who can't talk."

Samuel arched his brow. He'd seen many curiosities, but never someone who talked with his hands.

Captain Jackson produced a book from under a pile of newspapers and showed it to him. Drawings of hands and fingers filled the pages.

"They say this priest, Pedro Ponce de Leon—fitting, isn't it?—started the first sign language to allow monks who were observing periods of silence to communicate. I think you need to know how to read first before learning it."

Samuel flipped through the pages. He didn't understand the words under the drawings, but the signs were clear. People talked with their hands! It would be wonderful to be able to ask questions and be understood.

There was a knock on the door, and they both tensed.

"It must be Lady Vivienne, but just in case it isn't, go to the bedroom."

Samuel closed the door to the bedroom, his heart beating faster. If the police came for him, he would put up a fight. He'd rather die while fighting the police than return to Murdock. But if it was Lady Vivienne, his heart would burst with emotion anyway. She'd saved his life, and he didn't know how to thank her.

A breath remained trapped in his chest when he heard Lady Vivienne's sweet voice.

"Samuel," Captain Jackson called. "Come here."

He inched the door open as a sudden shame washed over him. He tugged at his shirt and ran a hand over his face, not sure how he should greet a lady. Without his hair and beard, he felt oddly naked. His body seemed suddenly too big for the room and he fought the urge to hide somewhere.

His gaze on the floor, he took a tentative step forwards, nearly dragging his feet.

She let out a delighted squeal when she saw him. "Heavens, Samuel. I'm so happy to see you up and about."

He raised his gaze. Her blue eyes sparkled. The dark green gown she wore exalted her raven hair and gave her a royal look—a reminder of how distant they were.

Even Dobkins looked at him with approval. "How do you feel, darling boy?"

He mouthed, "Good," hoping she understood.

Dobkins nodded with a smile.

Vivienne stared at him with her head tilted slightly back. "I seriously doubt anyone would recognise you. Even Cade wouldn't know who you are."

He flashed a smile before mouthing slowly, "Thank you."

She became serious, her eyes shining. "You don't have to thank me. We did what any decent person would do."

Then he must have met only not-so-decent people.

She sidestepped the clothes and empty bottles on the floor to come closer to him. The rising worry couldn't be fear, could it? There was no reason to be scared of Vivienne.

She stopped in front of him, tears welling up in her eyes. "You are so brave."

He didn't feel brave, only lucky.

She reached out, maybe to take his hand, but withdrew her arm.

Likely, the way he'd reacted the last time she'd touched him discouraged her from touching him again. Perhaps he should make her understand he didn't mind her touch.

He inched his hand towards her, shaking with irrational fear. His stomach clenched. The worst that could happen was Lady Vivienne would recoil, and he would understand her reaction. Or maybe he was doing something he wasn't supposed to do.

He offered her his hand, palm up, incapable of controlling his shivering.

When she slid her hand into his, he barely contained the storm of sensations inside him. She closed her hand around his, and he became painfully aware of how rough his skin was, how big his hand was compared to hers, and how homely it looked.

"It's a pleasure to meet you, Samuel," she said in a low voice.

He had to lower his gaze because her clear blue eyes held too much compassion and saw too much. He pulled back his hand slowly, staring at the tips of her shiny boots. Surely that had been the first and last time he would ever touch her. While that made sense and sounded right, it was also sad.

"While we are here." Captain Jackson showed Vivienne the book on sign language. "Samuel needs to know how to read and write so he can learn this."

She flipped through the pages, her fine eyebrows drawing together. "Sign language. That's perfect." She looked up and gave Samuel a warm smile. "We'll start immediately."

ten

The hours Vivienne spent with Samuel were the best of her week. They gave her the strength to endure Mother's worries. If Father hadn't intervened and convinced Mother to let her go every time she wanted to go out, she would have spent all her days at home.

In a few months, Samuel had learnt the letters of the alphabet and composed his first sentences. Learning to use sign language, writing, and reading was a difficult task, but he never complained and worked hard.

What she complained about was the state of Captain Jackson's flat. Bottles and glasses were everywhere, dirty plates filled the sink, and the stuffy air bothered her. Perhaps she was a spoiled brat, but Samuel deserved a decent place to live in, and because she had given the captain her bracelet, she felt she had a right to request he not live in squalor.

That afternoon, she entered the flat, welcomed by a smiling Samuel. She smiled back. The change in him was incredible. His gaunt cheeks had filled up, and his gorgeous hair had a shiny hue that glinted with gold in the sunlight. His skin was still a bit pale, and sadness lingered in his lion eyes, but her heart stuttered every time he showed his hunger to learn or when he smiled. He stared at her as if she'd lit the stars, and while his adoration made her warm and fuzzy, she didn't deserve it.

She removed her gloves, walking over a bottle. "Where is the captain?"

Samuel pointed to the sofa where Captain Jackson slept soundly, an empty glass in his hand.

Dobkins opened the window, not bothering to be silent as she stomped across the room. "He passed out and left you on your own."

Samuel took his time before signing, "No police."

A flare of annoyance swelled in Vivienne's chest. "It doesn't matter if the police aren't around anymore."

The circus was still in London. Cade's obsession was to find Lion Boy—he'd put up a reward. A thousand pounds for who found Lion Boy.

The smell of cheroot permeated everything, and the dirty shirts draped on the chairs drove her mad.

Dobkins shook the captain's arm. "Wake up, for heaven's sake."

Mumbling, the captain blinked his eyes open. The glass slid out of his fingers, but Vivienne snatched it before it smashed against the floor.

"What?" he drawled.

"This needs to stop." Dobkins balled her fists on her hips.

Samuel withdrew to a corner, his amber eyes widening. Perhaps Dobkins's raised voice disturbed him.

"What do you want?" the captain repeated, sitting up. One of his braces hung low on his arm.

Dobkins waved towards the room. "You can't drink yourself into a stupor and leave Samuel on his own. The flat is a pigsty, and it stinks."

He raked a hand through his dishevelled hair, yawning. "I don't see where the problem is."

"The problem is that this young man," Dobkins said, "deserves better from you, and we paid a nice sum to take care of him."

Samuel lowered his gaze, working his jaw.

Worry hung heavy in Vivienne's chest. She glanced at Dobkins and gave her a slight shake of her head. Mentioning the payment might bother Samuel.

"And you should buy fresh food for him more often," Dobkins continued. "For you as well. Have some dignity." Her voice shook.

The captain's bloodshot eyes narrowed. It didn't escape Vivienne's notice that he was still sitting. Not that she cared, but he was letting himself go.

"Wait a moment," he said. "You recruited me for a job, and I did it, and I did it damn well. Samuel is alive and healthy. My life and my flat are my own business."

Samuel hunched his shoulders as if he wanted to disappear.

"What life?" Dobkins gestured at the empty bottles. "The one you're wasting away on cheap whisky and tobacco? Whisky doesn't solve anything."

"Nor does milk."

Dobkins glowered at him. "You were an army surgeon once. What happened to you?"

"Her family happened!" The captain pointed to Vivienne. "They accused me of murder when I did everything to save that girl's life." He stood, his voice stronger. "Doctors can't do miracles, not even for an earl's daughter. Her death broke my heart, too."

"I understand, Captain," Vivienne said. "No one understands you better than I do. But you must move on and find your purpose again."

Samuel had stepped back, almost into a corner, hugging himself and shaking.

She walked between the captain and Dobkins towards Samuel.

"You must clean up this flat." Dobkins scrunched up her face at a dirty shirt.

The captain replied with some rambling, loud words, but Vivienne wanted to talk to Samuel.

"Let's go to the bedroom while they talk."

He obeyed her without hesitation, which she didn't like. She didn't want to become his new master. She shut the door to block the captain's and Dobkins's rising voices.

"Samuel." She tilted her head to see his eyes, but he kept his gaze down. "Please look at me."

Again, he obeyed her.

"What is it? Why are you so upset?" She gave him the time to answer.

He consulted his notebook and signed a few times, making mistakes, but she understood what he meant—*the captain is kind to me.*

Yes, but she suspected something else troubled him.

"The loud voices disturb you, don't they?"

He nodded, gazing away.

"It's understandable."

He didn't sign anything.

"You shouldn't feel embarrassed."

He raised his gaze, but she didn't understand if he was grateful for her words of comfort, or if she was too bold, intruding on his private feelings.

"Stop playing the victim," Dobkins said from the other side of the door.

The sound of glass clinking came.

"I'm tempted to give you my nasty attitude, but you already have one," the captain rebuked.

"Oh, dear." She rubbed her forehead. "I didn't mean to cause all this."

Samuel skimmed the pages of his notebook before signing, "Who is the girl who died?"

"My sister Adele. She got sick with scarlet fever. My parents asked the captain to take care of her. The captain and my father were old friends. But Adele grew weak quite quickly and died."

"Sorry," he signed.

"My mother blames him. My father wasn't convinced the captain was to blame, but between his grief and his love for my mother, who is grieving, he didn't really do anything." She stared at him. "If you're uncomfortable, you should tell me. The captain told me you don't sleep well."

He shrugged.

So the problem wasn't the communication. He had the means now to explain himself but didn't want to. Or she wasn't the right person for him to confide in.

"Is there anything I can do to help?"

Another shrug.

She sighed. She wouldn't bother him if he didn't want to talk to her.

"I'm just worried that Cade might barge in here and take you away from me," she said in a low voice.

He sucked in a deep breath, his eyelashes fluttering up. Then he searched his notes again and started to sign. "Cade isn't the..." He wrote something on a page and showed it to her. "Ringmaster." He signed again. "He's the muscle, not the mind."

"Cade isn't the one who drugged you?"

He shook his head and signed, pausing a couple of times to check the alphabet. "Murdock drugged me. He's the clever one. I grew up with him, following him and his minions from one place to another."

"Goodness. We don't even know what Murdock looks like. But no matter. You have us now. We'll do everything we can to protect you from whoever tries to hurt you." She stretched out a hand to touch him and hesitated.

He gently took her hand and held it as if he were handling a precious gem. Again, he gave her the adoring look that broke her heart.

Sudden silence came from the other side of the door. Samuel released her hand and averted his gaze.

She craned her neck. "Either they stopped fighting or they killed each other."

A corner of his mouth quirked up in a smile, which made her realise how rarely he smiled.

"Let's see what happened, shall we?"

eleven

After Vivienne and Dobkins left, Samuel closed the door behind them and took a good look at the room.

Captain Jackson was tossing the empty bottles in a box, smashing them.

Samuel picked up a few glasses from the floor and put them on the table. Vivienne's questions had left a trail of thoughts in his mind. He'd disappointed her somehow although he wouldn't know why.

Her smile never failed to make him acutely aware of her beauty. Not only her beauty, but her shining soul, too. Under normal circumstances, a man like him would never share the same room as she did. His inadequacy was on full display, but he didn't mind that; he was only sorry he couldn't be more for her.

The captain paused, wiping the sweat from his brow. "What do you think of my situation? Do you agree with Dobkins and Lady Vivienne that I must change my habits?"

Since there had been too many arguments for one day, he shrugged.

"Don't give me the bloody shrug!" Captain Jackson smashed another bottle in the box.

He flinched, and the glass he was about to place on the table fell to the floor, breaking into pieces.

"Hell..." the captain said, "I'm sorry."

He suppressed another shrug.

"I didn't mean to give you a fright."

He knelt to pick up the shards.

The captain crouched, too. "Leave it."

He insisted. He hadn't done anything to help the captain. It was his turn to be helpful.

"It's sharp. I'll do it." The captain swatted Samuel's hand away, cutting himself on a sharp piece. "Bloody hell!"

On impulse, Samuel recoiled and covered his head with his arms. When no pain came, he lowered them.

Captain Jackson slouched. "I truly am sorry, lad. I have a temper, but I would never hurt you."

"I know," he signed with trembling fingers.

"I'm an ass." The captain sagged on the floor, blood trickling from the cut on his palm. "You can be honest with me. I'm a bloody mess, right?"

Samuel sat next to him and searched his notes, which were very rudimentary sketches of a few signs and some scribbled words.

"I went through this," he signed.

What he wanted to say was that he understood what the captain was going through, and if he'd managed to get rid of the morphia, the captain could get rid of his whisky. But that was a speech too complicated for his skills.

Nevertheless, he beat a fist against his chest and then on the captain's.

"You're stronger than I am," the captain said.

Samuel laughed. A throaty sound came out, more chilling than joyful, but he laughed anyway.

"You are." The captain nodded. "I'm a coward. That's why alcohol is called Dutch courage. Not that I feel particularly brave when I'm drunk. I feel nothing, which is even better."

Slowly, he signed, "Adele?"

"I didn't drink back then. I was a paragon of virtue, convinced that, if you were honest and good, life repaid you in kind. My arse. Such a fool I was. But no matter what I did to help Adele, she died too quickly for me to save her. So small. So fragile. So many tears."

Samuel took his handkerchief and wrapped it around the captain's injured palm.

The captain let him do it. "The ladies are right. I need to change. You deserve better."

Samuel wanted to tell him he should change for himself, but if that was a good motivation, he wouldn't say anything.

"Is it true they paid you to rescue me?" he asked, signing slowly.

The captain exhaled. "Not my finest moment. But it's different now. I care about you."

He hugged the captain and patted his back.

The captain returned the hug. "We're friends."

They remained sitting in the messy room. A breeze from the open window swept through the room.

"Will you help me?" the captain asked.

Samuel squeezed his shoulder and signed, "You're my first friend. Of course I'll help you."

THAT AFTERNOON, Vivienne was sitting next to Samuel, reviewing the irregular verbs in sign language. His deep hunger for learning shocked Vivienne. The young men she usually met cared nothing about studying and learning, while Samuel would give anything to be taught something new.

The circus had finally moved out of London, after Cade had given up searching for Samuel, granting them a much-needed respite from the constant worry of being caught by the police. The newspapers had thankfully stopped talking about Lion Boy although countless sights of him throughout London had kept the readers entertained and the constables busy.

Some people had sworn to have been attacked by Lion Boy and demanded Cade pay them for the damage. After a few of those complaints, Cade had left London in a hurry.

The man who had enslaved Samuel, Murdock, was never mentioned. No article had reported his name, and even Cade had dogged journalists with a skill that bordered on magic. Not that she cared, but she wanted to see the face of the man who was vile enough to enslave a child.

"You don't pour the boiling water on the leaves," Dobkins said to Captain Jackson, "or the tea will taste bitter."

"Rubbish. It releases the fragrance better."

"You never listen to me!"

"I do. That's why I'm nervous."

Vivienne whispered, "They argue like an old couple."

Samuel smiled. Since his cheeks weren't gaunt anymore, his smile had become full, bright, and rather charming. His hair had grown and reached his jaw with dark golden curls. No trace of his sickness was left. Lion Boy was as unrecognisable as the captain's flat. Clean, tidy, and not a bottle of whisky in sight. The captain looked a bit worse for wear, but his eyes were sharper.

She spied on Samuel's profile as he moved his fingers while reading, slowing slightly on the most difficult words.

What pleased her was the fact his ordeal hadn't left traces on him, at least on the outside. He looked like any other healthy young man, strong and handsome.

His determination to learn impressed her. His will to work hard was admirable. Had she been in his situation, she wouldn't have been able to recover so quickly and focus on learning so many things. Her predicaments seemed so trivial compared to what he'd gone through.

He flipped his fingers in the air, signing, "I don't remember all of them."

"Take your time. You're doing an incredible job."

"An Englishman who can't brew tea," Dobkins said. "What's next? You making cucumber sandwiches without butter?"

"Pot kettle black," the captain replied. "You add French cheese, which is unpatriotic."

Vivienne chuckled.

Samuel smiled, and his face brightened before he focused on reading again.

"You should take a break," she said.

"Tea is ready." Dobkins served tea and sandwiches, explaining to the captain why French cheese was a great addition over English cheddar.

Vivienne lifted her tea cup. "Do you remember anything about your life before the circus?"

His smile disappeared as he returned his gaze to the book. "No. The earliest memories I have are about Murdock and travelling with him. Before joining the circus, he swindled people out of thousands of pounds. After one of his deceits, we would move to another place and start again. It was horrible."

When he didn't add anything else, she spoke again. "I'm sorry. I didn't mean to upset you. But I wonder if you have a family, parents, or siblings who are worried about you."

"I don't think I have. Why would my parents leave me with Murdock?"

Some words he signed were confusing for her because he was faster than she was. But his deep pain was clear.

"Maybe they had no choice, or maybe they didn't know where you were."

He pressed his lips in a hard line. "Murdock treated me like a beast, feeding me leftovers and locking me up in a cage when he wasn't with me. He called me only *Boy* back then. Then, when I was thirteen, he got the idea of turning me into Lion Boy and, with Cade, put up the Circus of Curiosities. What parent would leave their child in such desperation?"

A muscle of his jaw ticked, and his nostrils flared.

She ought to change the subject. "Have you thought about what to do once you finish learning to read and write?"

"No."

She didn't press him, but he might become an apprentice and learn a trade, or find employment in a rich house. With his height and build, he would be an excellent footman, granted if he found an employer who didn't mind him being speechless.

The sunlight streamed through the diamond window and lit his hair with radiance. He stared at the street outside as if mesmerised by the people walking along the pavements, the carriages, and the street vendors. It occurred to her he'd never left the captain's flat. While the circus had still been in London, it'd only been sensible to keep him hidden, but now there was no reason to.

"Would you like to go out? Take a walk? I'm sure the captain will agree."

He turned towards her, his chest heaving. "Yes."

twelve

G oing out was a terrible idea.

During the long period in which Samuel had been cooped up in the captain's house, he had never complained. Not once. As much as the flat could be oppressive, it was safe, and the fear of meeting Murdock or being arrested by the police had been the strongest motivation to stay indoors.

But now that the police had stopped searching for him and Murdock was gone, the sunlight was a temptation too big.

He wanted to feel the warmth of the sun on his skin and the breeze on his face. He wanted to be part of the colourful crowd on the pavement. Be someone normal.

But the moment he stepped out of the safety of the flat, he fought the impulse to rush back inside. His legs trembled, and his vision darkened at the edges.

The fear of making a fool out of himself in front of Vivienne forced him to pull himself together, so he swallowed past the lump in his throat and walked close to the captain.

Likely, she already had a poor opinion of him; he barely answered her questions about his past or his future, and her knowledge of books and the world, in general, was so vast it couldn't be compared to his. She often talked about famous poets or places he knew nothing about.

To her eyes, he feared he was an ignorant young man with no name and no past. He didn't want to be marked as a coward as well.

"Beautiful day." Vivienne closed her eyes for a moment in the sunlight.

Her long eyelashes overlapped at the tips against the perfect alabaster of her skin. When she opened her eyes and realised he was staring at her, he averted his gaze, feeling like a thief.

"Let's go." The captain put on a Bowler hat. "It was time to go out, lad."

"I'm not sure," Dobkins said. "It might be too soon for Samuel."

"I disagree," the captain said. "As usual."

Stepping onto the pavement, Samuel wished he could hold Lady Vivienne's hand to get some courage.

The deafening clapping of the horses' hooves against the cobbles startled him. People talked in loud voices and so quickly he found it difficult to understand what they were saying. Or maybe he was too nervous. The collar of his shirt had turned too tight all of a sudden.

When a boom and a flash of fire blazed out of a corner, he couldn't contain himself and made a dash for the house.

"Do not worry." Vivienne closed her hand gently around his wrist. "It's only the sound of a blast furnace. It makes steel. It's not dangerous. You must have heard that noise many times."

Yes, he had, and he also knew what the furnaces did.

He nodded. So much for not being a coward.

The feel of her soft fingers on his skin shot a riot of sensations through his body. He was petrified but not because of fear. He wished to lace his fingers through hers and hold her hand while he walked in this strange city he didn't understand.

The captain walked next to him as if ready to protect him, and Dobkins walked next to Lady Vivienne.

"Do you want to go home?" Vivienne asked.

He stared at her elegant fingers on his rough skin. "No," he signed.

"Would you like to go to the park? It's lovely and quiet." She withdrew her hand, and his heart thudded faster.

He took her hand, maybe squeezing it with too much energy. She whipped her head towards him, her blue eyes filled with surprise. His manners were non-existent, but he needed the contact with her.

Captain Jackson and Dobkins mostly tried to explain to him all the rules of civil behaviour, but he found it difficult to remember them. Still, even an uneducated man like him understood that grabbing a lady's hand wasn't something he should do.

He released her although it cost every ounce of his willpower. "Apologies," he signed slowly. "I'm nervous."

"Don't look at the people around you," she said. "Focus on one of us."

He walked along the busy pavement. If he ignored the noises and didn't get distracted by the crowd, he could control his reactions.

A man rushing past him startled him. Someone else bumped lightly into him, sending his heart into a frenzy.

"It's all right. You've nothing to fear," she said.

He sucked in a breath when she brushed his fingers. Surely a casual gesture. But when she slid her hand into his, his pulse spiked.

She was staring ahead, and he did the same. Her hand in his felt both reassuring and serious, like a responsibility. He hoped he wasn't holding her hand with too much strength.

His heartbeat slowed, and warmth spread from his palm to his chest. Slowly he breathed normally, inhaling the combination of different scents—coal dust, horse dung, and freshly baked bread.

No one paid him the slightest bit of attention. People rushed past him, busy with their errands, without stopping to sneer or point at him. Crowds had always been given to insults and cruelty. The lack of interest in him was a welcome change. He'd never been happier to be ignored.

"Better?" She tugged at his hand.

He nodded.

The park distracted him again. Tall, leafy trees swayed their canopies in the breeze. Green grass stretched in front of him seemingly forever, and birds sang while flying across the sky—the ultimate freedom.

She let his hand go, and the loss of her touch was as painful as one of Murdock's beatings.

"This is The Regent's Park." She gestured around. "One of the most famous parks in London, but not the largest. Richmond Park holds that record."

"Is there a park bigger than this one?"

"Much bigger. The main path in Richmond Park is more than seven miles long."

Seven miles. He wasn't sure how much that was, but for her sake, he pretended to be impressed. The end of the park wasn't visible. London was big indeed.

She tugged at his sleeve. "And that circular stone thingamabob is the Griffin Tazza, also known as the Lion Vase."

He stopped in front of the statues of four winged lions balancing a large bowl over their backs. Red flowers grew at the base while blue flowers sprouted out of the bowl. So many colours!

"Sorry." She rubbed her forehead. "I didn't think about... you're probably tired of hearing the word *lion*."

"I'm not hurt," he signed slowly, wanting her to understand. "I trust you."

She gave him a graceful nod.

The breeze caressing his cheeks and ruffling his hair was the best gift of his newfound freedom. The gravel path weaved through trimmed bushes and fountains. Maybe the view was mundane for Vivienne, but the variety of colours, scents, and lights overwhelmed his senses in a good way. Life pumped through his veins, and for once, the energy flowing through him wasn't fear, anger, or the result of a potion.

They stopped where a crowd had gathered around two street performers. An actor in a fine tailored suit played the role of a lord while the other his clumsy servant.

He laughed as the servant kept dropping the tray with the tea cups or tripping on his feet. But when the lord raised his walking stick to hit the servant, he stopped breathing for a moment.

Cold sweat trickled down his back. He winced every time the lord hit the servant, even though the beating wasn't real and the servant's groans sounded phoney.

A phantom pain burned his back, and the familiar anger and sense of impotence crawled over him like an army of ants.

The face of the actor became that of Murdock, twisted in anger, his beady eyes glinting. The laughter of the audience mocked him. The sunlight vanished, replaced by the darkness of his cage.

No, he would never, ever go back to the circus. He'd rather die than be caged again.

He spun on his heels, crunching the gravel, and ran away. A buzzing noise rang in his ears, turning into Murdock's icy voice.

You belong to me.

No, he didn't.

You're a beast.

No. He was a man, not a creature. He was free to live his life. No more beatings. No more performances.

He sped up, but the crowd's mocking laugh followed him.

"Samuel." Vivienne swept into view in front of him, a hand on his chest. "Please stop."

He hadn't even noticed her.

Her touch shocked him into reality. His heart pounded against her palm, and his attention focused on her worried eyes.

She removed her hand quickly. "Are you all right?"

"No."

"It was the performance, wasn't it?"

A bitter taste filled his mouth. Not only fear but shame as well caused him to shake. He must have looked as deranged as Murdock had always said.

Footsteps came from behind him.

Captain Jackson squeezed his shoulder. "There's a bench over there. You'd better sit down."

He didn't move, and he didn't know why.

"Samuel." Vivienne took his arm and gently led him to the edge of the path. "Please listen to us."

He followed her, his body moving mechanically. He sat on the bench under a large tree from where he couldn't see the performers although the audience's laughter reached him, bothering him.

"What happened?" Dobkins asked.

"Something I've seen among soldiers too many times." Captain Jackson sat next to him. "Take deep breaths and focus on something happy."

He raised a sceptical eyebrow at the captain. A happy memory couldn't have any power over his fear.

"It works. Try it." The captain nodded encouragingly.

No, the trick didn't work because Samuel didn't have many happy moments to recall. The first happy moments of his life had happened recently, and even those were entwined with fear, shame, and pain.

"Perhaps he doesn't have many happy memories," Vivienne said, seemingly reading his mind.

"I'll fetch you something to drink." Captain Jackson rose. "A lemonade with a lot of sugar." He started to walk off.

"Wait, I'll take one for Lady Vivienne as well." Dobkins followed him.

Without saying anything, Vivienne took his hand and stroked his knuckles. "Perhaps we can make a good memory." She sat next to him in a swish of fabric.

His head was light, but he forced himself not to faint. "How?"

She started singing softly a song about a boat sailing along a quiet sea, and how the thoughts of the sailor drifted towards the horizon as he was eager to see all the wonders of the world.

Her voice was like her—gentle, soft, and beautiful.

> *From sun-kissed shores to lagoons of emerald hue,*
> *From ancient ruins to bustling ports,*
> *A sailor's journey, always fresh and new.*
> *With weathered hands and a heart that holds*
>   *the sea,*
> *Through coral reefs, where vibrant fish swim,*
> *He sails to lands, his spirit always free.*

He imagined being that sailor, leading his ship towards wonderful, new places, away from the darkness of his past, somewhere he could start afresh and be only himself.

Her velvety hand over his spread calm through him. She had elegant, slender fingers with a delicate touch.

His dark thoughts drifted away with the song, sailing on a sea of enchantment. Freedom was the most intoxicating of feelings, and the fear of losing it was equally powerful.

When she finished, he couldn't help but smile, his breathing less troubled.

"Thank you," he signed. "I'll bring this memory with me forever."

She smiled back and withdrew her hand as Captain Jackson and Dobkins returned with the lemonade cups.

"Better?" The captain handed him the cup.

"Yes." He sipped the sweet drink, watching a group of children romping about on the grass.

They were playing with a hoop and a stick. Such a simple game, but the children laughed, delighted.

Vivienne glanced at him. "Do you like the lemonade?"

He put the cup down to free his hands. "Delicious. I've never tasted it before. Another happy memory."

Her smile dropped, and her eyes turned surprisingly shiny.

"What is it?" He worried he'd said something wrong.

Her hand was half an inch from his on the bench. She stretched out a finger to touch his thumb. The touch was barely there. A feather floating down on his skin would be stronger. But the reaction it triggered inside him was as devastating as a storm.

"I can't remember the first time I've drunk lemonade. I was probably two years old. It pains me..." She swallowed.

Reluctantly, he moved his hand from her to sign. "I'm here thanks to you. Do not feel sorry for me. I'm free now."

Another bout of laughter from the crowd distracted him. The two actors were bowing to their audience, the walking stick on the ground.

A chill slithered down his neck as the scene of the beating flashed through his mind.

Yes, he was free, physically, but he was carrying his cage with him.

thirteen

A s Samuel walked back home from the park, Vivienne's singing and his first glass of lemonade filled his thoughts. Feeling again the glimmer of joy would be his mission. He clutched it with desperation because he didn't want another moment of panic to overwhelm him, especially in front of Vivienne.

The wind picked up speed, and a torn piece of a poster rolled over his shoe. A drawing of his wild face appeared ripped in half. The words *dangerous* and *reward* were still legible.

He didn't recognise the angry, wide-eyed man staring at him with his teeth bared and his only visible eye narrowed. Yet he'd been Lion Boy for years. Lion Boy was his past and part of him.

The captain stopped walking a few yards in front of him. "Is something the matter?"

Vivienne picked up the piece of paper and studied it. Her pinched expression radiated sorrow. "It's over. This isn't who you are. You've never been Lion Boy. It was a lie." She crumpled the piece of paper and lobbed it to a corner. "You have a new beginning in front of you."

Which was scary—in a way, scarier than a cage.

For the rest of the walk, his breathing remained normal even when a man on a bicycle raced past him or when a couple of police constables tipped their hats at Vivienne and Dobkins. Controlling his rising emotions required all his energy.

"We're almost at the captain's flat," Vivienne said.

Fatigue rode him hard by the time he entered the flat, glad to be in a closed space. He was about to sit on a chair but stopped, remembering the captain had told him not to sit when standing ladies were present.

Vivienne waved him down. "Do not worry. You must be tired."

"Yes."

"And we must go," Dobkins said. "We'll come back as soon as we can."

"Likely the day after tomorrow, but please keep practising." Vivienne walked over to him. "I'm very proud of you. You're a brilliant, brave man. We'll help you get happy memories."

He couldn't sign any words, not even a 'thank you.' She held his hand between hers for a moment before releasing it, and yet he didn't thank her.

After they left, he sat at the table and flipped through his notes on the latest mathematics lesson he'd studied to better understand measurements.

"What bothers you?" Captain Jackson took out a stick of liquorice. Since he'd decided to give up whisky, he'd replaced the liquor with the strong taste of liquorice. "I have to see a patient, but I have time if you want to talk."

"I think I need a cage to feel safe." He moved his fingers as little as possible as if he were whispering.

"Cages trick you. They give you enough safety to make you scared of freedom. But there's safety in freedom as well." The captain handed him a liquorice stick. "Opportunities and choices mean safety."

He munched on the stick, just bitter enough to be pleasant.

They shared another stick until the captain picked up his leather bag. "I'd better go now before I start losing patients again."

"I'm proud of you, too."

The captain flashed a rueful grin. "It's too early to be proud of me. I've just started taking care of sick people again. I'm still lost in the woods." He donned his hat and left.

Finding the right path in the woods was more difficult than learning sign language.

Samuel sat in front of the window to watch the bustle in the street, and he wondered if Lion Boy would ever leave him alone.

MATHEMATICS, history, geography…Vivienne had taught Samuel the basics of each subject but she knew music and poetry deserved to be talked about as well.

She selected a book of songs and another of poetry to bring to him for their afternoon meeting. Or maybe she shouldn't mention singing since he couldn't sing. He could learn to play an instrument if he wanted to. They surely had time to expand his cultural horizons.

She rushed down the stairs to the hallway, where Dobkins helped her don her coat, and they were about to leave the house when Mother came out of the parlour.

"Out again? You're spending a lot of time outside." Mother eyed Vivienne's satchel.

"I'm going to the park with Dobkins. Would you like to come with us?" She regretted playing on Mother's feelings.

After Adele's death, Mother wasn't fond of walks in the park; she also was convinced certain flowers spread diseases. Where she got that belief from, Vivienne had no idea. One of the many quacks she consulted, likely.

Mother scowled. "You shouldn't spend so much time in the park. It's unhealthy, especially when elm trees are flowering."

"It's winter."

"I don't care. You went to the park almost every afternoon as of late. You aren't going out today."

Vivienne exhaled. Her trick had backfired. "I really want to."

"I'll be careful, my lady," Dobkins said. "I'll make sure Lady Vivienne gets a hot bath with kerosene when we're back."

Mother narrowed her gaze. "No."

Why hadn't Vivienne mentioned another place? "Mother, please. I won't catch any diseases."

The footman remained next to the door, glancing from Mother to Vivienne.

Dobkins didn't move.

"Go to your room." Mother pointed upstairs. "It's for your own good."

"No. I want to take a walk. Please, Mark, open the door," she said to the footman.

"Don't open the door, Mark." Mother straightened. "Vivienne, you'll go upstairs."

"Mother—"

"Don't make me say it again. I've been patient with you, but enough is enough. The more time you spend outside, the greater the danger of getting sick."

"This is ridiculous." Vivienne gripped the satchel, shaking. It was the first time she'd argued with her mother, and it was affecting her body.

Dobkins shifted her weight, and Mark removed his hand from the knob.

Mother quivered too, her cheeks paling. "Please. I can't lose you, too. It's cold. If you leave the house, you'll get sick. I'm sure of it." Her voice rose to a high-pitched, hysterical note that didn't bode well.

"My lady, you might want to sit down." Dobkins took Mother's elbow.

Mother was shaking so hard her teeth chattered. "Adele fell sick on a day like this," she whispered, as Dobkins led her to the sitting room.

"It's all right, my lady. Lady Vivienne will stay home." Dobkins gave her an apologetic glance.

Vivienne sagged against the bannister. Fear of living wasn't living at all.

"Sorry, my lady." Mark bowed and left the hallway.

She rushed up the stairs, angry tears burning her eyes. Mother was suffering, but so was she.

Once in her room, she tossed her coat and hat on a chair and paced. Giving advice to Samuel seemed so easy, but she shouldn't talk. She lived in a cage, too. But something pinched inside her chest. Being angry with Mother because of Adele's death tore her heart apart.

She dropped the satchel as well. Was it wrong of her to wish for a normal life?

"My lady." Dobkins entered the bedroom and shut the door. "Your mother sent for the physician, and Mrs. Lewis is with her now. I'm so sorry."

"Why does she have to be scared of everything?"

"Shush, my lady, please lower your voice. Your mother is at her worst during her crises. Winter is always difficult for her."

Vivienne wiped her tears. "I hate it here."

"No, you don't. This is your home and your family, and we'll see Samuel tomorrow. We'll think about something, a good reason to leave. Changing the day of our visit won't make any difference."

"Samuel is waiting for us today."

"I'll send him a message. It's not a tragedy."

She sat on the edge of the bed, shoulders stooping.

Dobkins patted her head. "I feel sorry for Her Ladyship."

"So do I. And guilty. But I'm not sure we're helping her. We're making her condition worse."

If Samuel found the courage to be free, so should she.

The next time, she would flee. No matter what Mother said.

fourteen

The next day, Vivienne knocked on Captain Jackson's door with eagerness. Guilt buzzed in her ears like an annoying mosquito. The only reason why she'd left the house today was because the physician had given Mother a strong sleeping potion, and she was now in her bed, drugged and unconscious. Father had urged Vivienne to go, telling her not to worry and to enjoy herself, and she'd seized the opportunity

The way she'd been allowed to go out left a bitter taste in her mouth, with her mother drugged and in bed. But Samuel was her responsibility. The more time she spent with him, the more she wanted to be with him, especially after what had happened in the park.

She shouldn't have taken him out. Or maybe she should do it again.

The fear and pain in his eyes had affected her deeply. She'd orchestrated his rescue, and while she didn't regret anything, she wanted to help him through his recovery.

"Your mother will probably be asleep tomorrow as well," Dobkins said. "But we have exhausted the excuses."

"Samuel needs me." She knocked again.

"Exactly." Dobkins angled towards her. "You don't want your mother to forbid you to go out completely. Do as she asks you now and then."

"I always do as she asks me."

"This is a particular moment. This is one of her deep crises."

She was about to say that the particular moment had lasted for years when the door was flung open.

"You're early." The captain scowled.

"Would you please greet a lady properly?" Dobkins said.

The captain shot his gaze skywards. "Please do come in."

The scent of wood polish teased Vivienne's senses, distracting her from her worries. No more smell of cheroot.

"Samuel?" She rose on her tiptoes to see past the captain.

"He's getting ready. Getting ready takes a long time because he doesn't stop hand signing now. Always chatting. I have to tie his fingers to make him stop." He laughed, hooking his thumbs into his waistcoat.

Vivienne gasped, and Dobkins glared at him.

"It's a joke," he said. "I would never do that."

Samuel came out of the bedroom, dressed in a dark brown suit that made his lion eyes stand out. He beamed when he saw her, and she admitted to a little, fluttery feeling in her chest. He bowed, keeping his stare on her.

"What would you like to study today?" she asked. "History, geography? Or literature?"

"The Regent's Park."

The captain paused putting the kettle on. "Are you sure, lad?"

Samuel nodded. "I want to try again."

"Isn't it too early?" she asked.

He signed slowly. "I don't want to let too much time pass."

Judging by the silence, Dobkins and Captain Jackson shared Vivienne's worries. But then again, she'd told him she would help him overcome his fears.

"Let's go."

As all four of them walked along the pavement, her hand brushed Samuel's. Every time their fingers touched, he would catch a breath.

Warmth stirred in her as well, but with it came worry. He was a pure soul, and she didn't want to make a mistake and hurt him.

He signed but stopped. He tried again and stopped.

"What is it?" she asked.

He signed slowly, "May I hold your hand?" He blushed but didn't gaze away from her face.

She was about to say *yes* when Dobkins searched over her shoulder.

"Is something the matter?" the captain asked.

"I thought I saw a man following us, and when I stared at him, he quickly turned around that corner." She pointed at the street.

"I'll check," the captain said.

"It might be nothing." Dobkins didn't sound convinced.

"Stay here." The captain strode towards the corner.

Samuel gripped her hand tightly. His chest rose and fell quickly. Tension caused his neck muscles to stand out.

She held his hand in both of hers. "It may be nothing. Don't worry. And no one would ever recognise you."

"I'm worried."

"So am I, but whatever happens, you have us now. We won't let anyone hurt you. Stay optimistic."

He shifted his weight as if ready to bolt away.

When the captain walked back to them at a rather slow gait, Samuel released a breath.

"I didn't see anyone." Captain Jackson kept searching the street.

"I was mistaken then." Dobkins gazed around, too. "I'm too jittery."

"No, you have sharp eyes." The captain tipped his hat at her, and she smiled.

Vivienne exchanged a glance with Samuel. Captain Jackson paying a compliment to Dobkins? Interesting.

"Perhaps it was a footpad who changed his mind." The captain clapped Samuel's shoulder. "I won't let anyone hurt you. I promise."

The deep affection the captain showed for Samuel was touching.

As they resumed walking towards the park, Vivienne wrapped her scarf more tightly around her neck. A chilly wind blew from the north, carrying the promise of snow. Dark brown and red leaves littered the path in the park, and the trees swayed their skeletal branches towards the grey sky.

Samuel stopped in the middle of the gravel path and tilted his head towards the golden-brown canopy of an oak tree.

"Beautiful, isn't it?" she said.

He seized a red leaf floating towards the ground. "I feel like I'm inside a painting I've looked at for a long time. I have loved autumn when the leaves turned red and float to the ground. I looked outside and wanted to be part of it."

"Part of it?"

He released the leaf. "Being a beautiful leaf, floating in a golden world. It's silly, isn't it?"

"No." She held his hand again. "I understand you. You were locked in a small world and that leaf was outside your small world, freely flowing."

She and Samuel sat on a bench in a quiet corner surrounded by evergreen bushes that protected them from the wind. The captain and Dobkins were busy feeding pieces of leftover vegetables to the geese at the Boating Lake.

Not far from them, a woman played with a toddler and a large, colourful ball. The child's arms weren't long enough to embrace the ball fully, so he fell and rolled with it, laughing. The mother scooped him up and scattered kisses on his chubby cheeks.

Samuel stared at them with sad eyes.

She touched his hand. His knuckles weren't as rough and calloused as they'd been weeks ago. His skin wasn't soft, but not hardened either, and had a healthier, rosier colour.

"Why are you so forlorn? You can talk to me if you want."

"I don't remember having ever been kissed. Maybe my parents kissed me, but I don't remember them, and when I was with the circus, no one ever got close to me unless it was Murdock or Cade, and that was to punish me. I don't remember anyone ever hugging me, either." He glanced at her hand. "You're the first person who has freely touched me for no reason. The captain is the first one who has hugged me. I wonder how it feels to be kissed."

He had never received a kiss.

Emotion tightened her throat because Samuel had known nothing but violence and ridicule all his life. Her mother might be anxious and controlling, but she cared about Vivienne, and Dobkins had always shown care, love, and affection to her. Father, as busy as he was, had always been wonderful to her. She'd grown up surrounded by love and comfort. Instead, Samuel had been lonely and scared for years.

She couldn't comprehend the extent of his pain but she could feel it.

She inched closer to him, waiting for him to acknowledge her. She signed instead of talking because it was more intimate. "May I give you a kiss?"

Shock flashed across his amber eyes, but then he nodded.

She checked Dobkins wasn't looking before moving closer. Her lips were an inch from his face. His warmth caressed her.

They both stilled for a moment before she kissed his cheek. She pressed her lips to his skin, finding it surprisingly soft and smooth. She lingered but a moment, catching a whiff of his scent, something fresh and pungent like bergamot.

When she moved back from him, it was as if the air between them had permanently changed, filled with tenderness.

He brought a hand up to cover the spot she'd kissed. His lips parted, and his eyes became larger. A flush coloured his cheeks, and even his lips reddened.

Had she shocked him? Embarrassed him? Maybe she'd been too bold. She ought to remember he lacked her life experiences.

"Are you all right?" she signed.

He nodded but didn't meet her gaze. Moments passed, and he didn't say anything.

Staring at the lake, he signed slowly. "It was the most beautiful moment of my life. If I ever start to panic again, it'll be my happy, precious memory."

Oddly enough, it would be hers, too.

fifteen

Samuel had a new reason not to sleep at night, but for once, it wasn't a bad memory or fear to keep him awake. Vivienne's kiss burned on his cheek as if she'd branded him. A week had passed since the kiss, and he wondered how it would feel to kiss her, if she wanted to.

Since he'd recovered, he now slept on the sofa in the main room. Captain Jackson had protested, but while Samuel had never slept in a bed, the sofa was a luxury, and he was a poor sleeper anyway.

Dawn was blushing the sky when he brewed some strong tea. Everything around him reminded him of Vivienne—the pink clouds were similar to her lips, the frost on the window shone like her eyes, and even the blast from a furnace reminded him of how his heart pounded when she was close to him. Her presence in his mind was a welcome change from his dark thoughts.

"Tea. Good lad." Captain Jackson yawned, coming out of the bedroom. "I'm ravenous."

Samuel buttered his slice of bread absentmindedly, even though butter was his favourite new food.

How his life had changed in the past months amazed him.

He'd gone from living in a cage to eating butter for breakfast and having been kissed. His first kiss.

The captain watched him from over the rim of his cup. "What's wrong?"

He arched his brow. "Nothing."

"Rubbish." The captain put aside his plate. "You have a distracted gaze and keep flushing. Are you running a fever?"

Before Samuel could sign anything, the captain put a hand on his forehead.

"Are you having a relapse?" The captain placed his thumbs under Samuel's eyes and pulled down the lower eyelids. "Relapse is normal if it happens, but you must tell me how you feel."

"I'm fine." He blinked.

"You aren't wolfing down everything as usual. Is your stomach upset?"

Samuel smiled. "No. I'm fine."

The captain studied him. "If it's not a disease then it's love, which is the same thing."

Love? Samuel rubbed his chest. He had no idea if the flicker in his chest was love.

"Samuel, listen to me." Captain Jackson's serious tone worried him. "I understand how you feel. You left a horrible situation where you experienced only fear and abuse. We are the first people who care for you. Anyone would feel confused."

He didn't see where the captain was going.

"But I have to be brutal. Lady Vivienne is the daughter of an earl. After her Season, she will probably have a queue of suitors, all wealthy men or aristocratic gentlemen, who wish to marry her."

Now he saw where the captain was going.

"She's sweet and pretty, and she's the first young woman who spends time with you. It's normal to...feel something for her. But after all the horrible things that happened to you, I don't want you to have any illusions about this matter. Once you're completely recovered, and you find a job, which I hope you will, she'll live her aristocratic life without us. Hell, if she marries a toff, she won't be allowed to spend time with us. Horrible, yes, but that's how society works."

Samuel hunched his shoulders and stared at his tea. Of course, Vivienne had a life full of opportunities and engagements that had nothing to do with him. His life had truly begun a few months ago. He couldn't expect her to dedicate more time to him than she'd already done.

"I'm not telling you that to hurt you." Captain Jackson searched his face. "It's the opposite. But the reality of our society can't be ignored. And..." He paused, scratching his beard. "Unfortunately, people don't trust someone who can't talk. They won't accept you easily."

He nodded. He should be grateful for being free, but if that was his future, then he would enjoy his time with Vivienne as much as possible. He would need the good memories for the days to come.

When she arrived for one of their frequent walks at The Regent's Park, a riot of emotions thickened his throat.

"Would you like to go to the lake?" he asked.

"No, sorry. I have a dinner party tonight, and I need to get ready. I came only for a quick walk."

"Is it a fancy party?"

"It is. Father ordered a Worth gown for me. It's golden and white with pink roses." She looked radiant. "Mother didn't want me to go, didn't want anyone to go, but Father insisted."

"Why didn't your mother want you to go?"

"She's recovering from one of her crises. The physician gave her Godfrey's Cordial."

"I know what it is." He'd drunk gallons of the sweet, syrupy potion that worked as a powerful sedative.

She exhaled, and her breath fogged in the cold air. "It pains me seeing her like that, weak, defeated, and sleeping all day. Father hates it when Mother takes sedatives, but he wants her to come tonight as well. He says she needs to get out more and that I need to make new friends, and I agree."

He knew why. As the captain had said, she would find a suitor soon, and she might be tired of being in the company of a frightened man who couldn't talk. "You must look lovely in this new gown. I would love to see you."

She trapped her bottom lip between her teeth before saying, "We could meet after the party. I can sneak out of the house somehow and come to the flat."

No, he didn't like the idea. She already took too many risks to see him. He'd seen shady people walking down the street under the window at night, and a couple of times, a brawl had started, waking up the whole neighbourhood.

"Or I could come to you," he said.

"Wouldn't it be too dangerous? What if someone sees you around my house at night and warns the household?"

"I'll be careful. I've been cooped up in the captain's house for months. Aside from the walks in the park, I don't leave the house." While he was grateful for everything Captain Jackson had done for him, he wouldn't mind a bit of an adventure. "I'll ask Captain Jackson to escort me to your house, but once I'm there? How can I see you?"

She craned her neck towards Dobkins and the captain. "There's a tree right outside my window. You could climb it, and if I leave the window open, you'll be able to jump into my bedroom easily, but it might be too dangerous for you."

Actually, no. If there was one thing he was good at, it was climbing. Cade had often forced him to perform while climbing the cage or the ropes to impress the audience.

"I lived in a circus. Climbing a tree won't be a problem, and I'm curious to see where you live." He must have said something offensive because she knit her eyebrows.

"I live in Mayfair," she said as if expecting a reaction from him.

"I'm sure it's a beautiful place."

"Yes, it is." Her worried tone left him puzzled.

AFTER THE PROMENADE in the park, Vivienne walked back to the flat, chatting with Samuel about the different types of social engagements.

He dedicated all his attention to her. "So there are dinner parties, evening parties, afternoon parties, garden parties, and tea parties...did I forget something?"

"Just one. I love balls the most." She twirled, and he followed her with his gaze.

"You must teach me how to dance."

"I will." She hooked her arm through his, and he beamed at her.

Dobkins cleared her throat, and even the captain grumbled.

Vivienne was about to leave Samuel at the flat to hail a cab home when the captain called her.

"A word, my lady?" His too-polite tone didn't bode well. "I'll escort you to the high street."

"What's wrong?" Dobkins said.

"Nothing." The captain stuck his head inside the flat. "Samuel, I'll be back in a moment. Put the kettle on, will you?"

"What is it?" She waved at Samuel who was looking at her from the window.

The captain closed the door behind him and started to walk. "What is this madness?"

"What?"

"Samuel told me you invited him to see you tonight after you return from your dinner party. He mentioned climbing a tree to reach your window."

"My lady!" Dobkins gasped.

Vivienne's face warmed. "Well, yes. He wished to see me wearing my new evening gown, and I offered to come here after the dinner party, but he thought it too dangerous and said he preferred to come and see Mayfair, where I live."

"It is dangerous. Both are too dangerous," the captain said at the same time as Dobkins said, "Inappropriate."

"I told him it could be dangerous, but he insisted, and he said he'd been cooped up in the flat for too long. I agree."

The captain frowned. "He's been cooped up in the flat for a damn good reason."

"Language," Dobkins said.

"Cade and Murdock left," Vivienne said. "The police aren't patrolling the streets anymore, and Samuel looks completely different."

"Sod Murdock. I was referring to his mind." The captain put a hand on his chest. "And heart. I know the chance that Murdock and Cade could find him is low, but Samuel is vulnerable to other types of dangers."

She rolled her bottom lip between her teeth. The captain was exaggerating.

"Lady Vivienne," Captain Jackson started patiently, "we know your future and his future travel in two different directions. With no family, connections, or status, not to mention with no voice, the best he can hope for is to work at the docks or on a building site. Good professions, but not enough for an earl's daughter. Officially, he doesn't exist. Tell me, what are his chances of spending time with an earl's daughter?"

She wrung her hands. "You're too grim. I could help him find employment in my house."

"Great. Wonderful. And then what? Will you take tea with the stable hand?" He inched closer. "How do you think he would feel when you marry a toff? That young man is quite smitten with you. Hasn't he suffered enough?"

"Captain," Dobkins said. "Lady Vivienne has no intention of hurting Samuel. Don't throw accusations."

"Lady Vivienne might hurt Samuel unintentionally. We often forget how different he is from us."

She rubbed her brow. "That's a good point." Although who knew what would happen? She was sure they would find a way to be happy.

"Put yourself in his shoes." The captain's tone became gentler. "He doesn't know much about love and affection, and then he meets you, pretty, kind, and caring. I would say it's inevitable that he falls for you, and that he falls hard."

"I care for him as well," she whispered.

"That's lovely, but for his own sake, let's end the feeling there."

"I agree with the captain," Dobkins said. "Samuel wouldn't understand why he can't see you if things between you two grow into something impossible."

She acknowledged the bitter taste of sadness in her mouth. "Exactly for that reason, I want my days with him to be filled with good experiences. He wants to see me, and I think he needs a distraction from his confinement and to see something else other than the park. Please, just for this once, will you let him go? He needs to explore London. Keeping him confined in the flat won't do him any good."

Captain Jackson exhaled. "Climbing at night into a lady's bedroom isn't the right way to start knowing London better."

Dobkins was flustered. "I agree. Again. I'm worried."

"You'll go with him." Vivienne stopped walking. "You know Mayfair well. If something worries you, and you think you should return home, then by all means, you'll leave. But Samuel needs something exciting to look forward to."

"Yes, getting arrested for trespassing is thrilling." The captain scoffed.

Dobkins chuckled but composed herself immediately.

"I'm sure you'll understand if the situation is dangerous or not," Vivienne said. "Dobkins could make sure the draperies on the ground-floor windows are well shut. Lest someone see him."

Dobkins didn't look pleased.

"Just this once," she insisted.

The captain worked his jaw. "At the first sign of trouble, I'll take him home."

She smiled. "Thank you."

"But please, keep in mind what I have said. He's too fragile. Another blow would shatter him."

sixteen

After five hours of preparations, which included a bath, styling her hair in a complicated chignon, and donning her new Worth gown, Vivienne was finally ready for the dinner party.

"You look lovely, my lady," Dobkins said, draping the train nicely.

The ivory-coloured silk enhanced Vivienne's eyes, and the coiffure left a few curls falling over her lightly rouged cheeks. Dobkins helped her arrange a delicate shawl on her shoulders.

Mother entered the bedroom; her black gown was in stark contrast to her pale cheeks.

"How are you feeling?" A high note crept into Vivienne's tone.

"Better." Mother's voice sounded drowsy. "So we're all going."

"It'll be a lovely evening."

No reaction changed Mother's features. "Remember to apply the sage salve under your nose. It kills germs as you breathe."

"Yes, Mother."

"I'll ask Lady Acton to give you a seat close to the fireplace. The fire will keep the air around you clean."

Where did Mother get those ideas from? "Of course."

"Your hair is lovely, and—" Mother frowned, regaining some of her colour. "Why aren't you wearing your diamond bracelet? I asked Gilbert to take it from the strong room."

"And I told him there was no need. I lost it."

Instant shock flashed across Mother's face. Finally, a reaction. "Excuse me?"

"I wore it while I was riding, and it must have fallen without me realising it." She hoped her voice didn't quiver too much.

"Why didn't you tell me?"

"I hoped to find it. I've been searching the park ever since."

Mother paled again and sat on the edge of the bed, gathering her black gown around her. "Is that why you went to the park every day?"

"I'm sorry."

"You put your life in danger for a bracelet." Mother reached out to take her hand. "Your health is more important than a diamond bracelet. I could have sent someone to search the park. You didn't need to breathe that poisonous air."

It was with an effort that she remained silent. Her instinct was to shake Mother by the shoulders and beg her to stop believing every stupid claim the quacks she listened to said.

"There's no evidence the air in the park is poisonous." Her tone sounded low.

Mother was flustered but didn't argue. A good sign, perhaps?

A half an hour later, the drive in the carriage was a quiet one, with Mother holding the silver box for dear life.

Father held Mother's hand. "Why don't you put the box away, darling?"

"Why do you always ask me to do that? I don't want to get rid of it."

"You can't spend the evening with that box in your hands."

Mother clenched the box more tightly.

"And couldn't you wear something else other than black?" He rubbed the spot between his eyebrows.

Mother pressed her lips together, and a silent tear slid down her cheek.

As much as Vivienne agreed with Father, seeing Mother so upset broke her heart. She squeezed Mother's hand, but Mother didn't acknowledge her as if there were an invisible barrier between them, as if Mother were trapped in her own world of pain, unreachable.

"I didn't want to come," Mother whispered.

"You need to spend less time listening to doctors and more time with the living." The furrows between his eyebrows deepened.

They remained silent for the rest of the drive.

Lord Acton's house swept into view when they turned a corner. Lights glowed around it and from within, turning it into a shiny, giant diamond. Despite herself, she stared up at the magical building in awe.

A short queue of carriages slowed them down. Through the window she saw the many footmen who helped the arriving guests from their carriages and up a flight of stairs covered by a red carpet.

"It's beautiful," she whispered.

Father tugged at her gloved hand. "I would like to see you meet someone you like. Lord Acton's son is a clever young man, and there are other gentlemen I would like you to meet."

"Oh, yes, of course." She didn't sound enthusiastic to her own ears.

Under other circumstances, she would have enjoyed meeting new people, but since Samuel was in her life...Captain Jackson's words echoed in her mind.

She still secretly believed they would find a way to be together, but Samuel's peace of mind and health were more important.

Mother wiped her tears discreetly. "It's too early for Vivienne to have a suitor."

"Not if she wishes to have one," he said.

"Please don't argue." She took one each of her parent's hands in her own. "Not tonight."

He patted her cheek, and Mother nodded.

It took them half an hour to actually enter the drawing room for drinks before dinner. Between the slog of the carriages, the crowded entry hall, a trip to the powder room to refresh her hair and gown, and the endless introductions and greetings, she was exhausted before she held a drink in her hand.

As her gaze swept around the wide room, she spotted several young women her age next to their eager mamas.

She smiled at each introduction although Mother's black gown attracted a lot of attention and grim comments.

Lady Acton gave Mother an assessing glance, lingering on the black gown. "Jane, it's a pleasure to see you again."

Mother jutted her chin out. "Mary."

"Many guests tonight," Father said in a cheerful tone. "I don't believe I know the gentleman over there."

"Oh, he's a new friend of mine. Dr. Tucker." Lady Acton stopped a passing footman. "Ask Dr. Tucker to come over here."

Vivienne groaned inwardly. Not another blasted doctor.

Dr. Tucker walked over to them, limping badly. His beady black eyes didn't reassure her at all.

The light from the chandelier glinted off his bald head when he bowed. "My lady."

Lady Acton beamed. "Lord and Lady Huntington, and their daughter Lady Vivienne, this is Dr. Robert Tucker. He's recently arrived in London from overseas, but has quickly become the favourite physician of many of my friends."

"My ladies, my lord." Dr. Tucker's gaze lingered on her for a brief moment.

Mother was staring at the physician with interest.

"Dr. Tucker has worked at some the most prestigious clinics on the Continent," Lady Acton said. "He's an expert in medicinal herbs and homeopathic medicine from the Americas to the Far East. There's nothing he can't cure."

Vivienne exchanged a desolate glance with her father. She could bet he was thinking the same as she.

They'd just met Mother's new obsession.

FOR THE WHOLE DINNER, Vivienne hadn't stopped thinking about Samuel's visit. At first, she'd agreed with enthusiasm to his proposal and defended it against Captain Jackson's complaints. Walking at night might be dangerous for him, but the captain would protect him, and she had no doubt he was a good climber.

But now, as she sat on the edge of her bed, waiting, the risks of Samuel being caught climbing to her room were real.

Also, she worried about what he would think of her opulent house. Huntington Hall had belonged to a few generations of Huntington earls; it was loaded with precious carpets, porcelain vases, and priceless paintings. Mayfair was the area where dukes and earls lived...and for the first time in her life, she'd been self-conscious of that.

What if Samuel became overwhelmed when he saw the imposing, white-walled houses, the manicured gardens, and the many tall windows? She looked down. The Worth gown was lovely, one of her best, but it looked ridiculously extravagant now.

He would think she was too different from him, that they came from two different worlds, which was true; he would think they shouldn't see each other.

She sat on the edge of her bed in a froth of ivory-and-golden silk and massaged her temples. Too many thoughts crammed her brain at the same time. Her emotions pulled her in two different directions. She wanted it all—to be with Samuel and keep her place in society, which was selfish of her. Samuel's happiness was more important than anything else. If staying close to her caused him pain, then she would respect whatever he chose to do.

"I'll help you undress, my lady," the maid said.

"No, not now. You may retire. Thank you." She glanced at the window, wondering if Samuel was already there.

The maid dropped a quick curtsy, narrowing her gaze, likely upset because she would need to brush and press the gown the next morning while she wanted to put it away now.

"Anne."

The maid paused at the door. "My lady?"

"I'll hang up the gown."

The maid gave her a slight smile, acknowledging Vivienne had read her mind. "Thank you, my lady." And she closed the door.

Vivienne crossed the room and locked the door. She'd asked Dobkins not to be present. Nothing untoward would happen, and the captain would wait for Samuel on the street.

But her time spent with Samuel was precious. She meant to give him as many good moments as she could.

A rock pinged against the glass.

She opened the window, shivering as the cold winter night caused her skin to pebble. The clouds hid the moon, so she stuck her head out.

"Samuel?" she whispered.

When he waved from the tree branch right in front of her, she suppressed a gasp.

He was almost invisible in his dark clothes.

She stepped aside to let him enter, and he landed on the floor with a soft swoosh.

It was too late to change her mind.

seventeen

Samuel had underestimated the strength the climb would have required and the effect of the freezing night on his body. But the discomfort was completely forgotten when he landed in Vivienne's room and stared at her.

Her raven hair was styled in curls, forming small roses around her head. The golden-and-white gown hugged her lovely waist, to give way to a flowing skirt with many folds. Small silken sleeves and large ribbons covered her shoulders. The neckline left her collarbone bare. The pink ribbons and embroidered roses matched the colour of her lips.

But what left him breathless was the shiny golden fabric. It made her skin glow as if she were a fairy, and glittering sparks flickered every time she moved.

"What do you think?" She twirled around, and the skirt lifted a few inches, showing her slender ankles, silk slippers, and white stockings.

What did he think? He was stunned. He'd never seen anything more beautiful. She looked like starlight wrapped in silk.

"Too much?" She smoothed down her skirt. "Perhaps it's too extravagant."

He swallowed hard. "You look so beautiful."

The word couldn't express how lovely she was.

She blushed, and it suited her. "It took me hours to get ready. Ridiculous."

"All worth it."

She averted her gaze, her eyelashes long and thick and dark as night. "This is my bedroom." She stretched out an arm.

Her bedroom was twice the size of Captain Jackson's flat. The four-poster bed had to be huge, but it looked tiny in the wide room. He wasn't an expert, but the furniture and ornaments had to be worth a small fortune. The shiny fabric of the bed curtains had to be expensive as well.

Now he understood Captain Jackson's words better. They were from different worlds.

"Did you have problems coming here?" she asked.

He shook his head and signed. "But I'll have problems leaving."

She tilted her head, and a dark curl slipped down the curve of her cheek. "Really?"

He hesitated. "I don't want to leave."

"Then don't." She sounded damn serious, and he was tempted to oblige.

Her tone killed the playful atmosphere from a moment ago.

"The captain is waiting nearby."

"Oh, I forgot," she said quietly.

They stood next to the window, staring at each other in the warm glow of the lamps until he either gathered the courage to tell her what he wanted or left. The clouds shifted, letting in the pale moonlight. Her eyes and gown were lit with tiny diamonds, and he couldn't contain himself any longer.

"May I kiss you?" he finally asked the question that had tormented him for days on end.

She stooped her shoulders, and her inner glow seemed to dwindle. "Samuel..."

"Sorry, I shouldn't have asked."

"No, it's that..." She took a few deep breaths. "I'm worried about you. I don't know what will happen to us. We can't meet in secret forever, and soon you won't need me to learn new subjects."

"I'll always need you." His words must have shocked her because her lips parted. "But I understand what you mean. We don't belong together."

"We do. But I don't know how, and I don't want you to get hurt."

A flare of frustration made him huff. "I'm not the fragile, poor soul you think I am. I appreciate your concern, but I'm not an idiot. I might not know a lot of the world, but even I understand you're the daughter of an earl whose future doesn't involve me."

"It's not fair."

"Trust me, I know a thing or two about unfairness."

She exhaled. "You're right."

He wasn't finished. "I'm not deluded. I know I still need everyone's help to understand the world, but I don't need you to protect me from my feelings. I'm not scared of the pain. I'm scared of having regrets."

She raised her sapphire eyes to him.

"That's why I asked you if I could kiss you." He slowed his fingers. "But I understand if you don't want a kiss from me. I'm so beneath you—"

"Don't say that. You aren't beneath anyone." Then she whispered, "Yes."

"Yes, what?"

"I want a kiss."

"Really?"

"Yes."

His world brightened like the dawn.

She moved closer, her dress swishing with each step. He took a deep breath and traced a fingertip over her cheek, wondering if the touch affected her as much as it affected him. Because he was shivering with unfamiliar emotions.

He dipped his head and kissed her cheek as gently as he could. She smelled of oranges and elegance, of starlight and happiness. The tremor going through him became an overwhelming sensation of joy he'd rarely experienced. Her cheek felt soft and warm under his quivering lips.

When he stepped back, he was surprised to find her frowning. A delicate crease appeared between her eyebrows.

"You didn't like it," he signed, forcing himself not to slouch.

"It's not that. It was very sweet." She lowered her gaze. "I'm glad you have another good memory to think of in a dark moment."

He wanted to run his fingers over her shoulders, neck, and cheeks and get lost in her scent and softness, but he was risking everything standing there, and Captain Jackson was waiting for him in the street below.

"Did you like it?" she asked, and put a hand on his chest, sending shivers through his body.

He could only nod because the shock of her touch was too great for him to sign.

A veil of sadness clouded her eyes. "I've never met anyone like you. You're different from the young men I know."

The men she knew were normal people. His mind was as broken as his voice box.

"You're..." He started to sign but paused, searching for the right words. "You're happiness and freedom." He winced inwardly. He should have told her how beautiful she was.

She hugged him, resting her head on his chest. He wrapped his arms around her awkwardly. His pulse thundered again.

She cleared her throat. "Samuel—"

A soft whistle came from the street. Captain Jackson was calling him.

"I have to go." Never had moving his fingers been so devastatingly painful.

The sadness didn't leave her face. "I'll see you soon." She followed him to the open window.

He was on the branch a heartbeat later and he paused, looking back at her for a shared moment. When he climbed down the tree, he left, carrying with him not her sad eyes but the feeling of his lips on her silky cheek and the lingering scent of her, so sweet, standing in her pretty room.

eighteen

Vivienne's lessons with the dance master had always been enjoyable and she had awaited them with anticipation until that day. Especially since Mother was watching the class from a corner.

Vivienne's feet had become clumsy all of a sudden. Her legs couldn't keep the tempo. Her mind was distracted. No matter how hard she tried to focus on the steps, her thoughts drifted to Samuel and the kiss—the chaste, sweet kiss they'd shared in the quiet of her room. If Mother knew about it, she would send Vivienne away and lock her up in the nearest, most hygienic convent she could find.

When Samuel had asked to kiss her, she'd thought he meant on the lips. She shouldn't have been disappointed, but she was. The kiss had been nice; but she'd wanted more. She'd been tempted to ask him to kiss her properly, but he'd looked so happy with the simple kiss, she hadn't wanted to overwhelm him.

If Captain Jackson knew about their innocent kiss, he would be disappointed. In a way, she was disappointed in herself. All her intentions of keeping Samuel safe had vanished the moment he'd kissed her cheek. But after he'd talked about regrets and being beneath her, she couldn't have ignored his request.

"With the left foot, Lady Vivienne," the master said.

She corrected the step but was out of time, and she made another mistake during the quick gallop; she tripped and almost fell on her face. To steady herself, she stumbled and tottered like a newborn calf.

Mother frowned. "Walker, please, I need a word with my daughter."

"My lady." The master bowed and left the piano.

"What's happening with you? You're stumbling all over the place," Mother asked. "Are you unwell?"

Vivienne caught her breath, leaning against the wall. "No. I'm fine. I'm a little tired."

"Anne told me you didn't let her help you undress last night."

Never a moment of peace.

"You're too often tired as of late, and distracted. You spent too much time outside."

She wiped the sweat from her forehead with a cloth.

"Are you warm? Do you have a fever?" Mother asked.

"No. Nothing is wrong."

"You look pale." Mother touched her forehead and neck. "I'm worried. Maybe you're too busy. The dinner party was exhausting. Your eyes are dark with fatigue. You need rest. I'll tell Walker the lesson ends here today. Go to your room and lie down." Mother left the room.

She thumped the wall behind her. Yes, the past few months had been challenging and tiring, and fewer engagements would give her more time to spend with Samuel. Their secret meetings couldn't go on forever.

Also, if a suitor wanted to court her, she wouldn't be able to see Samuel.

The thought crushed her chest.

Vivienne went up the stairs. Tired or not, she ought to be

more careful, or Mother would have another fit and forbid her to go out.

"Is something the matter? I thought you had dance lessons." Father stopped her in the corridor, lowering his glasses.

"I'm just a bit tired. I'm going to my room."

"Did your mother order you to?"

"Yes, I mean, no. I do feel a little out of sorts."

He narrowed his eyes so similar to hers. "Don't let your mother influence you. She sees diseases everywhere." He kissed her cheek. "Do you want me to talk to her?"

"No, it's fine. I'll lie down for a while."

When she entered her bedroom, she gazed at the window. A faint trace of bergamot lingered in the air, as did her doubts.

She lay in the bed face down. If her future had been decided and she'd accepted her fate, why did it hurt so much?

THAT AFTERNOON, after Vivienne rested and got ready to leave for the usual walk with Dobkins—ostensibly to go to the library— she found her mother at the base of the stairs, waiting for her.

In her black gown and under the dim lights of the hallway, Mother looked particularly gloomy.

"Is something the matter?" Vivienne asked, exchanging a glance with Dobkins.

"You aren't going anywhere today." Mother stretched out an arm towards the stairs. "You'll stay in your room and rest until you regain some colour."

"I'm full of energy. I just needed some rest."

Mother searched her face. "You've been busy all morning. Going out would be too much."

She wanted to see Samuel and tell him she'd enjoyed the kiss. She'd come to the conclusion she wanted a proper kiss. "I need a breath of fresh air."

"No." Mother's hands trembled. "You'll stay home until you're better."

"I want to go out."

"Not today. Please." Mother shook.

Not again. "I'm fine."

"It's too freezing today. There's frost everywhere. You might slip or catch a cold. And you look pale. You were not well during your dance lesson."

A comment on how she didn't have any symptoms of scarlet fever or anything else died a quick death in her mouth as Dobkins gave her the slightest nod.

Mother shivered and blinked a few times. "Please." Her broken voice hurt.

"I'll stay home," Vivienne said through clenched teeth. "Don't worry."

The last words were useless. Mother worried more frequently than she needed to breathe.

"Good. Good." Mother gripped her inseparable silver box.

"I'll do a few errands," Dobkins said. "Do you need anything, my lady?"

Mother touched Vivienne's wrist, checking her pulse. "Go to Harris's and buy a few vials of the primrose tonic to strengthen the blood."

Vivienne suppressed a sigh. That potion was a nostrum. But at least Mother hadn't sent for the physician.

Dobkins curtsied and left.

A weight pressed against Vivienne's chest when she went upstairs. She didn't want Mother to suffer from yet another crisis, but she didn't want to renounce her secret time with Samuel either.

She shut the door and removed her hat. The hatpin clinked against the floor.

From the moment she'd seen how strong and determined he

was to get his life back, she'd found all the rules of her life useless and burdensome.

Years ago, she'd looked forward to getting married. Marriage was the beginning of her life as the lady of the house, which meant having all the power. But as Mother had kept postponing her Season, she wondered if she could spend the rest of her life next to someone she didn't love, or worse, she didn't respect.

She could share a marriage with a gentleman who was her friend, but not with someone she had a low opinion of. She respected Samuel, and they were friends. He inspired her to fight for what she wanted.

She paced, hoping Samuel would understand and that he wouldn't think her absence had to do with their kiss.

The tree next to her window swayed its branches slowly in a sad dance. She sat on the stuffed seat next to the bay window.

Samuel had shown her that her life was more complicated than she thought.

Dusk was painting the sunset in dark tones when Dobkins returned. Vivienne shot up to her feet from the seat.

"Did you see him?"

"Yes. He was sorry not to see you. He gave me this for you." Dobkins handed her a folded piece of paper.

"Thank you." She waited for Dobkins to leave before opening the message.

His handwriting was all sharp angles and strong strokes. The message only said, '*Leave the window open, please.*'

She smiled for the first time that day.

nineteen

If Samuel didn't see Vivienne that night, he wouldn't sleep.

Seeing her had become a necessity, especially since he needed to understand if she was upset because of the kiss. Dobkins had simply said Vivienne's mother hadn't let her out, but perhaps she regretted having kissed him and decided not to see him anymore, or maybe she'd taken ill.

"This is madness," Captain Jackson said as they walked down the pavement next to him. "If you get caught in her room, there will be huge trouble."

"I'll be careful."

"Wonderful. I feel so much better now. Thank you."

"You're welcome."

The captain rolled his eyes. "That was sarcasm."

"Sarcasm. It's like lying."

"No, it's like realism." The captain shoved his hands in his pockets. "And it's bloody freezing."

They waited in a dark corner of the street until all the lights of the house had gone out.

"Don't be long," The captain grunted. "It's so cold my

bollocks have to be so blue and frozen we can hang them up on a Christmas tree."

He scowled. "Disgusting."

"Quick, lad."

He climbed the tree in a moment and leapt through the open window. Happiness burst in his chest. She wanted to see him.

"Samuel." Vivienne ran to him, and he caught her by the waist.

He meant to give her a quick hug, but the moment her arms were around his neck and her body was pressed against his, he couldn't let her go. She clung to him with desperation as if they hadn't seen each other in years.

He was hugging her. He couldn't believe she was in his arms. Hugging her had come naturally.

She stepped back from him. "I'm sorry I couldn't come. My mother believes I'm too tired. She worries about my health a lot."

"I missed you."

"Did you go to The Regent's Park?"

He raised his hands to sign. "It wasn't the same without you."

"I'm not sure my mother will let me out soon."

He caressed the top of her head, marvelling at how silky her hair was. "I thought you didn't come because of the kiss."

She flushed. "No, it wasn't the kiss."

She didn't add anything else, like '*Would you kiss me again?*' and he didn't want to be too insistent.

He stroked her cheek, happy to see her. "I'll leave before someone realises I'm here."

She nodded, lowering her gaze. "Of course."

He was about to get back to the tree when she took his hand. She didn't say anything, but her large eyes had a private conversation with his heart.

"Yes?" he asked when she didn't say anything.

"I'll find a way to see you tomorrow. I promise." She cupped his cheek, and he leant into her palm.

A sound like the hoot of an angry owl came from the street. Captain Jackson was growing impatient.

He kissed her hand before letting her go. She waved when he jumped on the tree. He went down slowly, thinking about going up again.

The emotions running through him turned cold when he was on the pavement, heading home with a brooding Captain.

What could he possibly offer to a lady like Vivienne?

He didn't have a legal name, and Murdock was likely searching for him. And she was used to living in a beautiful house and wearing expensive gowns.

He pulled the collar of his jacket up to fend off the chilly wind.

For the cold gripping his heart, there was nothing he could do.

Vivienne had had enough of drinking useless potions and resting to recover from a disease she didn't have. But Mother had decided she needed to rest more, claiming her complexion wasn't healthy.

In truth, she'd stayed up until late the other night after Samuel had left her bedroom. As she was sitting in her bedroom in front of the window, her thoughts kept going back and forth; one minute, she just wanted to live the moment with him without caring about the future; the next, she was too scared to hurt him as the captain had warned. Or to hurt herself.

"How do you feel today?" Mother tucked a shawl around her shoulders.

"More rested than yesterday."

"Shall I send for more primrose potion?"

"No need. Truly, I feel rested and well."

"It's very cold today. The pavements are frosted, and the Serpentine is frozen, and even the Boating Lake in The Regent's Park is solid ice. People are ice skating on it. Reckless."

Yes, but it was boiling in her room. The fire had been going on for hours. Mother had added more blankets to the bed, and Vivienne wore so many layers her shoulders stooped under their weight.

If she stayed in bed one more day, she would truly fall ill from the lack of sunshine, air, and activity.

"I have to leave this afternoon," Mother said. "I have an appointment with Dr. Tucker. He's quite brilliant and so knowledgeable."

Thank goodness.

"Will you be all right?" Mother asked.

"Yes. Don't worry. Enjoy your afternoon."

"I'll be back as soon as possible."

"I'm not dying!" She regretted her words the moment they left her lips.

Mother paled and seemed to have aged years in seconds. Her eyes clouded with hurt.

Vivienne rubbed her face. "I didn't mean to raise my voice."

Mother stared at the floor. "I only care about you."

How could she say, '*You're smothering me*' without sounding harsh? "You must trust me when I say I'm fine, and you must stop believing everything around us is trying to kill us."

"I'll see you later."

Vivienne pressed two fingers to her temples after Mother left. Mother's worry was understandable, mostly, but Vivienne should be free to live her life without being constantly stifled by her mother's fears. No one else in the family had fallen ill when Adele had contracted the scarlet fever. Surely that meant something.

Well, if Vivienne spent another day in her stifling bedroom, drinking that horrible potion, she would go mad. She changed into the dress she used to take long walks and put on a pair of thick boots. The sound of the carriage leaving brought her so much relief she felt guilty.

She left her bedroom and went downstairs with quick steps, enjoying the exercise.

"Dobkins?" she called.

Mark, the footman, came out of a door. "My lady, Dobkins is out for an errand."

"I need my coat, and maybe Anne can come with me?" She gazed out of the frosted window, anticipating the bite of the crisp air. She would find an excuse to tell Anne about seeing Samuel.

"I'm sorry, my lady, but the countess left us strict instructions. You can't go out today."

She whipped her head towards him. "Excuse me?"

"My apologies. We have our orders."

"Where's my father?" She closed her fists.

"I'm afraid he isn't home."

"I'm trapped in my own house."

Mark didn't say anything.

"It's not fair."

"Would you like a cup of tea, my lady?"

"No, thank you." She stomped back upstairs, angry tears blurring her vision.

The situation was her fault. She should have never pandered to Mother's whims and delusions. Her captivity was the result of years of saying *yes*.

She paced across the bedroom, nervous energy fuelling her anger. Seeing Samuel was only part of the reason she wanted to leave her house. She needed to get out.

The tree branches swayed as if wanting her attention. She paused in front of the window. How difficult could it be to climb down a tree?

A chilling gust froze her skin when she opened the window. Her breath turned into mist. The old oak tree had seemed a lot closer a moment ago. Perhaps she should find another way to leave her room.

No, there wasn't another way. The rear door would be filled

with maids and footmen at this time of the day, and when Mother was in that panicked state, even Dobkins never wanted to disobey her.

After getting her coat, hat, and gloves, she rubbed her hands and grabbed the closest tree branch before putting a foot on the windowsill. Without looking down, she hauled herself up and straddled the branch. Her heart leapt to her throat when she wobbled. But so far, so good.

Moving backwards while gripping the branch, she lowered herself. It was easier than she'd thought, like riding a horse. The ground didn't look far at all. Her foot slipped on a frozen spot on the bark, and she slid down at an alarming speed.

She couldn't stop a scream as she rushed down the tree, trying to slow her descent by grabbing the branches. She hit the ground with her foot before landing on her rear. A shot of pain went up her back and leg, but the worst thing was Mark sticking his head out of a window.

He stared at her in shock. "My lady?"

Oh, no. She hadn't risked breaking her neck to get caught.

She sprang up and raced along the pavement as fast as her throbbing ankle allowed. She must have twisted it.

Mark was tall and quick, but by the time he left the house, she had turned a corner, then another, till reached the high road and could hail the first hackney she saw.

Wheezing, she sagged in the seat, half-smiling and half-wincing. The escape had thrilled her, but her rear burned and her ankle throbbed. Not to mention Mother would punish her when she returned home. She was aware of that. But what was the difference between before or after her escape?

From now on, she would go against Mother more. She wanted to prove she was healthy and that Mother exaggerated her fears.

Vivienne was officially a rebel now.

twenty

Samuel was both happy and worried to see Vivienne.

She was alone, dishevelled, cheeks red, and limping, but she was smiling as she told him about her adventure to sneak out of her house against her mother's will and come to him.

Her enthusiasm was commendable, but she was going to be in trouble.

"…I fell and hurt my ankle, but I managed to escape from the footman." She chuckled. "And I felt so free!"

He scratched his chin. Seeing her so delighted was wonderful, but the idea of her sneaking out of her house, getting almost caught, and hurting herself left him conflicted.

She brushed a lock of hair from her flushed face. "Aren't you happy to see me?"

"I am, but you shouldn't have escaped like that. It was dangerous. You could have hurt yourself more seriously. Your mother will be furious. I've climbed that tree. It's not simple."

She pressed her lips in a flat line. "I thought you would understand why I did it. I want to be free and do what I want. You, more than everyone else, should appreciate that. I'm tired of following Mother's orders. Everyone in my house believes her hysterics are to be tolerated. I think not. If we keep doing whatever she says when she's in one of her crises, she'll never get better. I don't want to live like a prisoner, only because she constantly fears I might get sick."

"Yes, but...you won't achieve anything by defying your mother. She'll grow more worried. And you hurt yourself."

She frowned. "Fine. I'll go back home."

He exhaled. "Don't be so dramatic. I appreciate your presence. I'm worried."

"Everyone is worried, apparently." She shuffled her injured foot.

"Your mother won't understand why you left." He took her hand. "Don't be angry with me."

"How could I? I'd better go home anyway."

"I'll escort you."

The cold air chilled his lungs with each breath he took as they walked towards the high road to catch a cab to Mayfair. Patches of dirty snow made the pavement slippery, and frost covered the windows, street lamps, and benches.

He nudged her with his elbow. "Don't be angry."

"I'm not. You're right. Escaping like that was foolish." She winced every time she put weight on her right ankle.

"Does it hurt a lot?"

"I think it's sprained. At first, it wasn't that bad, but now it really hurts."

"Let me help you." He put an arm around her waist and helped her walk.

She leant against him, and warmth crawled up his neck. With her next to him, his fears were reduced to slight worries.

In the distance, the treetops in The Regent's Park were covered with snow, and the sunlight glinted off the white caps.

"I heard the lake in the park is frozen. People ice skate on it." She sighed. "I would love to. If my ankle heals quickly, we should go."

As they walked close to the entrance to the park, a sudden knot tightened in his stomach. His heart was pounding hard enough to drown out the noises from the street.

Cade, dressed in a dark coat, stood under a tree, watching the street with his keen eyes.

Samuel gripped Vivienne more tightly. Fear surged back to its full strength.

"What is it?" she asked.

"Over there," he signed slowly as if whispering. "The man with the top hat under that tree."

She drew in a breath. "Isn't he the man who presented the tour of the curiosities?"

"Yes, it's Cade. Murdock's right hand."

"Let's turn around and head for the park. We'll cross it and take a cab or an omnibus once on the other side."

A shiver rushed through him. His mouth grew dry, and his head felt light.

Not now. Not ever. He didn't want to return to the circus.

Cade's presence in London couldn't be a coincidence. He was Murdock's bloodhound, there to find Samuel. There wasn't any other explanation.

When Samuel had escaped years back, Cade had been the one to catch him.

"Stay calm." She stroked his arm. "He didn't see us, and even if he did, he wouldn't recognise you."

He wasn't so sure. The circus had left London a while ago, yet Cade stood in the same area as Samuel's house. Somehow, Murdock knew where he lived. Maybe Dobkins had been right and someone had followed them.

"He's here for me." He was so nervous his fingers trembled.

"It's not possible. Don't panic."

They weaved through the crowd towards the packed lake where people were ice-skating. Not an inch of the iced surface was visible. Entire families skated together, laughing and twirling around.

"Is he gone?" she asked, limping harder.

He glanced over his shoulder. "I think—"

Cade was marching towards him. His glacial stare caused Samuel to shake. There was no mistake. The lion had become the prey.

Samuel helped Vivienne to walk faster. "He recognised me."

She grimaced. "Leave me. I can't run. You must flee."

"Maybe we can hide in the crowd. Let's get closer to the lake."

He made his way through the people towards the lake. Cade was closer now, his fists clenched at his sides.

"We should keep close to the lake and get to the other side," she said. "He'll lose us once we're in the middle of the crowd."

His gaze met Cade's, and for a moment, time stopped. Even his heart stuttered. He was thrown back to the days he'd spent in the cage, living in constant pain, fear, and humiliation. The instinct to cower in front of Cade when he'd beaten him was almost overwhelming. A phantom pain sliced his back at the memory of Cade's baton while Murdock told him he belonged to him.

A vision of Murdock's face contorted with rage broke the spell, and panic seized him. Grabbing Vivienne's hand, he broke into a run.

"Lion Boy!" Hearing Cade's shout caused him physical pain.

Vivienne did her best to keep up, but she couldn't match his strides, so he hauled her up and soldiered through the people none too gently.

"Leave me, for goodness's sake." She squirmed in his arms. "He won't hurt me."

He held her more tightly. No, he wouldn't leave her behind. He didn't trust Cade.

"We're going in the wrong direction," she said.

In his hurry, he hadn't noticed he was running on the ice frosting the lake, or rather, he was trying to run. His feet slipped right and left, threatening his balance. People on skates jostled him.

"Careful!" a man said.

Someone bumped into him, and he lost control of his movements.

Vivienne dropped from his arms. She cried out in pain when she slammed against the ice, but he didn't have time to steady her.

A loud crack thundered like a boulder breaking in half after being struck by lightning. He caught a glimpse of all the people skating on the ice before they disappeared from view in a second, swallowed by the frozen water.

The ground cracked underneath him as well, and he and Vivienne fell into the icy lake.

twenty-one

The cold was so intense and the fall so sudden that Vivienne couldn't scream.

One moment, she hit the hard ice. The next, the ground disappeared and she was plunged into the freezing water.

People shouted all around her. The more they tried to get out of the cold lake, the more shards of ice cracked. The sounds of bodies splashing into the water terrified her.

Samuel wrapped his arms around her and tried to push her up. But the mud sucked them down, and she couldn't breathe because it was too cold. Their fingers didn't find purchase on the ice.

A chaos of screams and splashes erupted around her. She couldn't understand where the shore was.

Boats started to float through the broken ice, pulling crying people up. Samuel tried again to lift her, but she couldn't help him. Her wet clothes weighed her down, and the water, heavy and sticky with mud, ice, and sludge, blocked her. Her feet didn't reach the bottom. She couldn't haul herself up.

He flipped his fingers quickly in front of her, repeating, "I'm sorry."

But it wasn't his fault. If her ankle hadn't been sore, she would have escaped with him. She'd slowed them down although he'd panicked.

Her teeth chattered as she shook her head to tell him it wasn't his fault the ice had broken. There had been too many people.

She didn't feel her body anymore. Even her throbbing ankle stopped bothering her.

He hugged her, but his warmth wasn't enough to bring her comfort. Her eyelids became heavy. Fatigue washed over her. He tried to pull her up again but didn't find a grip on the slippery shards of ice.

A shadow loomed over her, and she blinked the fatigue away.

"Miss, we're going to take you out." Two men on a boat grabbed her arms.

Samuel thrust her up as well. Mud and water splashed everywhere as she dropped on the boat where other drenched people were shivering. She took a deep breath and tasted the mud on her tongue. Her muscles spasmed with the cold.

The boat rocked hard, threatening to capsize.

"We're too full," the man said. "Sorry, mate. We'll pick you up next."

What? They were leaving Samuel.

"No!" She meant to shout, but only a feeble sound came out. "Don't leave him." She stretched out a hand, but the energy to pull herself up deserted her.

"We'll capsize, miss," the man said. "Do you want to go back into the water?"

"I'll get out." She reached out to touch Samuel, but he swatted her hand away.

"Go," he mouthed. "Go."

"Miss, stay still or we'll all fall." The man shoved her back none too gently.

"Samuel." Her voice didn't want to come out.

He shook his head with determination.

She lost sight of him as the boat sailed through other boats and people stuck in the cold water, begging for help. Even her tears were frozen. So many people were still drowning.

Once the boat reached the shore, she scrambled out of it, muttering, "Thank you," to the people who had saved her.

The men barely nodded before returning to the lake for another round.

Shivering, she sat on the muddy ground, craning her neck to see Samuel through the people, but she couldn't find him. Too many arms waved, and too many people shouted.

A woman in a nurse's uniform wrapped a blanket around her shoulders. "Come with me, miss. We're taking everyone to the hospital."

"No, I can't. I'm waiting for my friend to be rescued."

"We must clear the shore to let the rescuers do their work. You can't stay here."

"I can't leave him."

"You'll see your friend at the hospital."

"No."

"Miss, you must move."

"No."

The nurse and a man grabbed her, lifting her with brutal strength that was no match for her weakened state. She tried to shrug herself free, but her lack of energy didn't allow her to oppose any resistance.

When they stashed her in a cart with other moaning people and closed the doors, she started crying.

BY THE TIME Samuel was pulled out of the lake and sent to the hospital, he'd almost lost consciousness twice because of the cold.

He had no idea where Vivienne was, but she'd been rescued quickly. She should be safe. She had to be because he would never forgive himself if something had happened to her.

He was sitting on a wooden bench in a white room with a dozen people. Everyone had thick blankets wrapped around them and a mug of hot tea in their hands.

A stove spread warmth through the crowded room, and the humidity lifting from the soaked clothes turned the air heavy and smelling of wet wool.

Every time the nurses brought in someone new, he sat bolt upright, but Vivienne was nowhere to be seen.

The scare had made him forget about Cade and Murdock, but as he grew warm, the sheer panic of seeing Cade caused him to shiver all over again. Fear left a metallic taste in his mouth, and visions of Cade catching him flashed across his mind. The more he tried to control his reaction, the more difficult breathing became.

He squeezed his eyes shut not to faint. If he lost consciousness, he would be vulnerable.

"Samuel!" the deep voice of Captain Jackson boomed in the room.

A wave of gratitude overwhelmed him as the captain ran over to him. When the captain hugged him, the visions faded; they didn't vanish, but he breathed better.

"Bloody hell, lad, I can't leave you alone five minutes before you nearly die," Captain Jackson said, taking him by the shoulders.

He couldn't stop himself from hugging the captain again. Captain Jackson returned the hug immediately.

"It was scary, wasn't it?" the captain asked.

The ice, the cold, and the water, yes, but he wasn't shivering from that.

The captain patted his back. "It's all right, and I'm a doctor. That's your lucky day."

"Vivienne," Samuel signed. "I lost her."

"We'll find her. The survivors have been sent here to Marylebone Infirmary or St. Mary's Hospital in Paddington. First, you need to get warm and change your clothes. Then we'll search for her. Let's go home."

He took the captain's hand. "Cade, Murdock's right hand. He saw me. He chased me. That's why Vivienne and I fell into the lake. We were escaping from him."

Captain Jackson's eyebrows plunged into a deep crease. "How did he find you?"

"I don't know." He swallowed. "He called me Lion Boy."

The captain ran a hand over his face. "Dobkins was right. Someone was following us. Maybe Cade doesn't know exactly where you live, but I won't take any chances. Can you walk?"

He nodded.

"We'll go somewhere else tonight. I know a flat we can use."

By the time Samuel entered an anonymous flat in South London, he was shivering again, and dusk cloaked the city in darkness.

Captain Jackson lit the cast-iron stove and a few oil lamps. "This place belongs to a friend of mine. He helped me during my darkest days." He cast a glance at him. "Needless to say, you aren't going anywhere else tonight. You're running a fever."

"Vivienne." He moved his fingers slowly.

"I'll find her, but you'll stay here and sleep after I get you some dry clothes and something to eat."

Samuel sat next to the stove and hugged his knees. A fear stronger than any he'd ever experienced poisoned his mind. Danger lurked in every shadow, and thoughts of Vivienne, pale and nearly dead, tormented him.

Murdock knew where he was, and Cade had been sent there to take him back.

Samuel would have to choose between being free and staying in London...between freedom and Vivienne.

twenty-two

Vivienne held her warm cup of tea with both hands.

She must have drunk a record number of hot cups of tea in the past three days, because her body didn't only need the warmth but the fluids as well. High fever and cold shivers had plagued her. She didn't stop coughing, and her lungs seemed on fire.

Dr. Tucker visited her every day, the maids never left her alone for more than a few minutes, and Mother essentially slept in her bedroom. She didn't mind the attention and care, but being always with someone didn't allow her to get news about Samuel from Dobkins.

The Regent's Park skating disaster had killed more than forty people. Countless others were suffering from pneumonia or high fever; some were severely sick, and she had no idea if Samuel was safe.

The fever wasn't her only problem. Her ankle was the size of a melon and burned every time she tried to walk. The damage wasn't irreparable, but at the moment, it limited her freedom further. She needed help to walk to the water closet.

Cade's presence in London topped every other worry. Hopefully, Samuel was all right and his silence was due only to him hiding from Cade.

Dobkins and a maid were cleaning the room—a daily occurrence—and she exchanged a few glances with Dobkins. Mother had blissfully left a few moments ago.

"Catherine, brew more tea for Lady Vivienne." Dobkins gathered a basket of dirty laundry. "And take this downstairs."

The moment Catherine left, Vivienne sat upright, wincing as her body hurt. "Do you have news?"

"I saw the captain briefly this morning. Samuel is well."

She sagged against the pillow. "Thank heaven."

"They moved to another flat in case Murdock and Cade surprised them."

"As soon as I'm better—" She coughed. "I'll go and see him."

Dobkins's eyebrows lowered. "My lady, I'm not sure it will be possible."

"Why?" Her voice quivered.

"For starters, you aren't well. The captain didn't say anything explicit, but he hinted at the possibility for Samuel to leave London, at least for a while."

"But he'll come back, won't he?"

"It wouldn't be wise for you to see him now, and you are too ill to try. The captain doesn't want to attract attention, and if someone is watching them, it's safer if he and Samuel don't get any visitors."

The speech was reasonable, but her heart didn't care. The last time she'd seen Samuel, he'd been half-buried in a freezing sludge, unable to move. The last word he'd told her was '*go!*'

She couldn't allow that exchange to be their last one. "Can you give him a message?"

Dobkins squeezed her hand. "I can't. I don't know where the captain and Samuel live now, and unless the captain comes here, which is too dangerous, I have no means to contact him."

"I'm here, darling." Mother went straight to the bed and took Vivienne's hand. "How do you feel?"

"I'm tired. Aside from that, I'm fine."

She wasn't. Her muscles lacked strength, her breathing was laboured, and sometimes she couldn't stop coughing until she fell asleep from exhaustion. And she couldn't even cross her bedroom with her ankle.

Mother caressed her head, her hand trembling. "I'll do anything to make you feel better."

"Darling." Father walked over to the bed and hugged her gently. "You're still warm."

"I'm better. Really." Another coughing fit belied her words.

The fear in Father's eyes struck her harder than Mother's concern.

"Good afternoon." Dr. Tucker limped inside, carrying his black leather bag.

Mother nodded at Dobkins to leave, but before she did, she gave Vivienne an apologetic glance.

Mother sat on the bed. Her puffy red eyes were a stab to Vivienne's heart. She hated seeing Mother so distraught. The pain was a rehash of what had happened with Adele.

Father kissed Vivienne's cheek. "I'll come back and check on you later, darling."

She held his hand for a moment before facing the doctor's beady eyes.

"How are you today, my lady?" Dr. Tucker opened the bag. His crooked smile didn't reassure her.

"I feel stronger." She coughed in her closed fist.

"Good." He walked over to the bed with his uneven gait. "Let me check your pulse."

"You shouldn't have escaped," Mother said.

"I truly am sorry, but I was tired of being cooped up in the house."

"Do you realise the gravity of what you did?" Mother's voice cracked.

"I do, and I'm sorry to have caused you such pain."

Dr. Tucker examined her eyes and throat, and auscultated her heart. A coughing fit shook her, and sweat dampened her forehead. Heat and shivers coursed through her, a sign the fever was rising again.

He frowned. "You're developing a double winter fever."

Mother gasped.

"What is it?" Vivienne asked.

"Both your lungs are affected by pneumonia," Dr. Tucker said. "Nasty, serious business. I won't deny that. It is life-threatening."

Annoyance more than fear caused her to jerk to attention. She'd met many physicians, but none of them had ever been so dramatic. Down-to-earth, yes, dramatic, no.

Mother looked as if she would crumble into a thousand pieces. There was a haunted look in her eyes. "She can't die. She can't! What can we do, doctor?"

"Absolute rest to start with. I'll prescribe everything Lady Vivienne will need and treatments here. She can't be moved." He flashed his yellowed teeth. "But it could take weeks…or months."

Vivienne didn't respond. The constant burning in her chest, shortness of breath, and fatigue overwhelmed her and gave her the same diagnosis. She was losing weight quickly, despite the rich meals Cook prepared for her.

But she would be lying if she said she trusted Dr. Tucker completely. Or maybe she simply didn't like the news and blamed the doctor.

"Vivienne?" Father's deep voice came from the other side of the door.

"Come in," she said, coughing.

Father narrowed his gaze on Dr. Tucker. "How's my daughter?"

"Pneumonia, my lord, affecting both lungs. Extremely serious." Dr. Tucker sighed dramatically. "Not good news, I'm afraid, but I'll do my best to help her."

Father hugged her again, and for some reason, tears welled up in her eyes.

Maybe because she could be fragile and scared with her father. For the first time since she'd returned home from the hospital, a sense of fear chilled her.

She swallowed a couple of times, leaned against him and whispered, "I'm sorry, Father."

"It's not your fault." He hugged her more tightly.

Mother cried silently, holding her hand.

Dr. Tucker cleared his throat. "Lord Huntington, under my guidance, she can survive. But it would be unprofessional of me not to mention the risks of long-lasting impairments. A pneumonia so strong might cause lung scarring, and in general, other health problems with the airways. These conditions will cause persistent shortness of breath, fatigue, chest pain, and general weakness, increasing the risk of a cardiac arrest."

Mother sobbed in earnest now.

"What are you telling me?" Father sounded angry.

The doctor didn't flinch. "I mean, Lady Vivienne's health might be permanently damaged and her heart might stop beating without the right cure, granted she survives the pneumonia, that is."

Father tensed, his arms tightening around her. "Don't worry, darling. You will be fine."

She was overcome by another coughing fit and realised how serious this was, and for the first time she was scared.

twenty-three

After three days of staying warm and drinking hot soup, Samuel didn't feel any stronger, but at least he'd stopped shivering and coughing for minutes on end. Knowing that Vivienne was safe at home was the only ray of sunlight of the past few days.

The new flat creaked and squeaked every time he walked on the floorboards, and draughts blew from cracks in the walls and the roof. One greasy window completed the sad picture.

Not that the view outside was anything exciting—a dark cobbled alleyway closed by two tall brick walls. Mostly drunkards walked by. And the smell of rotting vegetables permeated the air if he cracked a window.

He'd been in worse places, and he wouldn't mind if not for his wish to see Vivienne.

Captain Jackson stepped into the flat, his nose red from the cold. "Bloody hell. It's freezing outside and inside." He touched Samuel's forehead. "No fever. Good. How are you?" He added another wooden log to the stove.

"Tired."

"I bet you are." The captain blocked the front door with a

chair before peeking out of the window, half hidden by the thread-bare curtains. "This flat isn't the healthiest of places."

He tapped the captain's shoulder before signing, "Is something the matter?"

"I didn't want to mention it till you felt better, but after all, what's the point? You deserve to truth." The captain exhaled. "I saw someone yesterday prowling around my flat. His behaviour was suspicious."

Samuel stiffened. His nightmare didn't want to end.

Captain Jackson sat on a chair that groaned, threatening to break under his weight. "At the hospital, there are people, who work for Murdock, asking about Lion Boy. There are people out there are raising hell to find you. There is a lot of money on your head. Bad news, yes, but on the other hand, I also heard that Cade, too, was sent to the hospital after having dropped into the lake."

He closed his fists then opened them. "I'm tired. So tired."

Captain Jackson put a hand on his shoulder. "I think we should leave London sooner than we planned. We'll go away and return when no one is looking for you. You need a new identity, a new life that doesn't link you to that swine. Start over. So he can't bother you."

Tempting, but what about Vivienne?

"It's better for Vivienne as well," Captain Jackson said, seemingly reading his mind. "Murdock wouldn't hesitate to hurt her to get to you. But if you start over outside of the city and live another life, get a proper job, no one will link you to the circus. And I don't know what Murdock is legally to you."

He frowned.

"Is he your adoptive father? Your legal guardian? Did he simply take you away with him? Did he kidnap you? We can't have a confrontation with him without knowing if the law is on his side."

"He abused me."

"Yes, but who knows what he said to the police? Maybe

you're considered mentally unstable and dangerous, and he convinced everyone that certain harsh treatments were justified. Doctors who work in an asylum would be sympathetic to his pleas, and if you're legally declared insane and he's responsible for you, a judge would order you to go with him. My point is, we must avoid him at all costs, as much as I would like to shoot him."

He sagged. The logic was solid. He had no idea if Murdock was his legal guardian. "Where do you want to go?"

"I have a friend who lives in New York City. He's happy to help us resettle and accommodate us for a while. A couple of weeks on a ship, and we'll be there."

"New York City?" A few months ago, he wouldn't have known where it was, but thanks to Vivienne and her lessons, his knowledge of the world had increased enough to understand New York City was over three thousand miles and a continent away from London. "I assumed you wanted to stay in England."

"Cade's circus travels around the country. By now everyone knows of Lion Boy, and Cade will provide a new description of you. I don't want to take any risks. We sail to the Americas, get new identities, and eventually we can return."

He raked a hand through his hair. Risking his freedom now would mean never seeing Vivienne again. "May I see Vivienne? Say goodbye?"

"I don't think it's a good idea."

"Please. One last time before leaving."

Captain Jackson pinched the bridge of his nose. After a tense silence he said, "I'll send a message to Dobkins."

SAMUEL WINCED at each step as he walked with Captain Jackson towards Vivienne's house.

His muscles were sore, and the night's chill didn't help soothe

the ache in his chest. His fever hadn't lasted, but it'd left him exhausted.

They stopped at the usual dark corner from which Vivienne's window was visible. His heart sank. The dark window remained shut. The oak tree branches swayed slowly as if desolate.

Captain Jackson frowned. "I delivered a message to Dobkins. She knew we were coming."

Maybe Vivienne didn't want to see him.

"We can't wait too long. Only a couple of minutes." The captain searched the street. "I'm sorry, lad."

He shifted his weight from one foot to another, pondering if he should climb the tree anyway. Poor health aside, he didn't want to cause her problems.

"Samuel." Captain Jackson poked him with an elbow. "We must go."

He nodded, an ache tightening his chest.

Right then, a woman wrapped in a hooded cloak came from around the corner. She looked right and left and sped up towards them. Samuel drew in a breath but released it when Dobkins's red hair appeared from under the hood.

"Dobkins," Captain Jackson said.

"I don't have much time." Her voice quivered. "I have bad news. Lady Vivienne isn't well. She's caught pneumonia and is delirious with fever. Her mother has not left her bedside."

Samuel glanced at the window.

Dobkins's voice quivered. "A physician comes every day to treat her. Her Ladyship sleeps in Lady Vivienne's bedroom, so worried she is. Maids and footmen are up and about during the night. That's why you can't see her."

The captain's frown deepened. "How serious is the case of pneumonia?"

"The physician said permanent impairment of the lungs is probable."

Samuel swallowed hard. This was his fault. If he hadn't panicked when he saw Cade, Vivienne would be safe.

"Hell." The captain lowered his voice and gazed around again.

"I have to go," Dobkins said. "I'm sorry."

Samuel wouldn't have the chance to say goodbye. He leant against the tree and tilted his head up towards the window.

"We can't stay. Murdock is searching for Samuel," Captain Jackson said. "We must leave London."

Dobkins tugged at her shawl. "Where are you going?"

"The Americas."

Her eyes widened. "So far away."

"Samuel needs to get away, far away. There he can create a new identity to start over and get rid of Murdock forever." Captain Jackson handed her a velvet bundle. "This belongs to Lady Vivienne."

Dobkins shifted her gaze from the bundle to Captain Jackson. "You didn't sell it. How did you carry on then?"

Captain Jackson smiled sadly. "It's surprising the amount of pounds one can put aside when not drinking."

She took the bundle, hands trembling. "You're a kind man."

The captain chuckled. "Not really. This isn't a goodbye. We'll be back once enough time has passed and Murdock stops searching for Samuel."

Dobkins hugged Samuel in a tight embrace. "Good luck. You deserve a new beginning. I'll tell Lady Vivienne you came. Send me your information when you're settled, and I'll make sure she knows you are safe."

Samuel glanced up at the dark window one last time, fearing that this was indeed a goodbye.

twenty-four

Eight years later

Travelling first class was the best way of travelling.

On his way to London from Canada, Samuel had bought a first-class train ticket to New York City, and then booked a luxurious cabin on an ocean liner, then another first-class train ticket from Southampton to London. And finally, he'd booked the best, most expensive suite at Brown's Hotel in the heart of Mayfair. A suite with three bedrooms, a sitting room, a study, and even a piano room with one of the most beautiful views London had to offer.

He could afford it.

And more.

If he wanted, he could buy the whole damned hotel.

After sailing to New York City years ago, he'd made his way even farther, to the Klondike region in the Yukon, where he bought a piece of frozen land for a handful of dollars, and by sheer, dumb luck become the owner of the biggest vein of gold found there in a decade.

With his new name of Samuel Lyon, he'd founded Lyon Gold Corporation, a name associated with wealth, prestige, and power.

The boy, who didn't have enough coins to buy himself a glass of lemonade, now could buy a thousand acres of lemon trees. He had returned to London as a free, rich man, there to see Vivienne again.

Captain Jackson walked into the bedroom, wearing an expensive, tailored dark suit that accentuated his glossy black hair. Only a few grey strands coloured his temples, giving him a sophisticated air.

"How do I look?" The captain straightened and adjusted his bow tie.

"Elegant."

Years of being sober and working hard had changed the captain deeply, both physically and mentally. A trimmed beard covered his face, and his skin had lost that pale, doughy quality from when he'd drunk heavily. He'd grown muscles, and even his posture was straighter.

"What about me? How do I look?" Samuel opened his dark grey jacket, showing a matching silk waistcoat.

"Like a filthy rich gentleman. When is your filthy rich house ready to live in?"

"We should leave the hotel in a day or two." And he wouldn't need to pack a single bag. He paid a small army of people for that.

"Are you ready to meet Lord and Lady Huntington?" the captain asked.

"I've been waiting for this moment for years. I'm ready."

He hadn't exchanged many letters with Vivienne. He'd moved through North America constantly before settling in the Yukon, so he hadn't had the chance to follow her progress as he'd wanted.

But something must have happened to her recently. In her last letters, she'd sounded dispirited, and her writing looked thin and frail.

The double pneumonia had healed but not completely, and her lungs didn't work as well as they should. He worried she hadn't told him the whole truth about the severity of her health.

"I'll come with you in the carriage," the captain said, "but after the coachman leaves you at Lord Huntington's, I'll head to Oxford Street. It's better if the earl and the countess don't see me."

In the carriage, as they drove towards Huntington Hall, they remained silent. Lyon Gold Corporation had made investment deals with Lord Huntington—Samuel had made sure of that—and when he'd mentioned his intention of going to London to manage his English office there, Lord Huntington had been enthusiastic about meeting him. Exactly what Samuel had wanted.

Vivienne knew about the whole affair thanks to his letters, but he didn't know if they would have the opportunity to be alone. He was about to find that out.

"I miss the..." Captain Jackson made a wide gesture with his arm. "Endless spaces America has. Here everything is narrow and constricted. I had never noticed that before."

"New York City is as constricting as London."

"Its architecture, yes, but what New York City lacks in space, it makes up for with freedom."

He tilted his head, acknowledging the captain's point. Had he stayed in London, he doubted he would have built the empire he controlled today.

At first, the money had made him dizzy and drunk with opportunities. Now it was only something giving him safety from men like Murdock.

He'd hired Pinkerton men to discover where Murdock was with no result. Cade had had disappeared from London after the ice-skating disaster. Murdock as well had pulled a trick worthy of an illusionist and vanished, and the circus didn't exist anymore. Samuel didn't shed a tear.

"Are you going to use your notepad, or will someone translate from sign language?" Captain Jackson asked.

"The earl found someone who will translate. Shall I tell Dobkins you say hello?"

The captain smiled. "Ah, lovely woman. Yes, if you can."

When the carriage rolled to a stop, he hesitated before getting out. The last time he'd been at Huntington Hall, he'd stared up at Vivienne's dark room, his heart broken. His life had changed drastically, but the pain of not seeing her lingered.

"Good luck." Captain Jackson didn't look out of the window although no one would recognise him immediately.

Samuel exited the carriage and straightened his fine coat and silk neckwear.

Huntington Hall hadn't changed. Its white walls shone with a fresh coat of paint, the bay windows were framed by the same plush brocade draperies, and the marble stairs shone as if recently scrubbed. But the beautiful oak tree had been ruthlessly trimmed. Its branches didn't reach Vivienne's room any longer. They were fewer and thinner, lacking the vigour he remembered.

A footman welcomed him and showed him to a sitting room where Lord and Lady Huntington waited.

"My lord, my lady, Mr. Lyon is here." The footman bowed.

Samuel bowed as well, one hand on his notepad.

All the breath was flushed out of his lungs when he saw Vivienne. For a moment, he couldn't move, think, or sign.

Her lips parted, and her blue eyes sparkled with starlight. He had to clench his fists not to run to her, hug her, and sweep her off her feet. Controlling himself was the most difficult thing he'd ever done.

"Lady Huntington, Lord Huntington." He wrote in his notepad. "It's a pleasure to meet you. Lady Vivienne."

She replied with a nod. Her gaunt face had lost its roundness, and her raven hair wasn't glossy anymore.

The countess had lost weight too, and her black gown contrasted with her paleness.

Lord Huntington nodded at the footman who left the room, and a moment later, a man entered, followed by Dobkins. She had changed, too. A few more strips of grey streaked her hair and wrinkles of worry crowned her gentle brown eyes.

She gave him a wide smile, then directed the tea service that arrived behind her.

"Take a seat, Lyon." Lord Huntington gestured at the armchairs. "We're eager to hear everything about your journey. Mr. Jones here is from the Deaf Institute."

"Mr. Lyon," Mr. Jones shook his hand. "I will translate for you."

Sometimes not being able to use his voice was a blessing, as it was now. He sipped tea while Jones translated his answers to mundane questions.

He had the opportunity to steal glances at Vivienne who glanced back at him. Not warm glances. There was a coldness about her that bothered him.

He gave her a pointed look, with his hand hidden at his side and he signed for her only. "How are you?"

She put her cup down, lowered a hand and signed back, but her movements were sluggish as if she didn't have the energy.

He didn't understand what she said. "I've missed you." He checked Lord and Lady Huntington were still listening to Jones. "When can I see you?"

She gazed away.

That was a punch in the stomach. If she didn't want to see him, he wouldn't impose his presence on her, but he'd hoped she would be as eager as he was to be together.

"You must come to our garden party tomorrow," Lord Huntington said. "We'll serve lunch and a few drinks, and raise money for charity."

The countess gave him a small smile. "Please say you'll join us."

He couldn't refuse, and it would be another possibility to see Vivienne.

The rest of the visit was about his business and his life in the Americas. The ladies didn't talk, and Vivienne rarely glanced at him. She seemed about to fall asleep, and he couldn't blame her.

When he was about to leave, he bowed in front of her and signed while Jones wasn't looking, "What happened to you?"

That got a reaction from her. Her cheeks flushed.

He bowed again, showing a written page to Lord and Lady Huntington. "My lord, my lady, thank you for seeing me."

Dobkins beamed at him again.

Samuel left the house with a sense of confusion draped around him like a cloak. He drove through Oxford Street to pick up the captain. He was eager to talk to him.

"How did it go?" Captain Jackson said once he was in the carriage.

"Vivienne. Something is wrong with her. She's thin, pale, and even her hair is lifeless."

The captain drummed his fingers on his knee. "The damage left by double pneumonia might be severe and long lasting. She's lucky she survived."

"For years?"

"Yes. In some cases, for a lifetime. The body remains locked in a battle with the latent infection, and it's an exhausting battle. If parts of her lungs don't work properly, she'll feel tired constantly. Her breathing will be shallow, and she'll be prone to catching colds and having respiratory problems, and even her heart could be affected. Progress has been made with severe cases of double pneumonia, but modern medicine hasn't found a solution to help a body recover yet."

Samuel shook his head. "I'm not convinced. Spending time with you and your patients, I learnt a thing or two, and I tell you, whatever afflicts her is more serious. I want you to examine her."

"Of course. I just have to march into her house, from where I was banned years ago for not having saved her sister, and ask her parents to trust the assessment of the man who, in their opinion, killed their daughter."

"Don't be so dramatic." He shot his gaze upwards. "I'll find a way to let you meet her."

twenty-five

Vivienne couldn't focus on her needlework after Samuel had left, and for once, her chronic fatigue had nothing to do with her lack of concentration.

Seeing him after so many years had been a shock, even though she'd been aware of his coming. Her body still trembled from the encounter, and dozens of thoughts piled up in her mind. She hadn't been able to exchange any words with him also because…she wasn't the same woman he remembered.

Her body had changed and not for the better. She'd never cared too much about her excessive paleness, gaunt cheeks, and straw-like hair. Not when her health was most important. But in the mirror of his deep amber eyes, she'd seen her reflection as a ghastly woman, more dead than alive, which was exactly as she felt.

Shame had paralysed her, especially in front of his now-charismatic presence.

Samuel wasn't as she remembered. He looked strong and handsome with his dark golden hair cut above his jaw and fine suit. He was taller and broader than she had remembered, and simply magnificent. Looking at him, he had nothing left of the shy, worried young man she had known.

He was a man who knew what he wanted and wasn't afraid to take it.

And she...she was afraid of everything.

"Are you tired, darling?" Mother sat on the armchair in front of her and picked up her own needlework.

"Not really."

"What do you think of Mr. Lyon?" Father asked, lowering his newspaper.

She thought the world of him. "Mr. Lyon is an interesting gentleman. He has seen much of the world."

Mother resumed her work. "His good luck is impressive. Such an adventurous life, but his health is strong."

She didn't say anything, worried she might say something wrong. Health was a delicate topic in her house. She loved her parents, but Samuel wouldn't have been welcomed in Huntington Hall if not for his ridiculous fortune.

Her father embraced the association he had developed with Lyon Gold Corporation, welcomed the prestige and notoriety. The *nouveaux riches* were no longer snubbed by the aristocracy. Their money meant power, and its influx was welcomed by those who had before consider it vulgar and parvenu.

"I admire Lyon," Father said. "He's a man with determination and strong will."

Mother arched her brow. "Doesn't his muteness bother you?"

"He earns more respect because of it," Father said. "Another man would let his inability to speak rule his life. He has flourished despite his situation."

Vivienne smiled at him. Father didn't care only about money.

"I'm going to be honest, Vivienne." Father folded the newspaper and grinned. "If Lyon should become your suitor, I would welcome the match."

She didn't say anything. Surely Samuel had better options than a dying woman.

"Edward, you can't be serious." Mother lowered her voice.

"Lyon isn't aware of Vivienne's condition, and she isn't strong enough to be courted by anyone. We agreed on that."

Vivienne hunched her shoulders. The words weren't cruel, but sometimes truth and cruelty were siblings.

"I have hope for a bright future for Vivienne." Father held her hand tenderly. "Given more time, I'm sure she'll improve, and maybe I'm a fool, but I'm convinced Lyon's vibrant energy is contagious and is what you need, darling."

Mother pressed her lips together, stabbing the fabric with the needle.

Vivienne didn't have the strength to be as hopeful as Father was.

After the skating disaster in The Regent's Park, her pneumonia had gone from bad to worse in a matter of weeks. She would have died if not for Dr. Tucker's dedication and expertise. Instead, she'd improved, but her health had never fully returned. Her lungs were scarred, and her heart suffered, too.

Some weeks were worse than others. Sudden fevers would torment her for days, tremors and stomach aches would force her to stay in bed, and catching a cold was a normal occurrence.

But her spirits had been damaged more than her body. Every time a disease afflicted her, her wish to live was eroded. Like the tiny drop that corroded the rock with its persistence, so the constant illnesses and aches were winning over her life.

She had nothing to offer Samuel aside from her fragility.

Her hand quivered, and she pricked herself with the needle. A ruby drop of blood blossomed on her fingertip. She sucked it before it stained the needlework. The blood itself didn't cover the flavour of the countless potions she took every day; their metallic tastes remained in her mouth forever.

"I hope you'll enjoy yourself at the garden party," Father said. "The fresh air will do you good."

Not according to Mother, whose list of things harmful to Vivienne's health had never changed.

Mother glowered. "I've never been convinced that fresh air is healthy."

Father ignored her. "After your complete recovery, all I want is to see you married and settled, and finally happy."

So did Vivienne.

SAMUEL STOOD STILL AS RICHARD, his valet, helped him dress for the Earl of Huntington's garden party. His residence at the hotel had been a short one, since he'd bought a fully detached house in Belgravia and filled it with his household staff, people he'd chosen personally when he was in the Americas.

Richard was missing a few fingers on both hands—a tragic carriage accident while he'd worked as the valet of a rich businessman—so buttoning and tying Samuel's suit required a bit of time. But he didn't care. The accident that claimed Richard's fingers had also shaken Samuel deeply.

If he hadn't employed him, Richard would live on the streets. And he'd proved to be a damn good valet.

All his servants were knowledgeable in sign language, something he was proud of. He'd hired tutors to teach them, and they'd been eager to learn...with some exceptions, like his footman.

"All done, sir." Richard brushed Samuel's dark jacket.

"Thank you," he signed, smelling, as Richard moved away, the lingering scent of the shaving cream.

A knock came on the door. "Sir?" It was his housekeeper, Mrs. Foster.

He nodded to Richard who said, "Come in. Mr. Lyon is ready."

"Sir..." Mrs. Foster took a step in, stopped, then took another step.

Her tentativeness signalled it had to be bad news.

"Tell me," he signed.

She stepped closer, and the sunlight lit her deformed face. One side was pulled up as if an invisible force pushed it, making her face asymmetrical. After working as a maid for years, her former employer had refused to promote her to housekeeper due to her looks. She'd then found employment as the Monstrous Woman in a circus similar to Cade's, and when he found her, he hadn't hesitated to offer her a job.

Mrs. Foster lifted her chin. "Sir, it's about William."

Samuel exhaled. "What now?"

"I found a few pieces of our silverware in his bedroom."

"I'll talk to him. Again."

"Sir, if I may, perhaps we should consider dismissing him."

He shook his head. He wouldn't give up so easily on someone who needed help.

While he didn't regret having hired Richard, Mrs. Foster, and other people who had been as desperate for a chance as he'd been, William, his footman, was another matter. The young man had a compulsion for thievery that had granted him more than one brush with the police.

A few minutes later, he knocked on William's door and entered, Mrs. Foster behind him. "What have you done this time?"

"Not what it seems, boss." William held up his hands. "I just wanted to test how safe your safe was, sir, if you'll excuse the play on words. A matter of research, not thievery, I promise."

"Give Mrs. Foster the silver, William." He pointed a finger at him before signing, "This is the last time. No more stealing in this house."

William bowed his head as the perfect penitent. "Absolutely, sir. It's that since you're about to get married—"

"Are you, sir?" Mrs. Foster said at the same time as Samuel signed, "What are you talking about?"

"That's wonderful." Mrs. Foster glowed. "A wedding. Sir, I need to know all the details."

Samuel shook his head.

William glanced from one to the other. "Isn't that why you dragged us across the pond? You want to marry that lady..." He snapped his fingers a few times. "Valerie, Vanessa..."

"Vivienne," he signed before scolding himself for having revealed her name to William.

"Vivienne." William nodded. "And I thought you wanted a safe place for your future bride."

"How do you know about her?"

William smirked. "You can't stop talking about her, and you leave your private correspondence on the desk, sir."

"Yes, and it's called private for a reason."

"You shouldn't trust just anyone, sir."

"No more snooping and no more stealing. I'm serious." He left the room, annoyance turning his steps heavy.

William. He knew he was too soft with the cheeky footman... although the thief had just voiced something that had been lurking in his mind since he'd met Vivienne.

twenty-six

The day of the garden party was sunny, with a fresh breeze carrying the scent of flowers. A good start for Vivienne.

Mother had drastically changed the garden, eradicating all those plants she believed to be poisonous or unhealthy, and planted everything Dr. Tucker had told her to be beneficial. That doctor had lasted longer than any other. If she didn't believe he was very competent, her own recovery being clear proof, she would think he'd put a spell on Mother.

Still, walking in the sunlight and feeling its warmth on her cheeks was wonderful. She followed the elegant flight of a butterfly fluttering its blue wings over the bushes of white daisies. Before her illness started, she hadn't appreciated how important little moments like a butterfly's flight were.

Guests wandered through the manicured hedges and bushes, going from one marquee to another. Each gazebo offered a different type of refreshment, from hors d'oeuvres to smoked fish and caviar. A small orchestra played in a corner, making her smile for the first time in...she didn't remember.

She had to thank Father for her entire presence at the garden party. Mother wouldn't have let her stay for more than five minutes. It was a miracle that Mother had agreed to have so many guests in the garden, although the people were evenly distributed not to form large groups that were unhealthy.

Of course, Vivienne had to take her potions religiously. All the concoctions Dr. Tucker prepared for her were part of her day. Syrups, mixtures, and drops marked her day like a clock. Her stomach was filled with more drugs than food.

She knew when Samuel had arrived from the quick stir going through the guests.

Excited whispers echoed from the gazebos as Samuel stepped into the garden. Ladies stared at him with boldness. Gentlemen regarded him with respect.

Another thing that had changed about him was his confidence. His presence demanded attention and obedience. An aura of authority surrounded him. His lion gaze helped give him a hint of menace that added to his charm.

He surveyed the crowd with disinterest but bowed at every introduction to a lady and shook hands with the gentlemen. Father was glowing as he talked to him.

When Samuel's gaze fell on her, it ignited like warm brandy. Her chest heaved as her breath sped up. For the first time in years, she'd felt desirable, a sensation she'd completely forgotten.

She returned the stare. Father had told her he would welcome Samuel as a suitor.

He strode across the garden with predatory menace, an attitude new to her. The man in front of her was a warrior who didn't care about anyone's opinion.

"Vivienne." His signing was fluid and elegant with a certain... smoothness, almost a lilt?

"Samuel," she whispered, worried someone might hear her using his Christian name.

"I need to talk to you."

Years ago, he wouldn't have been so direct. Not that she was complaining.

She gazed around, a cold shiver going through her. "Behind those hedgerows. No one will see us."

He offered her his arm. "Perfect."

She slipped her arm through his. The contact with his strong arm brought her back years to when they'd spent the afternoons studying and learning sign language together.

Maybe Father was right about Samuel's energy being contagious because a shot of warmth coursed through her veins, and for a moment, her illness didn't weigh her down.

They walked through other promenading couples and footmen balancing full trays of food and drinks on their hands.

He signed quickly. "I'll go straight to the point. What has happened to you?" His eyebrows knit with concern.

"My body has trouble flourishing again. The situation is more serious than I let you believe in my letters. I didn't want you to worry."

He paused behind the hedgerow. In the shadow, his frown was deeper. "What does your physician say?"

"He tried everything he could and likely saved my life after the incident. I got better, but it didn't last. And I think..." Emotion choked her.

Telling him she feared she would eventually die terrified her, which didn't make sense because she'd come to accept her fate. Death didn't scare her, but now, standing so close to Samuel and the vibrant vitality he radiated, she didn't want to accept her fate. She wanted to get well.

"You think what?" he prompted her.

"I think I'm dying," she whispered.

It was the first time she'd confessed to her fear. Her low voice sounded like thunder in their small, quiet corner.

He cupped her cheek with infinite tenderness. His fingers quivered. "No, I don't believe it. I refuse to believe it."

"Dr. Tucker is considered the best physician in the country. The freezing water and the fever weakened my body, and I couldn't recover fully. Ever. No one told me I'm dying, but I feel it in my bones."

His eyes flared wide, and anger—not worry—flickered in them. "I want the captain's opinion." His fingers moved with sharp gestures.

She chuckled bitterly. "I respect the captain, but he can't be more knowledgeable than Dr. Tucker."

"If you really think you're dying, which I don't, then why not listen to another opinion?"

"Even if I want to, how can I let him visit me? My parents will never agree. Not to mention they have no idea Captain Jackson is your friend and mine."

"I'll find a way. You see obstacles everywhere."

"I'm being realistic."

He shook his head. "I was like you. When I was in the circus, I was scared of everything and had nightmares. I didn't believe I could ever be happy until I met you. Trust me, if there's someone who understands what you're going through, it's me. You became my friend, even though I was frightened and weak. You saved my life in more ways than one, and I'll be honoured to return the favour."

She took his hand, smiling. "I've missed you so much."

He kissed her knuckles, sending a jolt of sensations down her back; it was like waking up after a long slumber.

She hugged him, sighing when she rested her head on his chest, hearing the strong thumping of his heartbeat. They held each other for a long moment.

His amber eyes glowed from within. He held her hand in his. "Vivienne, will you marry me?"

She tilted her head. "Excuse me?"

"Marry me. Leave this house. This horrible life of illness. Stay with me forever."

"Forever? You might become a widower in a matter of months."

She'd meant to say something else, like why on earth did he want to marry her after they hadn't seen each other in years? But her first thought had been about her death. Perhaps he had a point when he said she saw only obstacles.

"No, I won't be a widower." He started to sign with sharp gestures. "I'm not a doctor, but I learnt a lot by standing close to Captain Jackson, and I know something about drugs. I'm sure we can help you."

"But Dr. Tucker—"

"Sod him!" He snapped his fingers angrily before stopping again. "Sorry. I didn't mean to..." He laughed softly. "Raise my voice."

She gave him a little smile.

"If you marry me, you won't have to worry about lying to your parents or how we can see the captain."

She arched her brow. "Are you telling me I should marry you so that I can see the captain?"

He flashed a charming smile that made his eyes more intense. "No. I want you to marry me because I know with all my soul that I'll make you happy."

Happy. She couldn't remember the last time she'd been happy. No, actually she could. She'd been happy with him.

They walked along the gravel path through the flowerbeds of violets without talking. He didn't press her further, which she appreciated because she needed a moment to fully understand the meaning of his proposal.

She, married to the golden king. But above all, she would be next to him and his radiance every day. Her heart gave a quick kick, and her cheeks grew warm. Her vision became sharper for a moment. Had the flowers in the garden always been so colourful? She didn't remember all those peonies, roses, and geraniums to be so vivid.

If she was truly dying and her end was close, then she wanted to live her last months free and happy. No, that wasn't the only reason why she wanted to accept his proposal. His energy was contagious, and his optimism gave her hope. A small, timid hope, but it was there. And she'd missed him terribly. She'd never stopped thinking of him.

She cleared her throat. "Father will accept you, happily. But I'm not sure my mother would approve."

"If there's one thing I learnt during the years I worked hard across Northern America, it's that everything is possible if you have the right attitude, mind, and will. Also, I don't have a title, but I'm one of the wealthiest men in the world. I'm not bragging... well, I am, but if I can't brag, then who can?"

She laughed, surprising herself with the sound of her happy voice. "I'm looking forward to becoming Mrs. Samuel Lyon."

He seemed to grow taller. His whole face transformed with happiness. He was so happy it was difficult to hold his gaze. He held her by the waist and twirled her in a circle. Laughter burst out of her until she coughed.

He put her down. "Are you all right?"

She coughed in her closed fist. "Never been better."

He scattered kisses on her hand, lingering for a few moments. "Let me talk to your father. I'm sure everything will go smoothly."

twenty-seven

Vivienne wasn't a pessimist. Not in this particular situation, at least.

But when Samuel had said that everything would go smoothly, he'd been naïve. After the party was over and the guests had left, she'd had barely time to drink her purple potion before her parents summoned her.

So here she was, sitting in the drawing room with her father and mother without having any conversation with them. They were arguing with each other, and she waited for them to stop.

"Lyon is a robber baron," Mother said, pacing along all the lengths of the room. "A *nouveau riche*!"

"An extremely rich *nouveau riche*." Father stood next to the fireplace, as composed as Mother was agitated. "And he isn't a robber baron but a tycoon."

"I don't care what you want to call him. He can't marry Vivienne."

"Why?" Vivienne and Father said together.

Mother glanced from one to the other. "Vivienne is too sick for starters. The last thing she needs is a wedding."

Father huffed. "Exactly because she's sick, she needs a wedding.

Something to look forward to. If she is..." He didn't need to end the sentence.

She understood him. Since she was dying, why not let her enjoy herself and marry Samuel?

Father rubbed his forehead. "What do you think, Vivienne? Is your health an impediment to the wedding?"

"No. I'm getting stronger." It wasn't true, but she believed Samuel. "And I like Mr. Lyon. He's an interesting man."

"He can't speak," Mother said.

"I'll learn sign language."

"You're too weak." Mother clenched her fists, shaking. "You can't leave the house. Where are you going to live? New York City? You'll be dead before you cross the ocean—"

"Jane!" Father raised his voice. "That's enough."

"But it's true." Tears welled in Mother's eyes. "Don't you see it? She's dying like Adele, in front of our eyes."

Vivienne stared at her hands folded in her lap. Samuel made her doubt her grim future, but she wasn't fully convinced. Her symptoms were real. She desperately wanted to believe him, hoping against hope.

Still, she could use her sickness to her advantage. "Then marrying Mr. Lyon is my last wish."

Silence dropped in the room. Mother came to a halt, and Father stopped rubbing his forehead.

She tilted her chin up. "If it's true I'm dying, then I want to spend my last months as Mrs. Lyon."

"And I will honour your last wish." Eyes shining, Father held her hand gently. "I have no objections to the marriage, especially if it makes you happy."

"Thank you, Father. This is what I want."

"No." Mother pressed her lips hard. "I won't let you. It's madness."

Father worked his jaw and straightened. "I've never imposed my will on this family. I've always believed in having a discussion.

I've always listened to everyone and respected your opinion, Jane. But this time, it's different. Vivienne will marry Mr. Lyon, and I don't want to hear a single complaint from you."

Mother paled, her eyebrows lifting to her hairline.

It was the first time Father had blatantly ordered Mother to do something...or not do something.

Mother regained her composure. "You'll have her death on your conscience." She ran out of the room, shaking with sobs.

Father didn't go after her but sat next to Vivienne. "Forget what that know-it-all of a physician says. I want to know your opinion. Do you really feel you're dying?"

A few hours ago, before her conversation with Samuel, she would have said *yes* without hesitation. But now she wasn't as sure as she'd been that morning.

"Mother is too scared. She's trapped in the past and wants all of us to be, as well. Sometimes I feel I don't have much time to live, but I would be lying if I said that Mr. Lyon doesn't spark my interest. He gives me hope."

"You know very little of him."

Not really. "Yes, but he possesses an aura of vitality that draws me to him."

"He spoke to me. He is in a hurry to marry you. When he asked me for your hand, he went straight to the point, chose a date for the wedding, quickly discussed your dowry, and shook my hand as if the business was done."

She smiled. "American tycoons."

He barked a laugh. "I guess you're right, but are you happy to have a quick wedding?"

"Yes. Soon. Just in case my strength diminishes, and he's a busy man. He doesn't like to wait."

He grinned. "American tycoons."

Samuel hated bureaucracy.

Not even his money could save him from filling and signing an endless number of documents at the Doctors Commons. The fact he was officially American—thanks to some forged documents acquired years ago—complicated the procedure. But finally, he had everything he needed to marry Vivienne immediately.

Her father had helped him navigate the intricacies of the marriage law, but her mother had barely talked to him.

He didn't care. What he cared about was Vivienne.

He was eager to show her his beautiful house close to Buckingham Palace in the heart of Belgravia. Not that he cared about closeness to the royal family, but the house had a stunning garden with tall, old trees and a great view from the top floor. Also, he didn't plan to stay in London forever. He wanted to travel around the world with Vivienne once she recovered.

And he ought to introduce her to his household, which was today's plan. She might want to hire her own maids.

He waited for Vivienne and Dobkins in the hallway of Huntington Hall. The wedding was a couple of days away, and time seemed to slog to a crawl.

Once he made a decision, he wanted things done as quickly as possible, although Vivienne wasn't a business deal. His eagerness came from wanting to see her happy again.

"Samuel." She went down the stairs, gripping the bannister for dear life.

Her steps were slow and uncertain, and she looked paler than the last time he'd seen her. Even her breathing sounded shallower.

A moment of panic seized him as the fear she was right, that she would die in a matter of months, sneaked into his heart. Something was killing her, yes, but he would be damned if he didn't stop it. What was the point of being one of the wealthiest men in the world if he couldn't help her?

Her smile lit up her sapphire eyes. "I'm sorry if I let you wait. Getting ready took me longer than expected."

He shrugged and offered her his hand.

Dobkins beamed and went to hug him but stopped, hiding her joy behind a cough. "Mr. Lyon." She bobbed a curtsy for the benefit of the footman and maid present, he guessed.

Vivienne barely took his hand before her mother came out of a room. In her austere black gown and black hairnet, she looked like a giant crow and just as cheerful.

He bowed to the countess, staring at her unwelcoming scowl.

"Mr. Lyon, I'm afraid my daughter can't leave the house," Lady Huntington said.

"I will go out," Vivienne said.

"You can barely walk." Lady Huntington sounded angry rather than worried. "I sent for Dr. Tucker. He will be here shortly."

He quickly wrote on his notepad, "I'll be careful. Vivienne won't get tired."

The countess flushed red. "You're killing her!"

"Mother!" Vivienne wrapped her arm around his. "You're exaggerating."

Before the countess could add anything, he bowed and opened the door without waiting for the footman. He'd had enough of waiting.

"You can't leave me." Lady Huntington's voice came from behind him.

Vivienne paused and faced her. "I'm not your responsibility anymore. Samuel is going to take good care of me."

You bet. He nodded.

Lady Huntington clamped a hand over her mouth and ran up the stairs in a flutter of black fabric.

As much as he didn't approve of the countess's suffocating love for her daughter, her pain was palpable, and he didn't enjoy seeing her distraught.

"I apologise for my mother's words." Vivienne needed his help to sit in the carriage, her breathing short. Dobkins followed.

"Don't apologise." He didn't care about what her mother said. "I'm not offended." He started to enter the carriage after Dobkins when a movement caught his eye.

A short man with a top hat and in a dark suit pivoted when Samuel craned his neck to take a better look. The man hailed a hansom and vanished. Samuel could have sworn the man was limping.

"Is something the matter?" Vivienne asked.

"There was a man on the other side of the pavement. I was sure he was about to cross the street in our direction but changed his mind so quickly he seemed to be fleeing from something."

She gazed around. "I didn't see anyone."

"Never mind." He climbed into the carriage, troubled by something he couldn't point out. "You are quite pale."

She lowered her gaze, and he didn't like it.

"The captain will take a look at you," he said before holding her hand and stroking her fingers.

"Is the captain all right?" Dobkins said.

"He's been sober for five years, and it shows."

Dobkins squeezed his hand. "It's so good to see you, and I'm looking forward to seeing the captain—" She composed herself. "Well, he doesn't need to know that."

He chuckled.

Vivienne brightened when the carriage stopped in front of the house. "Is this your house? Heavens, it's huge. How many servants did you hire?"

Speaking of which. "There's something I have to tell you." He helped her out of the carriage.

"Yes?" She put both hands on his shoulders, and he held her by the waist to help her out.

When she stepped onto the pavement, she stood so close to him he got lost in her sapphire eyes. Beautiful, but for the missing spark of vitality he desperately wanted to see.

She leant into him when they walked to the front door.

He forced himself to focus. "My household includes people who were former servants but were dismissed because of physical problems. I found some of them in the streets or in circuses similar to Cade's."

She paused. "Are there more awful circuses like Cade's?"

"Some aren't terrible. I mean, in some circuses, the workers are happy to be there. But others aren't. A few of my servants have... disfigurements." He paused before knocking. "I just wanted to warn you."

She nodded.

The door swung open, and Bernard came into view in his impeccable dark suit.

"Lady Vivienne. Mrs. Dobkins. This is Bernard, my butler," Samuel said.

Vivienne gave him a graceful nod.

Bernard bowed and stretched out an arm towards the hallway.

Samuel handed him his coat and hat. "Bernard is deaf and doesn't talk, so make sure he sees your face when you're talking to him. He reads the lips very well, and of course he signs."

She looked surprised. "Read the lips?"

Bernard nodded, smiling.

Samuel tensed a little when he had to introduce his house-keeper, hoping there wouldn't be any gasps. "Lady Vivienne, Mrs. Dobkins, this is Mrs. Foster, my housekeeper."

Mrs. Foster bobbed a curtsy, her gaze on the floor. She whispered, "Welcome, my lady."

Vivienne didn't flinch at Mrs. Foster's face, nor did she ask the housekeeper to speak louder. "I'm looking forward to knowing you better, Mrs. Foster. I've never managed a house so big. I'll need your help once I'm Mrs. Lyon."

Lyon wasn't Samuel's real name; he'd chosen it because he wasn't afraid of his past, but when she said it, his chest expanded.

Mrs. Foster raised her gaze. "It'll be my pleasure, my lady."

Vivienne's smile didn't falter. Even Dobkins remained stoic. If anything, she seemed distracted, searching around.

Samuel touched a series of thin ropes running along the wall. "These are for Potter, my cook. He's blind. He uses the ropes as a guide to move around the house. Each rope is different and leads to a specific room. He's a shy man. You probably won't see him around much."

She ran a finger along the ropes. "Very clever."

"Mrs. Foster, where is Captain Jackson?" he asked.

Dobkins straightened.

"He'll be here soon. He went out on an errand."

"Where is William?" He arched a brow, nearly worried to ask.

"I'm here, sir." The footman stood nearby, close to the hall that led to the kitchen, suddenly alert and brushing some bread-crumbs from his uniform. He bowed with enthusiasm and a smile that was all mischief. "My lady. I'm William, first footman." He eyed Vivienne's gold brooch with too much interest.

"William," he warned, signing slowly.

"Sir, I didn't do anything." William tugged at his jacket, all innocence.

Samuel wouldn't talk about William's criminal past in front of anyone. Not that William's former profession was a secret, but he didn't want to embarrass the young man.

"Bernard, call for tea please." He led Vivienne upstairs to the drawing room. "Are you all right with my choices? You'll hire your maids if you want."

She put a hand on his arm. "I'm more than happy about your choices, and I'm sure Dobkins will come with me."

"Of course." Dobkins nodded.

She sat on the sofa. "Quite proud of you, actually."

"And the house is beautiful," Dobkins said.

"How do you call your butler?" Vivienne asked.

"We have bells that warn other servants to call Bernard and other bell ropes that, instead of making a ringing noise, have some long, colourful ribbons that attract attention. If you need something, ring the bell, and someone will come. Sometimes Bernard doesn't show up immediately. Be patient, please. He's an excellent butler and a good man."

A servant brought in the full tea with a tower of sandwiches, fruit and tarts, various cream cakes, and biscuits.

"Try these." Samuel handed her a brown nut tart. "They are my favourite. From America. Potter knows, so she makes them every week. Pecan tarts. We brought a supply of pecans with us."

"Pecan tarts?" She bit into one and was assailed by its deep sweetness, and closed her eyes. "So sweet. It's delicious."

Dobkins tried one as well. She leaned over and quietly asked, "Are you worried Murdock might find you?"

"Even if he does, what can he do? I'm officially Samuel Lyon, born in New York City. He can't prove I am not."

"Lady Vivienne." The captain entered the room, carrying his leather medical bag and beaming. "It's a pleasure to see you."

Dobkins shot up to her feet, choking on the tart. Gagging noises came out of her. Her face reddened.

The captain grabbed her from behind and pressed her abdomen until she let out a loud gasp.

"Heavens." Vivienne put a hand on her chest.

The captain smiled, still holding Dobkins. "Next time you want me to hug you, just say it. No need to risk your life."

Dobkins slanted him a glare.

Captain Jackson helped Dobkins sit down. "Did you miss me?"

Samuel handed Dobkins a cup of tea. "Have some."

"Goodness." She glanced at the captain. "You caught me off guard. But yes. I missed you a little."

They smiled at each other with a tenderness new to Samuel.

Vivienne took Captain Jackson's hand. "Dear Captain."

The captain's smile vanished as he studied her. "Lady Vivienne." He hugged her.

"You took very good care of Samuel," she said.

"Sometimes I think it's the other way around." The captain sat in front of her and opened his bag. "Samuel has told me about his concerns regarding your health. I'm aware you got sick with pneumonia and suffered from permanent lung damage?" He opened his medical bag.

She nodded. "I have respiratory problems, and my heart isn't strong."

Samuel dismissed the only servant and Dobkins got up and closed the door.

"May I examine you?"

"Yes." A little shiver went through her.

"Do I need to leave?" Samuel asked.

"Stay. Tell me about your symptoms, Vivienne." The captain held her wrist and checked her pulse.

"Well, mostly I'm tired. Fatigue never leaves me. I feel weak and sleepy. I have a constant ache in my chest, difficulty breathing, and dizziness."

"She suffers from itchy skin and rashes as well," Dobkins said.

The captain auscultated her back and asked her to cough a few times.

"And I run a fever oftentimes." Vivienne exhaled.

"Hmm." The captain studied her eyes for a long time. "Push out your tongue, please."

She did as told.

After the captain examined her mouth, he used a magnifier to study her fingernails, her scalp, and her hair. "What drugs do you take?"

"Many potions Dr. Tucker prepares." From her pocket, she took out a vial filled with a dull purple liquid. "This one I always carry with me. I need to take a few sips every two hours."

Captain Jackson uncorked it and sniffed. The tendons in his neck stood out. "Does Dr. Tucker prepare this?"

She nodded.

"The bastard!" The captain sprang to his feet and paced, startling Vivienne.

"What is it?" Samuel stood and signed right in front of the captain's face to attract his attention.

The captain rummaged through his bag. "I need to do further tests, but I'm quite sure Lady Vivienne isn't sick. Pneumonia, my arse. My lady, you're being poisoned."

twenty-eight

Poisoned. Samuel's brain was stuck on that word.

Silence dropped in the sitting room for a charged moment.

"Poisoned?" Vivienne clamped a hand over her mouth.

Dobkins gasped and sat back in her chair.

Samuel's first thought was to throttle Dr. Tucker, whoever the man was. His hope had been vindicated. Vivienne wasn't sick and dying.

Captain Jackson selected an empty vial from his bag and compared it to the one Vivienne had given him. He repeated the process until he found a vial identical to the one with the purple liquid. "Dobkins, please take this to Mrs. Foster and ask her to fill it with blueberry juice."

Dobkins took the vial. "Is it poison?"

"It's belladonna, mainly, but I think Dr. Tucker gives Lady Vivienne other drugs."

Vivienne didn't flinch. "Isn't belladonna frequently used in medicine?"

"In small doses, yes, but this potion isn't meant to make you feel better." The captain pocketed the full vial. "I'll examine it and let you know what I find, but I don't have any doubts."

Vivienne leant back onto the sofa. "You don't think Dr. Tucker made a mistake, do you?"

"Mistake, my arse. Pardon me." The captain gestured at her. "Do you have itchy red spots similar to nettle rashes?"

"On my back."

"You have all the signs of poisoning. I would bet Dr. Tucker asks you to take another potion, a yellow one, and to replace it with the purple one for a week or two every month."

Her eyes widened. "Yes!"

"What's the second potion for?" Samuel asked.

"To make sure Lady Vivienne doesn't die." The captain rubbed his face. "Dr. Tucker is certainly a fraud, but he knows how to use potions and poisons."

She gasped. "Did he keep me sick all these years on purpose?"

"I'm sure at first, after the ice-skating incident, you were truly sick," Captain Jackson said. "People who contract a severe bout of pneumonia do suffer from permanent damage to their lungs. But you aren't one of them. I don't believe your lungs are damaged, or that you didn't recover from the pneumonia. Once you stop taking Dr. Tucker's potions, all the symptoms will disappear."

Vivienne blinked a few times. She opened her mouth, but no words came out.

Dobkins returned with the vial of juice and sat next to Vivienne. "Is Lady Vivienne going to be fine?"

In a flask, Captain Jackson combined a powder with a liquid he took out from his bag. "I'm optimistic. From now on, until the wedding, you'll drink only the blueberry juice in the vial I give you. Do not take anything else Dr. Tucker gives you." He handed her a glass with the mixture. "This is an extract from a fruit that grows in North America. A good antidote for poisons similar to belladonna."

Vivienne's hand trembled, spilling a few drops of the drink.

Samuel held her hand and helped her sip. Anger burned his chest and the back of his throat. She'd suffered for no reason.

She drank with small sips, shaking.

He knelt next to her and caressed her cheek. "You aren't dying," he signed softly.

The good news soothed his anger but not his desire for justice.

Tears slid down her face, and he hugged her. The moment his arms were around her, she sobbed on his shoulder.

Dobkins cried as well, hiding her face in a handkerchief.

Captain Jackson rubbed the back of his neck. "It's shocking. But look at the bright side. You don't have any fatal disease."

She cried harder. Samuel brushed his lips against her temple, regretting the fact he couldn't whisper any words of comfort while she buried her face into his chest. When her crying stopped, she wiped her face.

"I can't believe I've suffered for years for no reason." Her voice sounded strong.

"Lady Vivienne," Captain Jackson said, "when you return home later—"

"Rubbish." Samuel leapt to his feet, his blood seething. "She'll stay here. She can't return home."

"Lady Vivienne will be your wife soon. A night in her house won't change anything."

"She can't stay here," Dobkins warned.

He signed furiously. "The doctor will kill her."

"Why would Dr. Tucker want to poison me?" she asked, her eyes red.

"I don't know," Captain Jackson said. "One reason is money. The longer you're sick, the more money he pockets. You surely aren't his only patient."

"And my mother..." She lowered her voice. "Do you think she knows?"

"No," from what you have said, she has her own health issues."

The captain hesitated. "I think your mother has her own problems, and that Dr. Tucker took advantage of her."

Samuel wasn't convinced. "You don't believe the countess has her responsibility?"

The captain made a gesture halfway between a shrug and a shake of his head. "I think the tragedy of losing a daughter compromised her judgement, and now taking care of Vivienne is everything that keeps her alive. If Vivienne heals and leaves the house, what will she do with her life?"

A sob shook Vivienne. She pressed a handkerchief to her mouth. "In a way, she wishes I were sick all the time."

Captain Jackson opened and closed his mouth before talking. "I don't know. It's more complicated than that. I can't believe your mother really wants you to suffer. Ask me about the maladies of the body, not of the mind."

"I don't care," Samuel signed. "Whatever Lady Huntington's reason for wanting Vivienne sick, I don't trust her."

Dobkins sniffled. "Her Ladyship suffered enormously when Lady Adele died. It's easy to believe her mind was damaged."

"I don't doubt that." Samuel moved his fingers slowly. "But Vivienne can't pay for the consequences of her mother's sorrow. Hell, Vivienne's life is at risk."

"I'm not going to let her die because the countess is overcome by grief."

Dobkins twisted her handkerchief. "You're right."

Vivienne drew in a deep breath. "I'm not sick."

"Well, you are, in a way." The captain patted her hand. "It'll take a while for your body to get rid of the poison, but after that, you'll be perfectly fine."

She started crying again. "I can't believe it. All this time..."

"You should stay here," Samuel insisted.

"She can't," Dobkins insisted. "We can protect her for two days,"

Captain Jackson spoke, "If we want to stop Dr. Tucker and

understand if there's more to the story, it would be better if Vivienne behaved normally. She'll pretend to take her potions without raising any suspicion, and I'll gather evidence of Dr. Tucker's misconduct. We'll bring the bastard to justice."

Samuel held Vivienne again. She rested her head on his shoulder and sighed. The anger flaring in his chest was a primordial force he had never experienced, not even when Murdock had abused him.

He'd finally found someone he hated more than Murdock.

twenty-nine

After Vivienne stopped crying, her chest felt empty. Her whole life did.

All those days she'd spent in bed, taken by a high fever or sudden sickness, had been a lie. She could have been healthy and happy and sailed to New York City to see Samuel as she had dreamed. Instead, she'd believed every word Dr. Tucker had said. She'd trusted him.

How stupid of her! She was angrier with herself than with Dr. Tucker. For years, she'd thought Mother's fear of diseases and germs was ridiculous, but she'd fallen into the same trap.

The sweet taste of the purple potion she'd taken every day for years still lingered in her mouth. Learning the truth had sent a bitter shock through her. She had been upset with Mother for being gullible. How ironic.

Samuel sat next to her on the sofa in the drawing room after the shocking news. They were alone. Dobkins was somewhere in the house, and Captain Jackson had gone to start analysing the sample, or so Vivienne believed.

Life made little sense now, and she didn't even care.

"How do you feel?" He stroked her knuckles with his thumb. The small gesture made her breathe better.

"Angry. Relieved. Confused." She wiped a tear. "I hope Mother isn't aware of what Dr. Tucker is doing, but her anger at knowing I was about to leave the house worries me."

"I disagree with the captain about keeping the truth quiet. If you want to stay here tonight, your room is ready."

She put a hand on his cheek. "I know, but I want to deliver Dr. Tucker to justice. One more night won't change anything, and I'll have the opportunity to collect all the potions Dr. Tucker prescribed me so the captain can examine them. If I stay here, I fear he might flee."

"Another happy memory." He brushed a curl of her hair from her face with infinite care.

"I'll never doubt your word."

The intense way he looked at her sparked energy within her, and above all, hope. One look from him worked better than any tonic.

"I so admire what you did with your household staff." She caressed his cheek again. "Those people wouldn't find employment easily, if at all."

"We have some difficult days, but with a bit of organisation, the house runs smoothly, and I'm not deluded. Hadn't it been for my good luck, I wouldn't have easily found a job either."

"You seemed worried when you introduced me to your staff."

He gazed down. "I wasn't sure how you would react. I have my own...problems here." He put a hand on his throat. "And here." He pointed to his head. "My problems added to a particular household full of people like me might have been too much for you."

"No, never. You aren't too much." He was, but not in the way he thought. "You're so strong and confident, I can only be proud of you."

He shook his head. "The fear is still here." He placed a hand over his chest. "Sometimes I can control it. Sometimes it controls me."

She placed her hand over his. "Perhaps it'll be easier if we control it together."

He kissed her hand, sending shivers dancing on her skin. "I'm looking forward to it. I want to start a new life with you. I want to show you the world."

Her heart gave a quick kick that stole her breath, and she hugged him. A few hours ago, she wouldn't have believed she had the opportunity to take a holiday and leave London. Samuel made her dream again.

"Thank you."

He held her, his arms around her, so he couldn't sign. But it didn't matter. His warmth said it all.

WHEN VIVIENNE RETURNED HOME, the atmosphere was glacial at dinner.

Even the footmen serving at the table seemed stiffer than usual.

She took small spoonfuls of her soup while Mother barely touched it, twirling her spoon without pause. Father sported a permanent frown.

Mother dropped the spoon and waved at the footman to take her bowl away. "My appetite is gone."

Father straightened, assuming the pose he reserved for meeting with his business partners. "Are you *unwell*?"

Even Vivienne detected the sharp, sarcastic note in Father's voice.

"As a matter of fact, yes. I'm worried. I can't believe you left the house like that today," Mother said to Vivienne. "After I explicitly asked you to stay."

"Jane." Father shot Mother a glare. "I don't want to hear another word."

Mother put a trembling hand on the table. "You don't care about her. You'll let her die as you did with Adele."

Father shot up, scraping his chair back. "How dare you!"

Vivienne winced. The footman did, too.

"Adele meant the world to me." Father's voice cracked, and his pain thickened the air. "I was patient with you because we were both mourning our daughter, but enough now! Vivienne will leave this house tomorrow, and I can't honestly be happier for her."

"She will die!" Mother raised her voice.

"Then she'll live her last days doing whatever she wants, and we'll support her as parents who love her should do." His voice boomed in the dining room.

Mother's nostrils flared. "Her death will be on your conscience."

"Mother, please." Vivienne shook her head. "How can you say something like that to Father?"

He dropped his napkin on the table and left in such a hurry the footman had barely time to open the door for him.

Mother hunched her shoulders and cried silently, pressing Adele's silver box against her chest. It pained Vivienne to see her parents fighting, but she couldn't find the strength to be understanding. Mother had let her grief destroy their family although she and Father had their own faults. They'd always pandered to Mother's delusions, and this was the result. Her brothers and sisters rarely visited them in London, and their relationship with Mother was strained.

Vivienne had been poisoned, forced to stay home, and had been ill for a long time.

"Compose yourself," she said.

"How can you leave me?" Mother's voice sounded high-pitched and hysterical.

"Why can't you be happy for me? I've been cooped up here for years. I want to go out and have new experiences. I want my life back."

"You're sick!"

Enough. Father was right and she didn't have the patience or the energy to argue with her mother. Their separation would benefit Mother as well. Perhaps she would realise that her life could go on.

Vivienne pushed her chair back and rose. The footman's reflexes were once again put to the test by her speed. After she left the dining room, she didn't go far. Her energy dwindled, and she slowed her pace to pause at the base of the sweeping stairs. The world tilted, and she took deep breaths. Her dizziness was nothing new, but since she knew the real reason behind it, anger exacerbated it.

"Lady Vivienne."

She gasped at hearing Dr. Tucker's voice. He came from the hallway towards her, carrying his leather bag.

She forced herself not to shiver.

He adjusted his round glasses. "I heard the news."

Her legs quivered, and she put a hand on the bannister to steady herself. "What news?"

He leant closer and whispered, "You tamed my lion."

Her breathing stuttered with fear. "What an odd choice of words."

"You're getting married to Mr. Lyon, the golden king. Tomorrow. How quick!"

She inched back from him. "Not that it's any of your business, but why should we wait?"

"Love at first sight?" He stepped closer, and the light from the gas lamp glinted off his bald head. "Aren't you too weak for a hasty wedding? A wedding is so demanding."

"I have plenty of your remedies to give me strength. Isn't that what they're supposed to do?"

He smiled, but the result chilled her blood. There was no joy in that smile, only machination. "How comforting for me to know you'll take care of yourself with my remedies." He took another step closer.

Her breathing became more erratic. Curse the purple potion. She hadn't drunk a sip of it since that morning, but as Captain Jackson had said, her body would take a while to get rid of the poison.

Dr. Tucker stared into her eyes as if aware of her fear, as if he relished in it. "I think your decision to leave the house is too hasty. You aren't ready." He closed his clammy hand around her wrist. "I think you need to be taken care of in a proper clinic for a few weeks. I know one, a lovely place out of the chaos of London, immersed in nature. Plenty of rest and my constant visits will do you good."

A clinic? She shrugged her arm free, hurting her wrist. "Leave me alone."

Her words didn't come out as strongly as she wanted. She sounded small and weak, and she hated that.

"But I can't. I promised your mother I would do everything to save you. Apparently, icy baths and flagellation are the latest frontiers of medicine."

"You mean torture."

He seized her arm again. "Then tell Mr. Lyon you changed your mind and that you don't want to marry him anymore."

"Why do you care?"

"I'm afraid you don't leave me any choice." He gave her a yank, making her wince.

Dobkins stepped between them, seemingly coming out of nowhere. She shoved Dr. Tucker with one strong push. She towered over him, and his bad leg wasn't in his favour.

Dr. Tucker staggered a few feet back, his beady eyes growing wide with anger.

"Lady Vivienne needs to go to her room." Dobkins put an arm around Vivienne's shoulders.

"I'll come with you." He insisted.

"Absolutely not." Dobkins used a growling voice Vivienne had no idea she could produce.

"But see…" He fished out a folded piece of paper from his pocket. "I have a formal request to escort Lady Vivienne to a clinic, signed by her mother, who is very concerned about her daughter's health."

"I don't care if it's signed by the queen. Mark!" Dobkins called the footman who arrived promptly. "Escort the doctor out immediately."

Mark stretched out an arm towards the front door, but Dr. Tucker didn't move.

"The countess sent for me. I won't leave until I see her," he said. "I'm sure she wants to know if her request to hospitalise her daughter is going as she wants."

Vivienne shouldn't be surprised, but the news hurt. Mother would rather see her locked up in a clinic than married and happy.

"Fair enough," Dobkins said. "Go and see Her Ladyship. Lady Vivienne will retire now."

Mark stopped Dr. Tucker from going upstairs. "This way, sir."

Vivienne avoided glancing at him. The fright had robbed her of the last ounce of energy.

Dobkins helped her up the stairs, half-supporting, half-dragging her.

Vivienne panted by the time she arrived at her bedroom. "He wanted to take me away."

"Over my dead body. Your father wouldn't have allowed that."

"Why can't I breathe?"

"You've been taking that poison for a while, and that monster gave you a fright. I guess your body is too weak to endure too much excitement." Dobkins shut the door and released Vivienne. "I apologise for not having understood the truth earlier. I feel like an idiot."

Vivienne took deep breaths. "I didn't understand it either. It's not your fault."

"It is. Like your mother, I feared you would die as Lady Adele, and sometimes we fear something so deeply that our judgement is impaired." Dobkins sniffled. "But this is a conversation we'll have another time."

In a flurry of activity, she opened the armoire and took out a few clothes.

"What are you doing?" Vivienne sat on the stuffed stool in front of the vanity, her head light.

"We're leaving. Now. I'll pack only a few things."

"But we agreed I should sleep here tonight."

"Because we thought Dr. Tucker was unaware of the fact you knew the truth. It's obvious he isn't."

"He said something weird...you tamed *my* lion."

"Why is it weird?" Dobkins rummaged through the chest of drawings.

"Because he didn't say *a* lion or *the* lion, but *my* lion."

"Who knows what he meant by that?"

"What about my father? I can't leave him."

"He left for his gentlemen's club." Dobkins stuffed a shirt and a skirt into a carpet bag. "Write a letter to him. Tell him...what you want. The wedding is tomorrow. Your parents will find a way to contain the gossip for a night, but I won't take the risk of that evil doctor kidnapping you in your sleep."

She swallowed hard, opening the drawer of her escritoire. If Dr. Tucker knew she discovered his treachery, it was plausible to think he might want to get rid of her, not merely lock her away.

She addressed the letter to Father, telling him the truth, that Mother had authorised Dr. Tucker to send her to a clinic, and she had no intention of going anywhere. So she'd decided to go to a nearby lodge for accommodation.

"I've finished it." She folded the letter.

"I'll put it on his bed." Dobkins left the room with the letter.

From her pocket, Vivienne fished out the vial Captain Jackson had given him and took a sip. In the past few years, she'd been patient—too patient—with her weakness. Now she wanted to get better immediately.

Dobkins entered the room and closed the carpet bag. "Let's go." She carried the bag and helped Vivienne stand up.

"I can walk on my own." She could, but not quickly.

They went down the stairs slowly. The staircase darkened as she gazed down.

"We'll hail a cab and be at Samuel's in a moment." Dobkins searched around, her chest rising and falling.

Her gaze shifted towards the dining room. Was Dr. Tucker there with Mother?

She expected him to come out of the dining room and seize her to drag her to an asylum. Her pulse hammered in her veins.

"Nearly there, my lady." Dobkins helped her speed up across the hallway.

The cold air cleared her head, but sweat damped the back of her neck. The shadows could hide anyone, and fear tightened her chest.

"Stay strong." Dobkins hailed a cab and helped her in. "We're leaving."

She exhaled when she sat in the cab. Her heart was racing, and shivers went through her. Her vision blurred as well.

Not for the first time, she feared she was about to die.

thirty

Samuel finished writing down the menu for the next few days. Whatever he asked, Potter would provide it, spoiling him.

Following Captain Jackson's suggestions on how to improve Vivienne's health, he'd ordered plenty of tangerines, oranges, strawberries, and fresh fish. The captain had said to buy all the food that cured scurvy, but Samuel didn't understand what the scurvy had to do with Vivienne's condition.

He watched the darkness covering the cobbled street. Uneasiness crept over him like the shadows spreading over London. A few more hours, then Vivienne would be with him forever, and no one would hurt her.

Since he had finished the menu list, he replied to unimportant letters. Sleep would elude him anyway.

Bernard entered the study and bowed. "Sir, Lady Vivienne is here," he signed.

"Vivienne?" Samuel shot up from his chair. "She is here?"

He followed Bernard and stopped in the entry hall. Vivienne, pale and panting, leant against Dobkins who seemed about to fall under Vivienne's weight.

He rushed to Vivienne's side. "The captain," he signed to Bernard.

Vivienne's eyes started to roll backwards into a faint, and a raspy noise came out of her mouth.

"We had to leave." Dobkins sighed when he took Vivienne in his arms. "Dr. Tucker came. Lady Huntington sent for him. He threatened to lock Lady Vivienne up in an asylum if she didn't change her mind about marrying you. He said Lady Vivienne had tamed *his lion*."

Samuel couldn't sign to ask what the hell Dr. Tucker—the realisation hit him like a punch in the head. The shock caused his step to falter, and he had to thank his reflexes for not letting him fall.

Dr. Tucker had become Vivienne's physician after the ice-skating disaster; he was an expert in potions and drugs; the circus didn't perform anymore. Could he be Murdock?

He gathered Vivienne in his arms, and she rested her head on his shoulder.

Her breathing sounded shallow. Once upstairs, he laid her in the bed in the room that was supposed to be hers after tomorrow.

Dobkins wasn't faring better. She was wheezing, too.

"Describe Dr. Tucker," he signed angrily.

"Short, bald, piggish eyes, yellow teeth, and he walks with a limp."

Even if Samuel could have talked, he would be speechless at the moment. He should have suspected something.

"Murdock," he signed with effort as if his fingers were tied together.

Dobkins's cheeks paled further. "But...it can't be."

"Only I've seen him. We need evidence, but I think it's him."

"Good Lord." Dobkins wrapped her arms around herself. "There should be a photograph of him in *The Times* of last Tuesday. I remember spotting him in the crowd of a group of Harley

Street doctors for the inauguration of a new hospital in Chelsea." Samuel pulled the call bell and waited for his servant.

"He's like a disease that goes from one victim to another to find fresh energy."

He caressed Vivienne's cheek as a chilly shiver of fear crept down his back.

Murdock had been close to Vivienne for these past years, hurting her, and he was thousands of miles away and hadn't done a damn thing to help her. The thug had found the worst possible way to punish him for leaving the circus.

Bernard arrived.

"Bring me last Tuesday's issue of *The Times*."

The butler left quickly.

"I'm here." Captain Jackson strode into the room in his dressing gown.

Samuel moved away to give room to the captain. "She's barely conscious."

"Let me see." The captain checked her pulse and touched her neck.

Vivienne blinked a few times as if she had trouble seeing. Captain Jackson checked her pulse again.

"Samuel believes Dr. Tucker is Murdock," Dobkins said. "He wanted to take Lady Vivienne to an asylum."

Captain Jackson whipped his head towards them. "What the hell!"

"Dr. Tucker's description fits Murdock's," Dobkins said. "His timing in becoming Lady Vivienne's physician is suspicious as well."

"As if I didn't hate the bastard enough." The captain focused on Vivienne.

"How is she?" Samuel asked when he couldn't stand the silence any longer.

"Too much excitement. But nothing that a good night's sleep

and a tonic won't cure. Her pulse is slow, but I guess it spiked earlier. I'll be back in a moment." The captain left the room.

Samuel lit the fire. "How are you?" he asked Dobkins.

"Agitated."

"Thank you for bringing Vivienne here."

"I failed her all this time. It won't happen again."

"What happened isn't your fault."

Dobkins shook with a sob. "I should have understood Dr. Tucker was a fraud. He took advantage of the countess's feeble mind and Lady Vivienne's pneumonia."

"The important thing is that Vivienne will be better." He covered Vivienne with the quilt and caressed her hand.

She heaved a sigh and opened her eyes. A fleeting smile graced her lips. "Samuel."

He kissed her knuckles. "You're safe."

"I know."

"Here we are." The captain came back, twirling a spoon in a large glass containing an amber-coloured liquid. "Vivienne, you're awake. Good. Drink this. There are ginger, lemon, turmeric, dittany, and a lot of activated charcoal. I can't guarantee the taste is good, but I can guarantee the effect is great."

Samuel held her up and helped her sip the tonic, worried about her pale complexion.

She scrunched up her face after a few sips. "Horrid stuff."

"You caught me unprepared." Captain Jackson clicked his tongue. "I'll prepare something sweeter for tomorrow. Now drink it up."

She did as told, her cheeks flushing red. "Its strength is the disgust. I already feel better."

"Excellent." The captain checked her pulse again. "It'll take time, but your strength will come back, although you'll need to drink that tonic every day."

She sagged against Samuel, and he welcomed her weight, vowing to take care of her.

Dobkins hadn't failed her. He had.

Vivienne swallowed hard. "I'll force myself to feel better just not to have to drink this anymore."

"You should rest." The captain glanced at Dobkins. "So should you."

Bernard came back with the newspaper. "A few pages are missing because the flame-keeper uses them to start the fire."

Samuel flipped through the pages and stopped at the article about the inauguration of a children's hospital in Chelsea.

There was Murdock. Polished, with fine clothes, but with the same evil eyes. "Bloody hell."

"It's Dr. Turner." Dobkins pointed at a man in the first row of doctors.

His blood seemed to freeze, and the phantom pain of Murdock's cane stung his back. "It's him. Murdock."

Captain Jackson cursed under his breath.

Vivienne's eyes flared wide. "Dr. Tucker..."

"That thug." Dobkins tottered on her feet and grabbed the bedpost.

"Careful." The captain steadied her.

The back of Samuel's mouth grew tight as if a hand were choking him.

Dobkins rubbed her temples. "It was an exhausting evening."

"I'll ask Bernard to prepare the room next to this one for you," Samuel said to Dobkins.

"I'll do it." Dobkins walked on unsteady legs. "I think I left the luggage downstairs."

The captain was next to her in a moment. "Let me help you. A footman will bring it up. And I might need to check on you as well." He took her elbow and led her out.

Samuel touched Vivienne's hair.

She put the glass on the nightstand and squeezed him tightly, as much as her energy allowed her. "I felt it, that he was...evil, but I didn't listen to my instinct. He saved my life when I got sick after the fall into the lake, and that muddled my judgement. But deep down, I knew he wasn't to be trusted."

"I'm responsible for all the pain you endured. Murdock targeted you because of me."

"No, please. Don't say that." She pressed her face against his chest. "Please don't feel guilty."

He scattered kisses on her cheek. "Drink your tonic."

She let out a dramatic sigh. "Fine." She finished the tonic and scowled at it. "Every day to have to take this awful drink. But it serves me right. Dr. Tucker's potions have always tasted delicious. That alone was suspicious."

"I'll ask Mrs. Foster to help you get ready for the night."

"Thank you." She took his hand.

"I didn't do anything."

"I wanted to leave my house, and you helped me." She snuggled closer to him. "I'm looking forward to being your wife, feeling better, and travelling with you."

"Where would you like to go?"

Her cheeks had regained their colour, and her eyes shone more brightly. "May I choose any place?"

"Of course."

"Anywhere? Even Bath?"

"Bath?" It was his turn to scrunch up his face. "You can choose any place on Earth, and you want to go to a glorified spa?"

She laughed. "It's lovely and ancient."

"I was thinking of Paris, Rome, Madrid, New York City...or something less crowded, like Malta."

Her smile was broad and brightened her face. "I would love that."

"Malta?"

"Everything. It's a dream."

"No. It's a plan."

She wrapped her arms around his neck and hugged him. Her muscles lacked strength, and once again, he suppressed a flare of anger against Murdock. But she was safe in his arms, and he didn't want to think of anything else but her.

"I'm scared," she whispered, pressing her face to his chest.

He had to disentangle himself from her embrace to sign. "So am I. Money can do a lot of things, but not protect you from the pain of losing someone you love. I'm glad the captain is here to help you."

"I'm glad *you're* here."

He wanted to talk about a few things regarding their imminent wedding. Dire circumstances had brought them together, pushing them towards a hasty marriage, but that didn't mean he didn't care about her. She would have complete freedom as his wife, which included her choice about their being together.

Discussions for another time.

He kissed her forehead and gently disentangled himself from her. She fell asleep in a moment, breathing softly.

thirty-one

Vivienne expected a huge wave of relief and happiness after escaping her house, but instead, fatigue was the only thing she felt the next morning, despite a good night's sleep.

She was happy to be with Samuel, but for now, she didn't have the energy to show it.

After a maid helped her get washed and dressed, she had breakfast in her bedroom in front of the orange glow of the fireplace.

Everything she ate, from the tea to the scones, tasted like the concoction Captain Jackson had given her last night.

"My lady." Mrs. Foster entered the bedroom, carrying a fresh glass of Captain Jackson's drink.

Speaking of the devil.

"Wonderful."

Half of the housekeeper's face was normal, but the other half looked as if a brutal force had pushed the facial features up, distorting them. Her left eye was pulled up. The left corner of her mouth was twisted up as well, and in general, her left side was deformed. Her brown eyes were uncommonly kind.

Mrs. Foster curtsied. "Is there anything else you need?"

"Nothing, really."

"I'm sorry we had to wake you up at dawn. You need to get ready for the ceremony." Mrs. Foster folded the clothes and unpacked the carpet bag efficiently and quietly.

"I'm looking forward to it." Vivienne watched the housekeeper work around the room.

"Are you happy here?" she asked, vaguely aware she was crossing a line with a woman she barely knew.

Mrs. Foster smiled. "Very much. Before meeting Mr. Lyon, I worked as a maid for a wealthy family. My employer didn't want me to become his housekeeper, despite my years of service, because my face wasn't to his liking. So I joined a roadshow. It was honest work, but not the most rewarding, either in coins or in happiness. I played the role of the deranged monstrous woman and used a frying pan to fend off my attackers. People would always laugh. The show was silly, but I learnt a thing or two about fighting. When Mr. Lyon offered me a job, I didn't hesitate to accept it."

"Samuel is a good man."

"He is. I'm happy for you," Mrs. Foster said in a motherly way.

When Mrs. Foster left, Vivienne couldn't deny a hint of nervousness at the thought of her wedding. There were plenty of reasons to be nervous. It was her wedding, after all.

She wouldn't be surprised if Mother didn't show up, and maybe even Father might decide not to come after her last stunt. Her brothers and sisters wouldn't be present as well. She hadn't given them enough notice.

And there were things she wanted to discuss with Samuel. Things they hadn't mentioned, like what he expected from her. Selfishly, when she'd agreed to be his wife, her only thought had been to leave her house. He deserved better from her.

She resigned herself to drink the potion.

Loud voices coming from downstairs distracted her from her breakfast.

"...what was I supposed to do?" That was Captain Jackson.

Someone else answered but not loudly enough for her to understand who the speaker was.

Footsteps pounded closer. She tensed as her door was flung open.

"Vivienne." Father swept into view and crossed the room with quick strides.

"Father." She hugged him.

He searched her face. "I read your letter this morning and came immediately."

That explained the loud voices. Father must have met Captain Jackson.

"How are you?"

"Better. I'm sorry I left without seeing you, but Dr. Tucker scared me. And Captain Jackson—"

"Why is he here?"

"Heaven." She exhaled. "It's a long story. Take a seat. I'll start from the beginning."

Dishevelled and with his shirt wrinkled, Father listened patiently to her escapades from a few years ago, raising an eyebrow at her visiting Samuel regularly for months. He narrowed his gaze when she told him about Murdock and Dr. Tucker being the same person.

"Captain Jackson has been nothing but kind to me," she said, taking her father's hand. "I know it's difficult for you, but please, it would be wonderful for me if you could avoid arguing with him, especially today. I need you by my side."

He squeezed her hand. "Is it true? You aren't dying?"

She shouldn't be surprised he was interested only in that part of her whole speech.

Tears stung her eyes. "No. Captain Jackson said with time and the right food, I will fully recover."

Father hugged her again, shivering. "I confess I understood very little of everything else you told me. But that's the most wonderful news I've ever heard and the only thing I care about."

She rested her head on his shoulder as they cried and laughed together.

He caressed the top of her head, as he'd done when she was a child. "There's no hurry to get married then, since you aren't dying. You can have a one-year-long engagement, an engagement party, and we can plan a proper reception."

She dropped her smile. "But Father...I really want to—"

He laughed. "Only a jest. I know you well. You wouldn't have agreed to marry Mr. Lyon if you didn't like him. I'm happy for you."

"What about the captain?"

Father returned serious. "I was angry with him when Adele died, but after the pain diminished, I realised he wasn't at fault, but I was too proud to search for him. And he's helping you. I don't want to argue with him or bring enmity to this moment that is so important to you. You're happy and healthy. I don't care about anything else." He rubbed his beard. "No, there's something I care about. Rest assured, Dr. Tucker, Murdock, or whatever his real name is, will face justice. I've never liked him, and I should have followed my instinct."

"What about Mother?"

Father's facial lines tensed further. "I made the mistake of indulging her hysterics, because she was grieving. Not anymore. Because of her delusions and my being weak, you nearly died. She must face the consequences of her actions, too. Sometimes loving someone means not letting them do everything they want." He kissed her forehead and rose. "Now get ready. Your groom is waiting for you."

～

BETWEEN THE COMBINED efforts of Dobkins and Mrs. Foster, Vivienne was ready in about three hours. Almost ready.

After her hurried departure from home the other night,

Samuel had sent his footman, William, to retrieve her belongings, but somehow, the gown she'd planned to wear that day had been left behind, and all her accessories matching a few of her gowns had been mixed up. William had claimed the gowns and accessories looked all the same, even though a maid should have helped him.

She opted for a pale green dress with long sleeves hiding her thin arms and bony shoulders although the colour didn't complement her pale complexion.

Dobkins kept blinking as she fixed Vivienne's chignon.

"Don't cry. I'll cry, too."

"They're happy tears." Dobkins wiped her face. "I've always dreamt to see you happily married with a man you loved, and you couldn't have found a better man."

"True."

Dobkins's smile dropped. Her new tears didn't seem happy at all. "I can't believe I was so stupid to let that thug almost kill you. Captain Jackson saved your life. I don't want to think what would have happened to you without him."

Vivienne hugged her. "It's done. We can't change the past, but we can work together for a better future. And I have my share of fault, too." She stepped back from Dobkins and smiled at the woman who had been a second mother to her. "I'm glad you decided to come with me."

"Where else would I want to be?"

She poked Dobkins teasingly in the ribs. "Unless you're here only for the captain."

Dobkins laughed and blushed. "As you said, the past is done. Let's think about the future. He certainly isn't the same man he was before, and I can't deny I'm proud of him. As I'm proud of you."

They hugged again, letting more happy tears fall.

Samuel would wait for her at the church, so she went down the stairs with Father.

The entire household was gathered in the hallway to see her

out. She didn't know them well, but their warmth touched her. Dobkins, Mrs. Foster, Richard, Bernard, and William clapped their hands when she stepped into the hallway. The man with a hand around one of the ropes on the wall had to be Potter, the cook. He stood half hidden in a corner, a shy smile on his face.

Mrs. Foster helped her don her capelet. "My lady, we'll be here to welcome you and Mr. Lyon after the ceremony."

William held the door open. "I'm coming with you to the church."

She climbed into the carriage with her father and Dobkins. The bright sunlight glinted off the elegant windows of the neighbouring houses, flashing golden sparks over her. She closed her eyes in the sunshine, enjoying the warmth on her skin.

Captain Jackson's awful potion was already working because her body didn't feel numb and the air had a crisp quality she'd missed.

"If you feel unwell," Father said, "I'll take you home immediately."

Home. It was curious how her mind flew immediately to Samuel's house at the word *home,* and not her parents'. She'd been in Samuel's house for a few hours, but she already felt safe and comfortable there.

"I feel better than yesterday."

"And hopefully, worse than tomorrow." He smiled.

When the carriage rolled to a stop in front of the church, she looked out of the windows. Beautiful white roses adorned the stone arch of the front door, looking like an angel's wings. Father helped her out of the carriage.

"Do you think Mother will come?"

He shook his head. "She won't be here today."

Nothing new, and it was better that way.

Captain Jackson bowed his head at their passage, and Father returned the greeting with a polite gesture.

The semidarkness in the church made her squint her eyes as

Father accompanied her to the altar where a radiant Samuel was waiting in a tailored morning suit.

Her heart raced, and for a moment, she feared she might have another fit out of excitement, but when he smiled, her pulse returned to normal.

thirty-two

"Stay calm," Captain Jackson said to Samuel next to the altar.

"I'm calm," he signed, craning his neck to see Vivienne walking down the aisle.

"You keep moving your feet. The priest will think you want to make a dash for it."

He remained still, smiling at his bride. She looked radiant from the inside out. As she walked the few steps separating them, all the moments they'd shared flashed through his mind. When she'd sneaked into the circus to see him; when she'd taught him how to read; when she'd kissed him while they sat together on a bench to give him a happy memory.

And soon she would be his wife.

The priest said something that broke the spell, and then she was offering him her hand. He held it against his chest to make her feel his heartbeat. Her smile was so wide and bright his pulse raced further

They both faced the priest, and the ceremony began. He didn't care if there were only a few people or that Vivienne's Mother wasn't present. That day was the best of his life.

"Will you, Samuel, take Vivienne Elizabeth to be your

wedded wife?" the priest asked, "to have and to hold from this day forwards, for better, for worse, for richer, for poorer, in sickness and in health, to love and to cherish, till death do you part?"

Samuel signed quickly, "I do."

Captain Jackson would translate. "Mr. Lyon says—William, what are you doing?"

Everyone turned towards the footman standing in a corner next to a shrine.

William stood on attention. "Nothing."

The captain scowled. "Apologies, Father. That wasn't what Mr. Lyon said. He said 'I do.'"

Vivienne seemed to fight a chuckle as Samuel finished his vows.

When she said, "I do," Samuel would have loved to sweep her off her feet into a twirl. He was happy just smiling at her.

The priest took their hands. "I now pronounce you husband and wife."

Samuel kissed her hand and leant closer before stopping. They hadn't discussed the kiss, and he didn't want to embarrass her. So he kissed her forehead and hugged her, wishing he could whisper how much he cared about her.

But maybe words weren't needed.

THE CEREMONY HAD BEEN beautiful for Samuel, just because Vivienne had smiled the whole time, her cheeks had been rosy, and her eyes had shone. And because she was his wife.

She had many reasons not to smile—her mother hadn't come, the guests were only a few, and she wasn't wearing the gown she'd wanted. But the way her eyes lit up when she looked at him made up for all the rushed preparations.

Now that she was his wife, no one would hurt her.

Sitting next to her at the table of the wedding breakfast, he surveyed the dining hall.

Lord Huntington sat on the other side of Vivienne, studying the servants. The captain frowned at the glasses of champagne scattered around. Samuel would have been happy to ban any liquor out of respect for his friend, but Captain Jackson had refused the offer.

A wedding without liquor is like a joke without a punchline, the captain had said.

Potter had prepared all sorts of delicacies, from roasted Cornish game hens to a wedding cake of *dulce de leche* and pecans, and all his household was enjoying the celebration.

Vivienne took his hand. "Thank you. It's a beautiful reception."

He dipped his head, taken by the sudden urge to kiss her but paused an inch from her lips. Not because he didn't want to kiss her, but because their first kiss should be in private.

She gazed up at him, her lips parting. "You didn't kiss the bride."

"We didn't discuss the kiss, and I wasn't sure if you wanted to be kissed in front of everyone." He took her chin and stroked it with a thumb. "Perhaps in a more private place?" he signed for her only.

She nodded, and the nod was a tiny gesture that shifted the Earth's axis enormously.

The moment she rose from the chair, her father and the captain jumped up as well.

"Are you ill?" her father asked at the same time as the captain said, "Maybe you need to rest, Lady Vivienne."

She waved dismissively. "I'm fine. I just want to take a stroll with my new husband."

Holding her hand, he led her to the garden where a white gazebo towered among purple flowers and evergreen bushes.

She sighed when they were under the ornate roof of the

gazebo. "I know there are important things we'll need to face. Father wants to prosecute Dr. Tucker. He went to the police station last night to denounce him, and we should see the police soon, but today I want only to enjoy the party and be with you."

"I couldn't agree more." He stood next to her, lacing his fingers through hers.

For a moment, they listened to the birds singing and the sound of the carriages and carts coming from the other side of the fence.

She tilted her head up, her large eyes widening. "Do you remember the night when you came to my bedroom and asked to kiss me?"

"How could I ever forget?"

"When you asked me if you could kiss me, I didn't think you meant on the cheek. I was a bit disappointed but didn't say anything, not to sound petulant, but I've wanted a proper kiss since then."

Instant heat burst in his chest.

"It's time to correct past mistakes."

She parted her lips, and a new flush filled her cheeks.

She moved closer until her chest brushed his, and he didn't have time to think, breathe, or wonder.

They moved at the same time. His whole body tensed with anticipation and the fear of doing something wrong. He moved only his head, forcing his hands to remain at his sides. The distance that had seemed so short a moment ago was now endless.

She breathed faster, too.

At first, he simply brushed his lips against hers, and the delicate touch was like fire. He pressed his lips harder against hers, just to feel how soft and silky they were.

The kiss was nothing but a whisper, dancing on their breaths. He ran a hand from her shoulder to her waist and pulled her closer.

He savoured the perfect moment when the constant pain and

fear didn't matter, the world was beautiful, and he was just a man like any other.

Space separated them as he tilted his head back. Her blue gaze set on him for a long moment. Then they were kissing again.

Her lips moved over his, demanding everything from him. A little tilt of her head brought her even closer, and he parted his lips on pure instinct.

She shuddered when he darted out his tongue only to taste her lips, and that small taste awakened a hunger he didn't know he possessed; it must have lurked inside him all that time, waiting to burst out only for Vivienne.

Hell, his heart was about to explode with too many emotions.

They shared their breaths as he inched away from her, needing a moment to let his heart slow down.

"That's the kiss I wanted," she whispered against his lips.

He touched his forehead to hers and waited before signing because he liked his hands on her waist.

He swallowed a couple of times. "I don't want you to feel constricted by our marriage. You can do whatever you want."

"Good. Because I want to be with you, see the world next to you, and help you with the wonderful job you're doing."

He loved her answer, but did she mean she wanted to share her bedroom with him? Perhaps he should mention that when she recovered her strength fully.

He was about to kiss her again when William walked over to them.

"Sir, my lady." William bowed. "We're serving the sorbet. It's delicious, but no one wants to start eating it until you're back."

As the footman straightened, a glimmer of gold from his pocket didn't escape Samuel's notice.

"I would love a sorbet." Vivienne's cheeks were deliciously pink after the kiss.

He escorted her to the dining room again. "Excuse me." He

kissed his new wife's hand before beckoning for William to follow him to the sitting room.

"Sir." William stood at attention. "Everything is going smoothly. Do you want me to serve the biscuits with the sorbet? Mrs. Foster says they shouldn't be served together, but I think they taste—"

Samuel cut him off by holding up a hand. He pointed at William's pocket.

"What, sir?"

"What's in your pocket?"

"Nothing, sir." The young footman patted himself, faking surprise at the bulge in his pocket. "This? It's nothing, sir."

He opened his hand and wiggled his fingers. "Show me."

"It's a misunderstanding—"

"Now." He snapped his fingers.

William scoffed and pulled out a gold crucifix with a ruby on the top.

"You stole from the church?" Samuel snatched the crucifix from William's hand.

"No, sir. I meant to return it. I swear it."

He pointed a finger at him. "I thought I was clear. No stealing."

"You were very clear, sir, but you said *no stealing in the house.*"

He narrowed his eyes. "Then let me clarify. No stealing whatsoever, anywhere, for any reason. Is that clear?"

William returned the scowl. "I need to practise to keep the machine well oiled. My skills need to be honed, or I'll forget them."

"Then forget them. You don't need to steal. Your salary is more than decent."

"You're very generous, sir." William shuffled his feet. "But I miss my old life a little, and it took me years to sharpen those skills. You have no idea how difficult it is to lift a wallet without being noticed or to pick a lock in record time. I don't want to lose what I learnt. You never know, sir."

"No. More. Stealing."

"This is unfair, sir." William shoved his hands in his pockets.

"Is something the matter?" Captain Jackson walked into the room.

Samuel showed him the crucifix.

"Bloody hell, William. Yours is a nasty vice." Captain Jackson shook his head. "From the church, on your employer's wedding day, during the ceremony! What's next? Stealing the queen's petticoats? I knew you were doing something during the ceremony."

"You're overreacting." William huffed. "I meant to give it back."

"You will, right now, and I'll come with you."

"But the sorbet and the wedding cake!" William protested.

"Serves you right." The captain took the crucifix. "Let's go, William. Unbelievable."

Samuel had wanted to give the former cat burglar a second chance in life, after William had shown sincere regret for his crimes and the desire to change. But thievery was more than an addiction for him; it was a manner of living.

"Is everything all right?" Vivienne stepped into the room. She wasn't as radiant as he wished her to be, but she looked stronger, and he loved her smile.

He opened his arms, and she didn't hesitate to go to him. As he held her, fear gripped him by the throat. He'd been about to lose her, and the situation with Murdock wasn't solved yet. His position and status would protect him and Vivienne, but complete peace was far away.

She rested her head on his chest, and the thought of not being able to protect her sent a cold shudder through him.

She tilted her head back. "What is it? One of your moments?"

He nodded.

Holding his hand, she led him to the sofa. "What scares you?"

He took a few deep breaths before answering. "The same. Not being free. Not being able to defend myself and protect you." His fingers shook so hard he wasn't sure she understood what he was signing.

"A few years ago, I wouldn't have fully understood what you meant, but now I do. I'm scared as well. I've been trapped in a lie for years, but we aren't alone. The captain will help us, and you have loyal friends in the house."

"Friends I must protect." He loosened the collar of his shirt. "As much as I cared about my servants, none of them is prepared to face an emergency."

"Because you're talking about a butler, a housekeeper, a valet, and a cook, and a whole slew of footmen, maids, and grooms. They aren't soldiers."

He shook his head. "I mean, they're vulnerable."

"As everyone." She kissed him on the cheek. "Trust them. You've done it so far. And I trust you, husband of mine."

The simple kiss brought him back to that time in the park when she'd kissed him to give him a good memory. That kiss was still a good memory.

They held each other for he didn't know how long, but his fear had cowered in a dark corner of his mind.

He dipped his head to stare at her. She didn't look away.

He ran a finger over the curve of her cheek. "We didn't discuss the details of our married life."

"What do you expect of me?"

"Many things." He hated that he couldn't sign and caress her at the same time. "First, that you're strong and healthy again. Second...second..." He lowered his hands.

"Yes?"

"I didn't think past that point. What do you expect of me?"

"That you let me help you when you need me and that you don't worry too much about me."

He chuckled although only a soft sound came out. "Not worry about you? It'll be easier to find another vein of gold. What else?"

"I want to spend a lot of time with you. Are you always busy?"

He was, but who cared? He was rich. He could retire and spend the rest of his life sitting on the sofa with his beautiful wife.

"I'll always find time for you." He kissed her knuckles.

She parted her lips as if meaning to say something else, but no word came out.

"Yes?"

She shrugged. "That's all."

thirty-three

At the end of the wedding breakfast, Vivienne's body was sore, and her conversation with Samuel hadn't gone as planned. She'd lacked the courage to ask him if he meant to visit her at night, sleep in her bed, and have children one day. But maybe she should make sure her health was good before making any proposals.

Father hugged her for a long minute when he was about to leave after the reception ended. "I'm sorry about your mother. She loves you. You know that, don't you?"

"I do."

He kissed her forehead. "Don't hate her. Please."

"I don't."

"I wish you all the happiness you deserve." He turned serious. "Something peculiar happened today. If a maid finds my pocket watch by any chance, will you send it to me?"

"Did you lose your pocket watch?"

"I can't find it." He patted his jacket. "I had it outside of the church, and I checked it in the carriage. So it must be—"

"Here." Captain Jackson, just returned from yet another

errand, handed the gold pocket watch to Father. "We found it on the floor, Huntington."

Father hesitated before taking it. "Thank you."

"Thank you for being here." The captain stretched out his hand, and Father shook it.

"We care about the same people, Captain, and I'm grateful for everything you've done for my daughter." Father slid the watch in his pocket. "I asked the police superintendent to send news to both of us."

The captain gave another nod.

William scowled as he held the door open for Father. "My lord."

The captain shook his head at him. "William."

"Captain." The footman shoved his hands into his pockets.

"Is something the matter?" she asked, glancing from one to another.

The captain smiled. "Nothing you should worry about. I suggest a nap before dinner."

Halfway to the stairs, she paused to catch her breath. The sensation of being about to die had been real; it tormented her even now, but knowing the fatigue wouldn't last changed everything. Now she had hope.

Samuel stopped next to her. "Tired?"

"A little."

"Allow me." He opened his arms, and she went to him without hesitation.

He gathered her up and carried her up the stairs. She pressed her ear to his chest, hearing the steady beat of his heart.

"Aren't you tired?" she asked.

He made a noise deep in his throat.

She tilted her head up. "So? Are you?"

He smiled and put her down on the landing. "I can't answer when my hands aren't free."

Warmth of shame flooded her face. "Yes, of course. I shouldn't have asked. How embarrassing."

He kept smiling and shrugged. Holding her hand, he led her to her bedroom. Bernard placed a large glass of tonic on her nightstand before checking the curtains of the four-poster bed.

"Good afternoon, Bernard," she said, only to remember too late the butler wouldn't understand her unless he was facing her.

She rubbed her forehead, feeling like an idiot.

Samuel took her chin gently and shook his head.

Bernard was surprised when he turned around and found them there. He bowed from the waist and signed at first with one hand, making gestures she didn't follow. Then he started again with both hands.

"Lady Vivienne, would you like a cup of tea later, after you rest?"

"Yes, please." At least she remembered to stare at him.

Bernard bowed again and left.

She sat on the edge of the bed. "Heavens. I'm a disaster."

He caressed her shoulder. "No."

"Bernard and you sometimes use strange sign language."

"American Sign Language. It can be signed with only one hand, while the British Sign Language requires two hands. Two different systems."

"I'll need to learn the American one. You really went far. King of gold and knowing multiple languages."

"Without you, I wouldn't have gone anywhere. If you had just freed me without teaching me how to read, I wouldn't have become who I am today. I owe you my life and that of all the people who work here for me. Good luck had a role, but I wouldn't have seized a successful opportunity without your teaching."

A lump swelled in her throat for no reason. His success and all the good he'd done moved her to tears. He'd accomplished so much in a few years.

"I'm so proud of you." Her voice cracked with emotion.

He sat next to her and wiped a tear with his thumb. "I'm proud of you, too."

She wiped her face with a handkerchief. "Me? I didn't do anything aside from getting poisoned."

"As I said, without your help, Bernard would still live on the streets. Mrs. Foster would still work in a show where the spectators made fun of her, Richard and Potter might beg for a coin in the street."

"That would be a shame. I can't speak for your valet, Richard, but you always look impeccable. However, Potter's food is delicious. So good. Dinner is going to be another masterpiece."

"And you need to rest." He rose and kissed the top of her head. "Later."

Dobkins entered the room, discreetly clearing her voice. "Do you need help, my lady?"

"Yes, please."

Samuel kissed Vivienne's cheek again before leaving.

He lingered on the threshold to smile at her as if she'd given him a gift. It was the other way around.

SAMUEL LEFT Vivienne's bedroom and paused in the corridor behind the closed door.

Another moment of panic gripped him like a cold vine. The fear of Dr. Tucker hurting her made him dizzy. Maybe he should hire guards to protect her.

"Samuel." Captain Jackson jolted him. "We need to talk."

He followed the captain to the study.

"Let's start with the easy news. The crucifix has been returned, and William has been thoroughly scolded." The captain poured two cups of tea.

"The not-so-easy news?"

"A message has just arrived from the police. The superintendent said there wasn't enough evidence to prosecute Dr. Tucker. The few people he interrogated about the doctor's behaviour had sworn by him, claiming he was a genius."

He sat at his desk. Vivienne was more important. "I need to protect Vivienne until we can find enough evidence to lock Tucker away for good. We need to convince the police superintendent to press the matter further."

"We will. But in the meantime, on my way here from the church, I went to Harley Street. There's a practice registered to a Dr. Lawrence Tucker up and running. He's still in business."

"I don't understand. How much money can he make by selling remedies that make people worse?"

Captain Jackson scratched his chin. "He became the favourite physician of the most prestigious families in London. Many still swear by him. What we can find depends on how many people he's swindling. We need to take a closer look at his office, at his files, and at his patients."

Samuel had been around the captain for quite a long time to understand what he didn't say. "By closer look, you mean breaking into his office."

"Yes, and we know the perfect person for the job."

thirty-four

Dinner was served in a small, beautiful dining room with a soaring ceiling decorated by frescoes. The scene depicted puffy white clouds and doves, and had a soothing effect on Vivienne's mood, compared to her parents' austere house.

Samuel sat at the head of the table, taking small portions of his dinner.

"What is it?" She touched his hand.

He hesitated before signing. "I don't want you to worry, but at the moment, the police won't bring any charges against Dr. Tucker. There's no evidence he poisoned any of his patients, intentionally or otherwise. Many of his patients the police interviewed defended him."

"I hope my mother isn't one of them."

"I'm sorry for the bad news."

"This is the beginning. Don't be discouraged. And don't see obstacles everywhere."

His smile reached his eyes. "Fair point."

"Potter did a wonderful job," she said, finishing her perfectly seasoned veal hash with potato croquettes.

"He's the best."

"I would like to thank him."

Samuel nodded at William, who left the room immediately. "You can take care of the menu when you're ready."

Potter entered the dining room, his hand on one of the ropes lining the walls. "My lady, sir." He had a shy but genuine smile.

She dabbed her lips with a napkin. "Potter, everything was delicious. I'm impressed by your talent."

The cook bowed. "Thank you, my lady."

"Ask him if he can prepare the orange and almond cake for tomorrow," Samuel signed.

She reported the request. Of course, for Samuel and Bernard, communicating with Potter was a challenge.

"I will, sir." Potter bowed. "I'll need William to come with me to the market if you can spare him."

Samuel nodded, and Vivienne said, "Mr. Lyon has no objections."

Potter fiddled with his hands. "I feel confident with my knives, but I never leave the house without someone."

William raised a hand. "If I may, my lady, Potter is being modest. He moved to London a few weeks ago to get acquainted with the house and the kitchen before Mr. Lyon came in, but he already has a map of London in his brain. He knows every alley and backstreet like the palm of his hand, better than a Londoner."

"William is exaggerating." Potter kept fiddling. "But leaving the house frightens me, my lady."

"Whatever you need, we'll do our best to help you." She understood Potter's hesitation to venture from the house alone. Thugs could take advantage of him, and London's streets kept changing. "Where did you learn to cook?"

"I worked for a wealthy family in New York City until I lost my sight from a gas explosion. My former employer dismissed me, and I lived on the streets for a while. I have to thank Mr. Lyon for having trusted me and given me a job."

She cleared her throat as a lump tightened it. "You deserve your place here."

"I wasn't convinced at first," Potter said. "I was worried I would cut my fingers or burn my hands, but Mr. Lyon encouraged me."

She glanced fondly at Samuel. "Thank you for the lovely dinner, Potter, and the wedding breakfast was wonderful as well."

Potter bowed. "My pleasure, my lady." He left, guided by the ropes.

As the footman removed her empty plates, she wondered if there was a way that allowed everyone to communicate with Potter.

"You should see him chopping vegetables," Samuel said. "His speed is impressive. I would chop off my fingers if I tried."

She put her hand on his. "Another man, who went through what you did, would be full of anger and desire for revenge. Instead, you gave so many people hope."

He stopped smiling. "What makes you think I'm not angry and resentful? I want to bring Murdock to justice, not just because it's the right thing. I hate him for what he did to me, and I hate him even more for what he did to you."

"But you think of others as well."

"Because I know what they're going through, and I have the means to help."

She caressed his cheek. "You have a heart of gold."

After dinner, when she went to her bedroom, she admitted to a quick flutter in her chest. Her wedding night. Would Samuel come?

Dobkins helped her out of her dinner gown and into her nightgown. "Tired, my lady?"

"Yes. I'm a bit...confused. Surprised. But in a good way. And I love the household. Everyone loves working for Samuel."

Dobkins braided her hair. "Yes, but..."

"What?"

"It's not my place, my lady."

"Please tell me. Do you have problems with the people Samuel chose?"

"No." Dobkins frowned, tying a ribbon at the end of Vivienne's braid. "I'm worried about Dr. Tucker and what he might do. He's a clever, resourceful, and conniving swindler. He must have set aside a small fortune in the past years. I don't believe he'll be brought to justice without a fight."

"What do the servants have to do with that?"

"Well, with due respect, if someone sneaks into the house to attack us, their job would be easy. The butler won't hear anything, the cook won't see anything, William will loot the house and flee, and Samuel won't be able to give the alarm if something happened."

"Please don't."

"I apologise, my lady, and I mean no offence. I'm just worried."

"I trust Samuel to keep us safe, and these people have done remarkably well without incidents so far, and Captain Jackson is a former soldier."

"Yes, but ruthless men like Dr. Tucker won't hesitate to hurt any of us, and many of us are quite vulnerable."

That was true.

"I didn't mean to upset you tonight, my lady." Dobkins stoked the fire and drew the curtains. "But I confess I won't sleep well at night here. Do you need anything else?"

"No, goodnight." Vivienne slid under the covers once alone.

Dobkins was exaggerating. Why would Dr. Tucker attack them in their sleep? A confidence man wasn't necessarily a murderer, and he might just flee London if the police charged him. And she trusted Samuel.

The cosy room and the soft bedsheets, heated by the bed warmer, lulled her to sleep. But she sat bolt upright when the door to Samuel's bedroom inched open and he walked inside.

"Did I wake you up?" He was carrying a single large lily with dark blue petals tipped with yellow.

"I dozed off."

"My apologies." He put the lily on her nightstand, flashing a charming smile. "For you."

"It is beautiful. Thank you." She touched the velvety petals. "What is it?"

"A lion-heart lily, a species from East Asia." He flashed a boyish smile. "I was lucky to find them in London."

"Impressive."

"I'll put it in a vase."

She watched him as he walked around the room to take a vase and fill it with water. His expression was completely serene, which made her think she had never seen him so calm and happy.

Even during those months they'd spent together, tension had always bothered him, but now he was a different man. His rich brown dressing gown also added to the simple domestic night.

The candlelight played on the dark petals, igniting them with a warm glow.

"There." He placed the vase on her nightstand. "I just wanted you to sleep with a beautiful flower next to you."

"Will you stay here?" Her heart was torn in two. She wanted him to spend the night with her, but at the same time, she wasn't strong enough to do much aside from sleeping.

"Do you want me to?" He perched on the edge of the bed.

She hesitated to answer only because she wasn't sure how she could express herself without sounding petulant.

"I don't want to cause you more problems. Quite the opposite. I want to be someone who can help you solve them." He patted her hand. "Tell me what you want."

"Please stay." She lifted the covers. "But I would really like to sleep only."

He frowned. Then the lines on his brow smoothed. "Of course." He removed his dressing gown and slid under the covers.

The moment he wrapped his arms around her, instant safety enveloped her. She hadn't felt so safe in years. Her back rested against his chest, and his powerful arms formed a protective cocoon around her. She closed her eyes with the scent of the lily in the air.

A thud woke her up with a jolt. She flung her eyes open and sat bolt upright. The thud came again, like a fist hitting something.

"Samuel?" She touched around the nightstand until she managed to light a lamp.

Samuel was thrashing around in the bed. His clenched fists would hit the bedhead and the bedpost, causing the bed to shake. Low noises full of pain came out of him.

"Samuel." She shook his arm gently. "Wake up."

He flung his eyes open, panting. He gazed around as if he didn't recognise the room.

"A nightmare?" She caressed his shaking shoulder.

He crushed her into a tight hug, seeking comfort. She hugged him back and drew circles on his back.

"I know. I know."

He shivered. She kept stroking his back until his breathing calmed down. When he released her, she breathed better.

"Did I give you a fright?" he asked with trembling fingers as if he were stuttering.

"Don't worry. Does it happen often?"

He raked a hand through his messy curls. "Sometimes. I got better. At first, the nightmares happened every night more than once. Now they're rarer but powerful. Learning Murdock has been so close to you all these years triggered my nightmares again. I hate feeling powerless."

"You seemed in pain."

"I was." He shoved the covers aside. "I'll let you sleep. You're too tired to have to deal with my problems."

"No, stay." She took his hand and tugged at it.

The pain in his gaze made her regret her insistence. Perhaps he wished to be alone.

She let go of his hand. "If you want, of course."

"I don't want to disturb you. I'd better go to my bedroom."

"I'm fine."

"Goodnight." He kissed her hand and left.

She lay down, touching his side of the bed still warm and smelling of bergamot, wishing she could be able to chase his shadows away.

thirty-five

After a night of troubled sleep, Samuel rubbed the back of his tense neck. The nightmare had left his body sore and his heart cracked. He'd wanted to stay with Vivienne through the night, but she needed rest and quiet, and he might hurt her by accident.

"Preoccupied, sir?" Richard asked, helping him don his jacket.

"Yes." He stared at his reflection in the wall mirror.

The suit Richard had chosen was one Samuel had worn on other occasions. Best fabric, Italian cut, and well tailored. He was the rich Mr. Lyon, but the reflection lacked something that morning. Murdock was in his life again, and the oppression of an invisible cage pressed against his chest.

All his confidence seemed to vanish, or maybe the nightmare and the fact Vivienne had witnessed it had undermined his strength.

But then again, to understand who he was, living as Lion Boy had been necessary.

A knock on the door distracted him. "Samuel?" Captain Jackson peeked inside. "William is back. We need to talk."

Samuel nodded. "Thank you, Richard."

The fact William hadn't been caught breaking into Dr. Tucker's office was a good start and a testament to the footman's skills. He would never underestimate his footman again.

Samuel entered his study, forcing himself not to show his inner turmoil.

"You know," William said in a smug tone, "I find it curious that you two fellas asked for my help after everything you told me. After all the scolding and reprimands. After all the—"

"Yes, but what did you find?" Captain Jackson asked.

"Well…" William went to sit down, but the captain stopped him.

"You don't sit down when Mr. Lyon is standing."

Samuel didn't care, but William needed some discipline.

"Shall I remind you," the captain said, "that without Mr. Lyon you would be in prison?"

"Fine." William scowled. "My apologies. So the practice is obviously active. Dr. Tucker goes there every morning and leaves only to visit his patients. He started over years ago. But I found something interesting in his account book and ledger." He lowered his voice. "Lady Huntington paid him generous sums regularly in the past years, and I'm talking about large sums of pounds."

Samuel shrugged. "And? He's the family physician, and officially Vivienne was sick. What's extraordinary about that?"

"No, sir. These were large donations and too big to be the doctor's fees. There were other toffs in his records, people who gave him hundreds of pounds as donations to build a clinic near Coventry. I did a quick search, and I didn't find any trace of any clinic being built anywhere. No letters or contracts with builders, no layout of the building. Nothing. It's suspicious. My father was a builder, and building something requires many of documents and blueprints and fees."

The captain leant against the desk. "The donations would explain why Dr. Tucker didn't want Vivienne to leave. When was the last donation from Lady Huntington?"

"Weeks ago," William said.

"She hasn't given him money recently," Samuel said. "But the donations are legal."

"Yes," the captain said, "but if he poisons people to make them ill so that their families pour donations into his coffers to take care of them and to build a clinic that doesn't exist, that's fraud."

Samuel nodded. "We have to prove he poisons his patients."

"We should collect information on his other patients and find a pattern," the captain said. "There must be other people who realise he's a quack."

"I volunteer to collect information." William held up his hand. "I can sneak in and out of his office or into any patient's house unseen. I'm happy to put my skills to good use."

He smiled. "Good point."

William beamed. Perhaps they'd found a way to keep the former thief happy while leaving innocent people alone.

"Samuel?" Vivienne's voice came from the other side of the door.

He opened it. A hint of shame bothered him after how he'd left her bed last night. "I was about to search for you."

She craned her neck towards the captain and William. "You're busy."

"My lady." William bowed.

"Come in." Samuel waited for her to be seated. "William discovered your mother made generous donations to Dr. Tucker."

"Donations?" Her delicate eyebrows drew together. "I don't think so. Father and Mother discuss their donations together. Father has never approved of Dr. Tucker. He would never agree to donate money to him. Even before knowing Dr. Tucker was a fraud, Father didn't like him. He and Mother argued several times about him."

"How can your mother get those sums then?" he asked.

"She's always taken care of the expenses of the house. It would be easy for her to inflate the bills and set aside some pounds."

"We'll keep Dr. Tucker under surveillance," the captain said. "Then, when we have enough evidence, we'll strike."

"So we have to wait?" Samuel said. "Hell, no. I'd rather go there and drag him out of his office."

"And what will that prove? We need time and evidence." The captain clapped his shoulder. "We can't make mistakes caused by haste. William and I will take care of the doctor." He smiled. "You spend some time with your new wife."

Yes, but he was worried about that as well.

Vivienne glanced at him, and he tried to ignore the knot of anxiety in his belly.

When William and the captain left the room, he didn't have any excuses not to face his fears.

"You're nervous." She took his hand, lacing her fingers through his. "We're going to stop him. Don't worry."

He released her finger to sign. "I wish we could be quicker."

"Some things require more time than others."

He brushed a dark curl of hair from her forehead. "What would you like to do?"

"Can we take a walk in the garden? It's a beautiful day."

"Aren't you tired?"

"I feel better. A few days without the poison, and I already feel stronger." She straightened and jutted out her chin. "I could run a marathon."

He laughed and offered her his arm. "Let's go."

He observed her as they went down the stairs. Her cheeks were a nice shade of pink. The dark circles around her eyes were almost gone, but above all, her eyes were a bright blue. Even her hair was less dull.

Again, bitter anger at Murdock poisoned his blood.

"We'll have a proper honeymoon when you're better."

"The garden is lovely. I'm more than happy to take a walk there with you for now." She rested her head on his arm, and energy rushed through him.

In the sunlight with her smile shining upon him, his nocturnal fears seemed silly, but his desire for justice grew stronger.

She paused to sit on the bench under the shadow of an oak tree. He perched on the edge next to her with his back straight and his hands on his knees. The collar of his shirt chafed his neck all of a sudden. So his fears were still there, after all.

"Why are you so nervous?" She touched his knuckles. "Is it because of last night?"

He shrugged, following the flight of a sparrow.

"You were used to telling me everything. Or do you stop talking to me because I'm your wife? Isn't that a bit too early?"

He grinned.

"Don't you trust me?"

That got his attention. He turned towards her, and her large eyes stunned him for a moment.

"I do. More than anyone." But he also feared her opinion. More than anyone's.

"We're married, and we're friends. You can trust me."

He exhaled. Friends. He fiddled with his hands, searching for the right words. She didn't prompt him to talk.

He moved his fingers slowly, his way to whisper. "Only the captain witnessed my nightmares. They leave me exhausted. I don't want you to see me in that state. I don't want to wake you up in the middle of the night and scare you."

"And I want to help you, and there's nothing you should be ashamed of. Had I been in your situation, I would have nightmares constantly." She ran a hand through his hair with such tenderness that the tension riding his shoulders eased. "Will you sleep with me tonight?"

He nodded, under her spell and not at all sorry about that.

"Will you stay even if you have a nightmare?"

Another nod, although he was less confident.

She tangled her slender fingers through his curls. "Do you know what I was thinking this morning after I woke up alone?"

His mouth grew dry for some reason. "What?"

"You left without kissing me."

A flare of heat spread from his chest through his whole body. He cupped her cheek and inched closer. Only a short distance separated his lips from hers, but he took his time. Her sweet fragrance of orange blossoms intoxicated him. The warmth spreading through him made him dizzy.

She tilted her head, allowing him to press his mouth against hers more easily.

A shudder went through him as he tried to deal with the rough energy overwhelming him; it was a primordial force, more powerful than the anger towards Murdock that had always dominated his life; sweeter than the sense of freedom he'd experienced once he'd realised he wasn't Lion Boy anymore; more devastating than any blows he'd received.

He kissed her again, trembling from head to toe with a riot of emotions. After last night, he should control his feelings better, but the kiss was as shocking as the first one. The first one might have been the product of the spur of the moment, but this second one was deliberate.

She ran her fingers through his hair again and rested her hand on a sensitive spot on his nape.

Why the gesture made him shiver harder, he had no idea.

They opened their mouths at the same time, and the kiss turned quick.

Her tongue stroked his, sending his heart into a frenzy of beats. He liked it when she pressed herself against him or when her hand travelled from his neck to his chest. Matching the movements of her lips was natural.

He covered her hand with his, right over his heart, letting her feel how fast his pulse raced, only because she was kissing him.

They were both breathless and dazzled when they broke the kiss. Her sweet orange taste lingered on his lips.

He stared at her. His inner turmoil was reflected in her eyes. Her chest rose and fell in rhythm with his heartbeat.

She lowered her gaze. "I understand I'm not pretty now—"

"What? You're as beautiful as always." He rubbed her cheek with his thumb. "I'm only concerned about your strength. We don't have to rush."

She leant into his palm. "Then I'm looking forward to getting better." She ran the tip of her tongue over her bottom lip, and he caught a breath.

He dipped his head and was about to kiss her again when loud voices came from the path.

"I really don't understand why you have to be so stubborn!" Dobkins chased Captain Jackson along the gravel path.

"I'm not being stubborn. I'm showing common sense. Something you should try." Captain Jackson strode onwards, hands in his pockets.

"I am showing a lot of common sense." Dobkins came to a halt in front of the bench, her face flaming.

"What's the matter?" Vivienne asked.

Captain Jackson scoffed. "Dobkins asked me, no, ordered me to teach her how to shoot."

Samuel slanted a glance at the maid. "Why?"

"Protection." Dobkins folded her arms over her chest. "With everything that's happening, I would feel safer with a gun."

"Safer? A gun isn't a toy," the captain said.

"That's why I asked you to teach me."

"No. It's dangerous."

"Captain," Samuel said. "Perhaps you should consider Dobkins's request."

Captain Jackson pinched the bridge of his nose. "You, too? Since when do you approve of guns?"

"If you don't help her, she'll find someone else, and they won't be as good as you at teaching her. She might get hurt. Under your guidance, I'm sure she'll be safe."

Dobkins winked at him.

The captain exhaled. "All right. But she won't get a gun."

"What's the point of teaching me if I can't have my own gun?" Dobkins asked.

"That's the deal." The captain offered her his hand. "Take it or leave it."

Huffing, Dobkins shook the captain's hand. "Let's start."

After they walked away, Vivienne said, "I can't believe you agreed with Dobkins."

He watched Dobkins and the captain walking away. "I think the captain and Dobkins will enjoy their time together."

thirty-six

After a week of resting, eating, drinking the awful tonic, and sleeping, Vivienne had grown stronger. She didn't pant when she went up the stairs, and she'd gained weight thanks to Potter's delicious meals.

Even though it was well past midnight, she was still up, reading in her bedroom, waiting for Samuel. Between his work and his nocturnal excursions with Captain Jackson and William to get Dr. Tucker arrested, he went to bed late.

Every time a noise came from the corridor, she paused, hoping it was Samuel. But no. She'd almost finished the book by the time the door opened and Samuel entered on silent feet.

"Still up?" he asked.

"I was a little worried." She ran to him and hugged him. "Any news?"

"Not good." He gave her a quick peck on the lips before sitting on the armchair next to her. He smelt of soap, and his dressing gown had been recently washed because she caught a whiff of the laundry soap Mrs. Foster had ordered.

"Murdock fled. He hasn't been seen in a while, and William said his office is empty. He took his accounting books, potions, and ledgers." The dressing gown was open on the front, revealing his undergarment.

She eyed the way his nightshirt stretched taut over his chest. "I can talk to my mother. She might know where he is, and I wouldn't be surprised if he contacted her."

"Do you want to see your mother? She hasn't come here to visit us, even though we invited her." He gently took her face when he finished signing.

"It won't be easy, but if she knows something about Dr. Tucker, having to swallow my pride would be worth it."

He kissed her, his lips lingering on hers. The way he held her as if she were the most precious thing in the world made her feel confident and beautiful—two things she hadn't experienced in a long time.

She ran her hands over his chest. His warmth reached her skin, and his heart pounded faster when she darted out her tongue and caressed his lips.

He broke the kiss to stare at her with his usual soul-searching intensity.

She had no idea what he searched for in her eyes, but there was only love for him, his courage, and his kindness.

Then he kissed her again.

The kiss was a quick brush of his lips against hers at first. A mere touch, innocent and sweet. Yet a fire roared inside her, a fire that demanded to burn more brightly.

She slid her hands up his neck and to his nape before pulling him down for another kiss.

Only the feel of his body against hers and of his lips parting remained. They kissed, trying to devour each other's mouths, letting out their passion. His hands ran along her body from her waist to her breasts, never pausing and driving her mad with need.

The feeling of his gentle hands over her worked better than any tonic.

She explored his chest with urgent fingers, shoving aside his dressing gown and nightshirt until she found heat and smooth skin and hard muscles. With quick fingers, he unfastened her dressing gown.

She helped him, tugging at her sleeves with impatience. He cupped her face and stared into her eyes.

He mouthed, "Beautiful," with such strength she nearly heard the word.

He hauled her up and laid her on the bed. She expected him to shove her clothes out of the way, but instead, he caressed her cheek once more as if he couldn't believe she was real.

Then his mouth was on her neck, planting a sweet, careful kiss that made her moan.

The sweetness gave way to shuddering pleasure and throbbing need again. He slowly moved his hand down over her breasts. The nightgown and dressing gown formed a thin barrier, but she grew frustrated with the need to feel his hands on her bare skin.

She shrugged off the dressing gown, leaving only the nightgown covering her.

He lifted his head from the crook of her neck to stare at her. The longer he stared, the more achy she became. He dragged a hand over her breasts, pulling the nightgown down.

When she was bare to him, her first instinct wasn't to cover herself, but to feel more. More of his touch, lips, and heat. His mouth was around her nipple, sucking and teasing, and she reclined her head on the soft pillow.

She grabbed fistfuls of the bedsheets as his tongue teased her nipples to hard peaks. She was aching, her skin tingling with new sensations, burning with a new type of fever.

A breath tore out of her when he slipped his hand between her thighs, where she ached the most.

Her legs widened of their own accord to give him better access, and he took complete advantage of that. Slipping his hand under the hem of her nightgown required but a moment.

A growling noise came out of him when he brushed her. It was a sound filled with hunger that made her quiver more.

His mouth never left her breast as he rubbed her, and it didn't take long before her whole body shivered with a release so powerful she had to arch her back.

When the spasms died down, she lay boneless on the bed, grateful she hadn't experienced such a pleasure before because she wanted it to be him. Samuel—only he was supposed to give her so much pleasure.

He caressed her inner thighs for a long time, soothing a different type of ache inside her, for she craved his gentle touch as well. Now and then, he dipped his head to kiss her breasts until the fire returned.

He scattered kisses down her belly, nestling himself between her legs, and she had to watch. His golden hair tickled her inner thighs as he parted her thighs and grabbed her hips.

His mouth was on her, and her back arched again.

The sweet, gentle strokes of his tongue were a shock of heat and wetness. He kissed her deeply, holding her hips still because she kept writhing.

She had no idea—none—that a kiss could be so wonderfully pleasurable. The past years of sickness were blasted into oblivion by that kiss.

The longer he ran his tongue over her, the more she thrashed and couldn't hold back her loud moans and cries.

She'd stopped caring about being quiet when his tongue, lips, and fingers shocked her with pleasure. The second release was more powerful, stronger, and more intimate than the first, and it shattered her.

She screamed out her pleasure, or maybe she whispered. She had no idea.

She was certain only of Samuel's warm body next to her as he held her against his chest. She snuggled closer to him, so close there wasn't any space between them.

His heart beat a fast rhythm against her palm, surely matching hers.

thirty-seven

Samuel woke up rested, happy, and with his beautiful wife in his arms. Perfect.

A ray of sunlight sneaked through a narrow opening in the curtains to light her pert nose. Her dark eyelashes fanned over her cheeks, and her plush lips were slightly parted as she breathed softly over his skin.

The maid had come at dawn, but Vivienne had kept sleeping, and he was happy to hold her in the semidarkness.

He caressed her hair, trying to disentangle her long tresses the night of lovemaking had messed up. As it had his thoughts.

She blinked her eyes open, twitching her nose as if it were tickled by the sunlight. "Good morning."

He stroked her naked back, marvelling at the softness of her skin. He wanted to ask her how she was faring, but that would mean stopping caressing her, and he had no intention of doing that.

"It was wonderful." As she buried her face in his chest, her voice came muffled.

He agreed. The best night of his life.

"Will you stay with me tonight? Every night?" She gazed up at him. "Forever?"

He reluctantly stopped caressing her to sign, "If you want me."

"I do. And now I want a good morning kiss."

He kissed her gently when loud thuds ricocheted off the walls. He wrapped his arms around her and pulled her closer, ready to bolt out.

"What was that?" she asked. "An intruder? It sounded like the shutters were being slammed hard."

Footsteps thudded, and doors slammed.

"That woman is insane!" That was the captain.

"What's happening?" Vivienne asked.

Samuel had a good idea.

"Stay here." He kissed her and left the bed.

After he put on his nightshirt and dressing gown, he opened the door to find Bernard carrying a tray with tea, scones, and eggs. The scent of butter and vanilla teased his nostrils.

The butler bowed his head and lifted the tray, a serene smile on his face.

"Please serve breakfast to Lady Vivienne," Samuel said, wincing as another bang boomed.

The butler bowed again, blissfully unaware of the chaos unfolding downstairs.

Dobkins's and Captain Jackson's voices came louder, overlapping each other.

He rushed down the steps to the hallway. They talked together, raising their voices, as if it were a competition on who spoke louder.

Potter stood in a corner, wiping his hands on his apron, and Mrs. Foster looked out of the window. William yawned, stretching his arms over his head. Richard was pale and shivering.

"Silence!" Samuel signed with no effect whatsoever. He waved and stomped a foot on the floor.

They ignored him.

Mrs. Foster stepped between the captain and Dobkins. "Silence, you two. Mr. Lyon is here."

Silence dropped. Finally.

Captain Jackson and Dobkins turned towards him with matching scowls as if he were intruding in a private matter.

"What the hell is going on?" he signed with brisk fingers.

The captain pointed a finger at Dobkins. "She wants to barricade the house."

"There was someone lurking in the garden," she said, her face red.

"I didn't see anyone." The captain shook his head. "And even if there was someone, starting to panic and yell and slam every door wouldn't be the right thing to do."

"Is anyone hurt?" he asked, gazing around.

Captain Jackson waved a dismissive hand. "The noises were the most dangerous thing."

"You aren't listening." Dobkins jabbed a finger in the direction of the garden. "There was someone in the garden."

"I was listening, and I told you there isn't anyone in the garden." The captain glowered at her.

She was as tall as the captain, so if he was trying to intimidate her, it didn't work.

Samuel agreed with the captain. But it was better to be cautious.

"He was hiding behind the bushes," she went on, "and yes, I might have panicked a little, maybe I shouted and tried to barricade the garden doors with a chest of drawers, but the captain didn't want to take his gun when I asked him to."

"I don't want to shoot anyone unless it's absolutely necessary," the captain said.

"I was terrified, and you didn't believe me." She shook, her voice breaking.

"There was no one in the garden!" Captain Jackson pressed two fingers to his temples. "I never said I didn't believe you. I said that when I went out, I didn't find anyone. So the danger was gone."

"I won't let anyone hurt Lady Vivienne." Dobkins clamped a hand over her mouth.

Samuel frowned. "Neither will I. You need to trust me. All I want is to keep everyone safe."

"How? We aren't strong. Anyone can sneak up on us and slit our throats in our sleep." She wiped her eyes.

The captain frowned. "That's morbid."

While Samuel was sorry to see her so distressed, he didn't like her lack of trust in him.

"With due respect," Mrs. Foster said. "We're perfectly capable of taking care of ourselves."

Dobkins seemed about to rebuke but lowered her gaze.

"What's happening?" Vivienne came down the stairs in a lovely blue gown that fit her tightly, accentuating her small waist.

"Dobkins panicked after having allegedly seen someone in the garden," Captain Jackson said.

"Did you make all that noise? The scream and the bangs?" Vivienne stopped at the base of the stairs.

"I'm sorry." Dobkins curtsied and left the hallway in a hurry.

"Alice," the captain said, but she ignored him. "Hell."

"I checked the garden as well," William said. "I didn't see anyone."

"Sir, I think I saw someone." Richard raised a trembling hand. "A man in dark clothes."

"Where?" the captain asked.

Richard made a vague gesture towards the garden. "I'm not sure."

"Why didn't you tell me?" Captain Jackson looked out of the window.

"I was..." Richard swallowed a few times.

"It's all right, Richard." Samuel patted his valet's shoulder. "Why don't you go to the kitchen and have a cup of tea?"

"Let's have a look." The captain beckoned Samuel to follow him.

"I need a cup, but first..." Richard opened a cabinet and handed Samuel a coat and a pair of boots. "It's a crisp morning, sir."

They walked along the path weaving through the garden.

The sounds of carriages and hackneys came from the other side of the wall wrapping around the house. Climbing the wall didn't require any special skill, but the front and back doors and the windows were sturdy with anti-theft locks not even William could break.

He stopped next to the bench where he and Vivienne had sat the other day. The bush behind it had been flattened as if something heavy had dropped on it. A few footprints marked the soft soil.

He pointed them at the captain.

The captain clicked his tongue. "Yes, Alice was right. There will be no living with her after now."

thirty-eight

Vivienne's belly seemed filled with crickets when she walked up the steps to the front door of her parents, Dobkins following close behind.

After Samuel had found signs of an intruder, the urge to catch Dr. Tucker had grown. And she wanted to do something useful for her new family.

Before knocking, she took a good look at the house where she'd spent some miserable years for no reason other than a fraud who had taken advantage of her innocence.

She knocked on the door.

The footman who opened it froze for a moment before holding the door for them. "My lady."

Vivienne stepped inside. "Is my father home?"

"I'll tell him you're here."

"I need to talk to my father first, then will you tell my mother I'm here as well? Give me ten minutes with my father, then tell my mother."

"My lady." The footman bowed while the butler appeared and greeted her warmly before he led her and Dobkins to her father's study.

While they waited, Dobkins insisted on standing in a corner, pale since the morning's incident.

"Don't be so upset," Vivienne said.

"That's what everyone keeps telling me, even after we found evidence I was right. Someone was lurking in the garden."

Vivienne exhaled. "Nothing happened, and panicking won't help."

"I lost my temper, but I was frightened."

The door opened, and when her father entered, she ran to him. "Father!"

"Darling." He hugged her before taking her by the shoulders and studying her face. "I say! You look so much better, rosy and full of energy."

"I am. And look at my new gown." She twirled to show him how she'd put on some weight. "Can you see the—Father!"

He was swallowing hard, his eyes shining with tears.

She nodded at Dobkins who left the room.

"I'm so happy, but also I'm so angry with Dr. Tucker." He sucked in a deep breath and composed himself. "Superintendent Johnson said they don't have enough evidence to arrest him. I'll move heaven and earth to get that thug behind bars. He took advantage of our pain for his gain. He tortured Samuel. He must be locked up."

"About that...there's something I need to tell you." She glanced at the door. "Apparently Mother made some generous donations to Dr. Tucker."

He wiped his eyes with his handkerchief. "It's not possible. I would never approve..." He touched his forehead. "She gave him money without telling me. She lied to me."

"I'm afraid so," she said when he started to walk towards the door. "I understand you're angry, but I must ask you to rein in your anger for a moment. I'm here to talk to Mother about Dr. Tucker and understand if she knows where he is."

"Since they're accomplices," he completed.

"Right now, I need her to tell me everything. Let me handle the conversation."

He nodded and sat on the sofa, beckoning her to do the same. "I made so many mistakes with you." He hunched his shoulders as if tired. "I let your mother suffocate you and deceive me. What has our family become? We haven't spent happy days together in years. Your mother rarely sees her grandchildren, and we argue more than we talk. Adele's death destroyed us, instead of making us more united. I hope you'll forgive me one day."

"I'm sure we can be the strong family we've always been again. Mother will see reason once Dr. Tucker is brought to justice with evidence of his crimes."

He seemed to age ten years in a second. "When my Adele died, I lost my wife, too. I lost myself, too. I was too focused on my own pain not to see what was happening. I think..." He paused and lowered his gaze as if feeling shame. "I think I didn't want to see it. And even when you fell sick, my fear and dread of going through that pain again made me weak. I should have followed my instinct and order Dr. Tucker to leave."

The door opened, and he fell silent.

"Vivienne." Mother entered the room, looking like a ghost, she was so pale.

Father stood up, fists clenched. Vivienne gave him a shake of her head.

Her parents had a lot to discuss, but she wanted to know where Dr. Tucker was first. If Father confronted Mother about the money, she might refuse to say anything.

Mother fiddled with the silver box before sitting on the armchair next to the sofa. "I'm glad you came. And look at you. So beautiful."

"You didn't come to my wedding." Vivienne hadn't planned to start the conversation with an argument, but the accusation had come out before she could think.

"You left the house like a thief at night."

"For good reasons," Father said at the same time as Vivienne said, "You scared me."

"Scared you?"

"You authorised Dr. Tucker to lock me up in an asylum."

Mother was flustered. "I did not. I would not do such a thing. I would never, ever let someone take you away from me."

That made Vivienne paused. What Mother said was true. She'd never let Vivienne out of the house without a fight. Why would she send her away all of a sudden?

Mother lifted her chin. "Who told you that lie?"

"Dr. Tucker."

It was Mother's turn to remain speechless. Her lips parted as if someone had slapped her.

"He isn't the lovely man you think he is." She suppressed another angry comment. Otherwise, she wouldn't learn anything about Dr. Tucker.

"And as you can see, Vivienne is much better now," Father said. "No need for that quack anymore."

A smile brightened Mother's face as she eyed Vivienne. For a moment, she was the caring, happy mother Vivienne remembered, free from pain and the burden of the past.

"We know you made some generous donations to Dr. Tucker," she said in a gentler tone.

Mother glanced at Father, a tremor going through her.

"We'll discuss that later," Father said in a brusque tone.

"I want to know now, Father. Tell me the truth, Mother."

"He did everything to save your life and succeeded. Of course I wanted to support him and his work."

"Do you know where he is now?"

Mother stiffened. "Someone threw accusations at him, claiming he's a fraud..." She frowned, her gaze becoming lost. "Why would he lie?"

"Are you starting to realise now who he really is?" Father pinched the bridge of his nose.

Vivienne closed her eyes for a moment to collect herself. "Do you know his whereabouts?"

Mother folded her hands in her lap. "Well, I know he owns a flat close to St. Giles on Arrow Street."

"Does he live there alone?"

Mother wrung her hands as she did when one of her crises was imminent. "He has an associate, but I don't think they share the flat."

"Thank you." She rose. Her anger simmered under her composure, but if she was honest, pity more than anger filled her heart. "I hope you understand what he did to me was wrong."

Mother rubbed her temples, her cheeks paling.

"Father." Vivienne hugged him. "Talk to her. I think perhaps she is no longer under Dr. Tucker's spell."

"I'm happy you're safe." He kissed her forehead.

Not the reassurance she wanted to hear, but Father had every right to be angry.

~

THERE WASN'T much Samuel could do but let time pass.

William and Captain Jackson were searching Dr. Tucker's flat in St. Giles. He'd wanted to join them, but since Dr. Tucker was aware that Mr. Lyon was Lion Boy, the captain had dissuaded him from coming.

As for the guards he meant to hire, so far, he hadn't found anyone he trusted. Maybe he was too difficult to please.

So he was at home, spending time with his wife. Not that he was complaining. Quite the opposite.

Sitting on the piano bench next to her, he stared at her as she tried to teach him to play a tune. The sunlight lit the tips of her eyelashes with tiny glimmers of gold, making her whole lovely face glow.

She focused on the keys. "You need to press the keys like that to make the sound delicate and beautiful. Your turn. Repeat the sequence."

He plunked the music away, causing a sparrow perched on the windowsill to fly away indignantly.

Vivienne laughed. "You're doing it wrong."

Yes, he knew that, but hearing her laugh was worth the scolding.

"Like this." She gently placed her fingers over his. "Follow me."

Everywhere.

She gave him a mischievous smile, pressing her fingers against his.

A sweet tune filled the air. But he wasn't looking at the keys. He was looking at her intense face as she floated through the notes. Her radiance glowed again, like the full moon after an eclipse.

He didn't hear the music, nor did he see what his fingers were doing. His only focus was on the sensation of her hands on his and the sweet sound of her laughter. Finally, he heard it again.

"See? It's not difficult." She stopped playing but kept her hands over his.

Not difficult at all. Falling in love with her was the easiest thing he'd ever done.

He dipped his head and kissed her, meaning only to give her a quick kiss. But she trapped his face in her hands and held him in place.

As she moved her lips over his, he let himself go into the sensation of the kiss. Even his fears—always lurking under the surface of his emotions—dimmed and became nothing more than scarecrows.

He held her by the waist and pulled her closer. Her breathing sped up.

"Samuel," she whispered his name in a moan that triggered a shot of pleasure through him. "Can we go upstairs?"

He stood up, holding her hand, but Bernard entered the room, breaking the spell.

"The captain and William have just arrived and would like to talk to you, sir," the butler signed.

Samuel shouldn't complain, but...he did. He sighed and headed for the sitting room with Vivienne.

William and Captain Jackson were pacing and talking excitedly when Samuel entered.

"What is it?" Vivienne asked.

"We have him!" William waved a bunch of papers excitedly. "Everything you ever wanted about him." He kept waving the papers in the air.

"Stop this fuss. You didn't win at the roulette." The captain snatched the documents from William's hand and dropped them on the low table. "In a safe William opened with impressive skills, we found evidence of Tucker buying large quantities of belladonna, arsenic, and lead. We have his recipes written down, letters, and his notes on how to keep the patients sick without killing them. He kept records of every patient he treated. Ever. We also found a few angry people willing to testify against him."

William crossed his arms behind his head, a smug smile on his face. "We only have to inform the police. May I be the one? Please?"

"Wonderful." Vivienne beamed.

Samuel rushed to go through the documents. The captain was right. There was everything to build up a case against Dr. Tucker.

"No offence, Mr. Lyon," William said, "but I think I'll work for the police from now on. The job seems more thrilling. There's the excitement of the chase, the break-in, the tension, and all for a good purpose."

Samuel's excitement diminished when he went through the pages regarding Cade's Circus. And Lion Boy. There was a long list of all the mixture of drugs he'd taken while at the circus. Each entry had notes on how his body had reacted to the drug and which potion was the best to make him aggressive.

Dr. Tucker had played with him, experimenting on him and on other circus workers to make them stronger or fearless.

A lump of emotion swelled in his throat as he remembered those dark days when he hadn't been in control of himself. The walls closed in on him, and he couldn't breathe. Anguished noises came out of him.

"Darling." Vivienne closed her hand around his.

"Bloody hell, sir," William said, turning serious. "I'll stay here if you care so much. I must be the best footman you've ever seen."

"Shut up." Captain Jackson took William's arm and dragged him to the door. "Mr. and Mrs. Lyon need a moment."

When the door was closed, she wiped his tears with her delicate fingers. He hadn't even realised he was crying.

"It's over." She caressed his face and hair. "He can't hurt you anymore. You won."

"He's still here." He pointed a finger at his head. "I'll never get rid of him."

"Yes, you will. Once the police take him into custody and lock him up, we can forget the past and move on. Think about all the people we're going to save by catching him. He won't be able to hurt anyone else." She scattered kisses on his face. "Don't let him be here with us. He isn't welcome."

He held her, hating Murdock's power over his emotions.

"I trust you," she whispered. "You're strong enough to beat him."

"I'm not sure."

"Then you can borrow my strength." She kissed him again.

"You'll be left with none if I use it to defeat my fears."

"I have plenty. Don't you trust me?"

He hugged her. Just holding her slowed his quick pulse.

"You aren't alone," she whispered, caressing the back of his neck. "You have friends and a family that loves you. That's more powerful than gold. Trust me. Trust us."

He buried his face in the crook of her neck to hide from his fears. When he released her and stared at her face, he only found love.

She stroked his jaw. "I'm so proud of who you are and of what you've become. That's a stronger victory than getting Dr. Tucker arrested. We'll work on your fears, starting with you sleeping with me every night and not leaving after a nightmare."

Well, that sounded like a bloody good remedy.

thirty-nine

The visit to the police had taken longer than Samuel had expected because explaining Murdock-Dr. Tucker's crimes hadn't been an easy task, and they had to keep a few facts hidden.

He'd concealed his true identity as Lion Boy, just in case Murdock had documents about him, and they hadn't mentioned having broken into Murdock's flat or William's past.

It didn't matter. Murdock's crimes were plenty and well documented. His fate was sealed.

When Samuel arrived home, a sense of emptiness weighed him down. William was as bubbly as a freshly uncorked bottle of champagne, already seeing himself in a peeler's uniform. The captain instead was quiet, not as ecstatic as Samuel had expected.

Maybe they'd waited for that moment for too long.

"...and I'll catch criminals by the dozens," William said, his voice echoing in the hallway. "And everyone will know me as the defender of justice, William the Righteous."

"William the Footman who needs to take his master's coat," Captain Jackson said. "Chop, chop."

William's good spirits didn't diminish. He took Samuel's coat and hat and went down the corridor, humming a tune. Being so carefree had to feel good.

Captain Jackson squeezed Samuel's shoulder. "We did our part. Now it's up to the police although Lord Huntington would be on them like an eagle if Superintendent Johnson doesn't arrest Murdock."

He nodded.

"You should celebrate. Go to your wife. She must be worried." The captain searched around. "As for me, I'll inform Alice she doesn't need a gun anymore."

Samuel went up the stairs, his legs like rubber. Perhaps he needed to see Murdock behind bars before happiness overwhelmed him.

The door to his bedroom was ajar, and he paused to watch his wife. She was sitting in front of the vanity, singing a song while braiding her hair.

Her nightgown was of the best quality but quite modest with a neckline that covered her chest completely. The skirt didn't show any inches of her ankles, but it had a pretty lace at the hem. If he had to go through his miserable years with the circus only to live that moment when he was standing and watching his wife bathed in the warm light of the fire, he would do it without hesitation.

He stepped closer, being noisy on purpose not to alarm her. But she jolted on the padded seat and a bottle of face powder was tossed to the floor. A cloud of fine dust glittered in the room, like snow.

"Sorry," they said together.

He knelt to collect the shards of glass. "I didn't mean to scare you."

"My fault. I didn't hear you." She crouched as well and collected the powder with the help of a shallow bowl.

He touched her knuckles. "I hate what he did to you more than I hate what he did to me."

"I hate the fact you still have nightmares more."

He took her hand and helped her up. She set her large eyes on him, making him feel all her trust. He walked around her and paused behind her.

A shiver went through her as he lowered her nightgown.

The fabric slipped down her creamy skin with a swish of silk. He ran a hand along her fine spine, tracing its curves.

A few red spots marred her skin—an aftermath of the drugs she'd taken. They would be only a memory with time, as many things would. They were like slashes over a beautiful painting.

Whoever hurt her should be punished. He kissed the offending spots, taking his time to let her feel his lips and tongue on her skin. Soft moans came out of her, and he kissed his way up her neck.

Her sweet scent of orange blossoms teased him.

He cupped her breasts from behind, feeling their heaviness in his palms. She responded with another lovely moan, a sound so sweet and powerful it triggered his desire. He rolled her nipples between his fingers until she arched her back.

When she squeezed her thighs together, he slipped a hand between them to help her with the ache. As she writhed, he wanted to see her face.

He laid her on the bed and marvelled at the beautiful flush on her cheeks.

"You make me feel beautiful when you look at me like that," she whispered.

"You're always beautiful."

She lay on her back, widening her legs in an invitation he wouldn't decline.

He stretched himself over her, covering her body with his, but she wasn't content. She tugged at his clothes, unbuttoning his waistcoat and shirt, until his chest was naked.

"You're beautiful, too." She dragged a hand over his chest, leaving him breathless. "And brave."

He moved off her, only to complete the job and remove his clothes. She dragged him down again with a hand on his nape.

He stretched out over her, skin against skin, sharing his heat with her. He wished he could hold her, caress her, and touch her while telling her how beautiful she was, instead of needing his fingers to communicate with her.

Their kiss was slow and delicate as she rocked her hips. The friction of her heat against him made him quiver with need, but he wanted to take his time. He wanted to make her forget the pain and loneliness of those years she'd spent being abused.

He kissed the swift pulse in her neck, caressing her hip and thigh. Then he started to move forth, inching inside her with infinite care. She drew in a breath, moving her hips in slow circles.

He watched her face, enthralled by her expression of sheer ecstasy, and he was happy to be the one making her feel loved and cherished. Her inner muscles gripped him tightly as he slid deeper inside her.

She gasped for a moment, and he paused to sign, "Are you hurt?"

"No." She sounded breathy. "It's all right. Please."

He sheathed himself fully, feeling the strength of her grip.

Heaven. Perfection. Love.

They both exhaled. Then he started moving in and out of her as gently as he could, watching her face for her reaction.

There was no pain though. Her plush lips parted with a sigh. Her eyes became heavy-lidded, and her breath came out in quick pants. He paused only to kiss her neck and caress her lovely breasts.

He sped up his rhythm when he was sure she wasn't hurting. She threw her head back, exposing the slender column of her neck as he pounded faster.

Tension built up in his muscles, and all his blood flowed down. He was on the verge of a monumental release, but he forced himself to wait.

She sank her fingers into his shoulders when she found her release first, and watching her arch underneath him, scream his name freely, and close her eyes was too much. He followed her, shaking with a primeval force.

She held him tightly as if wanting to anchor him to herself. They breathed and shuddered in each other's arms until the spasms of pleasure left only ripples. He wanted to tell her he loved her, not sign it, but tell her. He didn't want to use his fingers.

"I love you." He put all his strength and effort into saying the words, but only an awful, grunting noise came out.

She held his face in hers, searching his eyes with her gaze. "I love you, too, Samuel."

He signed this time. "I love you. I wish I could tell you with my voice."

"There's no need. I feel it. Your eyes, your touch, and all your body scream how much you love me. There isn't a more profound way to tell me how much you care for me. My soul listens to yours all the time."

They hugged so fiercely one would have mistaken their hug for a goodbye.

forty

When Samuel woke up with Vivienne in his arms, his first thought was surprise. No nightmares had bothered him. No waking up, sweating and shaking. No palpitations.

Maybe knowing the police were after Dr. Tucker had calmed his inner demons. Or maybe Vivienne was the best cure.

But it was morning. He'd slept soundly through the night without waking up.

She stirred. "Good morning."

It was indeed.

"You slept for a long time." She stretched out her arms over her head. "I don't want to do anything today. Absolutely nothing. Just being with you."

"It sounds lovely. But I do have something else in mind." He kissed her neck.

She giggled and moved out of his reach. "Not so quickly."

"Why not?" He kissed her neck again.

She left the bed with surprising speed for someone who had just woken up. "They say lions are fierce predators."

He propped himself up on an elbow. "I can confirm it."

"I want you to prove it."

He shot forwards and seized her wrist. She cried out and slipped her arm out of his grip, like an eel. The sound of her laughter echoed off the wall of their bedroom.

She ran out of his reach. "Is that all you can do? The powerful, rich Mr. Lyon, the king of gold, isn't as scary as people say."

He pushed aside the covers, needing freedom of movement to catch his wife. She gave out a delighted squeal when he tossed the quilt off the bed. Then she was running again. He chased her, inhaling the scent left by her perfume. She opened the door to his bedroom and hid behind his escritoire.

"You're so slow—Ah!" She jolted when he made a dash for her across the writing table.

He barely brushed her wrist before she slipped away with expertise.

She went to the water closet, which meant she would lose the game. There was nowhere to go from there.

She stepped around the bathtub, using it as a barrier between them. "It's not fair. I can't escape from here."

He stopped at the door and stretched out an arm towards the other room. "You're free to go before I chase you again."

She narrowed her eyes but inched towards the door. "You are going to let me go? Really?"

He nodded, giving her a perfect gentleman's bow.

She kept her gaze on him while brushing past him. "I have to say you're tamer than I—" The rest of her sentence ended with a squeal as he grabbed her. "You cheated!"

He did, but so what?

He asked for her forgiveness by kissing that spot on her neck that made her tremble. She didn't sag against him as he hoped.

"You aren't going to conquer me so easily. This trick won't work."

He ought to be more persuasive then.

He pushed down the front of her nightgown with one hand.

She didn't help him but didn't stop him either. When he fully removed the nightgown, she remained uncooperative, but her breathing sped up and a lovely flush coloured her skin. He tossed the nightgown away, maybe with too much strength.

But the result was the spectacular view of her breasts. He kneaded them until she finally sagged against him with a sigh. Her rosy nipples hardened to taut peaks after he rolled them. He kissed her neck and grazed her earlobe.

She ran her hands over his chest, stealing kisses with him. Between kisses and touches, they were both panting. And somehow, they made it to the bed without breaking the kiss.

When he lay back, she straddled him, beautiful and fearsome like a goddess.

She stroked his jaw and neck while rolling her hips. He clenched his fists when she lowered herself over him.

If he had a voice, he would shout her name. He let her choose the rhythm, holding her hips to help her. She sped up, and he gritted his teeth at the ridiculous amount of pleasure coursing through him.

They found their releases together, her voice speaking for both of them.

As much as he loved making love with her, his most favourite moment was when she curled up next to him and he hugged her, and all his fears were finally silenced.

forty-one

The rest of the day wasn't as pleasant as the morning for Samuel.

The chief inspector in charge of Murdock's case informed them Murdock had hired a solicitor to defend him from the accusations, claiming the evidence Samuel had provided had been fabricated. A few of his patients defended him. Others attacked him.

In short, putting Murdock behind bars wouldn't be as quick and painless as Samuel had hoped.

"I hope Mother isn't among those people defending him." Vivienne sipped her glass of tonic without wincing.

"It doesn't change anything," Captain Jackson said. "Murdock's conviction will take a time. 'Tis all."

They were sitting at dinner, one of Potter's last masterpieces almost untouched. The spicy scent of pigeons *à la duchesse* filled the air.

"We should celebrate." The captain took a generous morsel of his pigeon. "We're too forlorn. And where's Alice?"

William moved from his position to the door. "In the kitchen, having dinner, sir."

"Call her. I want to propose a toast." Captain Jackson leant closer to him. "You don't mind, do you?"

Samuel shook his head. "Not at all. Vivienne and I always ask her to join us at dinner, but she refuses."

"My lady, sir." Dobkins bobbed a curtsy. "Is something the matter?"

The captain lifted his glass of cranberry juice. "I summoned you to make a toast."

"You summoned me?" Dobkins lifted her brow.

The captain stood up. "I want a toast to—do you fancy me, Alice?"

Silence dropped. Samuel exchanged a glance with Vivienne.

Dobkins frowned. "No."

"Why?" the captain asked, lowering the glass.

"You're rude, stubborn, and arrogant."

"Yes, but aside from that?" The captain handed her a glass of wine.

Dobkins hesitated before accepting it. A corner of her mouth twitched as if she were fighting a smile. "Well, you taught me how to shoot and can be quite charming when you want to."

"That's it!" The captain raised his glass again. "We toast to the fact that you won't need a gun ever again because we won."

"Almost," Samuel said.

"Don't be a pessimist." The captain took a sip. "Tonight is for happiness and hope only. We're happy and safe."

He barely finished saying that before a loud thud came from the corridor.

"What was that?" Vivienne rose to go to the door, but Samuel took her arm and stopped her.

The captain finished his drink. "I say to be happy and hopeful. It's probably nothing."

A muffled cry sounded.

Dobkins stepped back from the door as footsteps thudded closer.

"I'm sure the captain is right." William put a hand on the knob, but the door swung inwards.

Murdock stepped into the dining room, flanked by two men. One of them was Cade, wearing fine clothes that didn't hide the ugliness underneath. He held Bernard, twisting the butler's arm at a painful angle. Bernard's face was contorted in pain.

"Hello, Lion Boy," Cade said.

Samuel's blood flowed down from his head, and the floor seemed to turn into quicksand. His worst nightmare turned into reality.

"Let him go," Vivienne said.

Murdock gave a quick nod to his man who released Bernard with a shove. The butler bent over, clutching his arm.

Samuel rushed to him and helped him walk away from the thug.

"I'm not here to hurt anyone." Murdock smiled. In his tailored suit and Bowler hat, he could pass for a gentleman. "I'm a businessman, so I want to propose a deal."

Samuel shook his head, closing a fist.

Murdock eyed him with the usual contempt. "Although you wronged me." He shifted his gaze to Vivienne. "If you hadn't taken from me my main vein of gold—"

"Samuel is a human being!" Vivienne raised her voice. "You treated him beastly."

"Shut up." Murdock scoffed. "I wanted to kill you at first for what you'd done to me. Because of you, the circus doesn't exist. And I thought Lion Boy would have shown himself, knowing you were sick. But he didn't. Yet you turned out to be as profitable—"

Samuel shot forth, fuelled by anger. How dare Murdock speak like that of Vivienne?

"Don't." She stopped him by putting a hand on his chest. "Let's listen to whatever he has to say."

Cade shifted his weight, hand flying to his side.

Murdock waited for silence before speaking again. "If you

withdraw the charges and leave me alone, I'll tell you who your parents are. I'll tell you everything. Their names, your real name, and where to find your family."

Samuel drew in a breath. Captain Jackson stared at him in shock. Vivienne gasped.

His family. His parents. He had the opportunity to meet them. Finally, he wouldn't be a man without a past, but someone with roots.

Murdock slid a hand under his jacket, triggering Samuel's instinct. He pushed Vivienne behind him and hissed.

"I'm not taking out a gun." Murdock produced a piece of paper. "I have this document ready, double-checked by my solicitor. All you have to do is sign it, and I'll tell you everything you want to know."

Vivienne stepped around Samuel. "You're bluffing."

"I took him from his home," Murdock said. "I know everything about him." He tapped his temple. "It's all here. Sign the paper, go to the police, and tell them you changed your mind about the accusations, and I'll tell you everything about your family. Who knows, maybe your parents are alive. Maybe you have siblings. Maybe they're waiting for you."

A quiver went through Samuel. Seeing his family again, learning what had happened to them, and having the opportunity to be with them again were tempting. He had to admit that. His parents might need him, and he had enough money and power to help them.

Murdock's eyebrow spiked. "I don't want any trouble. Just do as I ask. I'll tell you where to find your family, and then I'll leave London. We won't cross paths ever again. You won't see me again."

Vivienne trapped her bottom lip between her teeth. Captain Jackson closed his fists tightly, seemingly ready to punch someone. Bernard rubbed his arm, shifting his weight.

All the people living in his house depended on him, but not

only them. The victims Murdock had hurt through many years deserved justice. He had to be stopped.

As much as Samuel's heart pounded faster at the thought of meeting his family again or knowing who his parents were, he couldn't let Murdock go.

He shook his head and signed, "You deserve to go to prison."

Captain Jackson translated, "Samuel said you can rot in hell."

A muscle of Murdock's jaw twitched. "I really didn't want to do this."

Cade and the other thug punched William and shoved Captain Jackson and Bernard away while Murdock lunged. Samuel leapt backwards, but Murdock wasn't aiming for him.

He grabbed Vivienne and pointed a gun at her head. "New deal. Sign that document, and I won't shoot your wife, which would be a shame, considering I was her physician."

Vivienne struggled in Murdock's grip, her face reddening. Captain Jackson moved closer to Samuel, and Bernard put a hand on his forehead from where blood trickled.

Samuel had been wrong. His worst nightmare wasn't seeing Murdock again—his worst nightmare was a gun at his wife's temple. There was no choice.

He picked up the pen. "Let her go."

Captain Jackson repeated his words.

"Sign first." Murdock pressed the gun harder against Vivienne's skin.

Samuel did as he was told.

Murdock gave her a shove hard enough to cause her to fall to the floor.

Samuel ran to her. "Are you all right?"

"Yes, yes." She shivered. Her pupils were so dilated the blue of her irises vanished.

Bernard was tottering on his feet. The poor butler must have received a hard blow to the head.

Murdock snatched the document and checked it. "You lost

everything, Lion Boy. You should have accepted my first deal." He clicked his tongue. "Now you'll never know who your parents are."

He moved towards the door but didn't have the chance to step out of it.

Armed with a frying pan, Mrs. Foster lunged at him from the corridor. The loud bang of the heavy pan hitting Murdock's head rang out.

Captain Jackson, Samuel, William, and Bernard all moved at the same time and jumped on Cade and the other brute. Dobkins wielded a poker and stood next to Mrs. Foster. Richard joined the fray, and the quiet dining room became bedlam in a moment.

Chairs were upturned. Dishes were smashed on the floor, and vases were broken.

In the chaos, as fists and kicks were thrown around, Potter came into view, but he wasn't alone.

Two police constables were with him.

"It's here." Potter pointed in the general direction of the middle of the room.

Samuel leapt back from the brute he was wrestling with to shield Vivienne as the police seized the two thugs and Murdock who groaned on the floor, a hand on his head.

"Thank you, officers." Captain Jackson wiped his forehead with a napkin. "Who warned you?"

"Mr. Potter came to the station to tell us there were intruders in the house," an officer said.

Holding Vivienne tightly, Samuel turned to Potter, surprised that his cook had left the house alone to warn the police.

Bernard pointed at the bells behind him. "I warned Mrs. Foster with the silent bells."

Mrs. Foster nodded. "I saw the thugs, and Potter volunteered to go to the police."

The whole household had fought back. Samuel had doubted them, thinking they wouldn't be able to defend themselves.

Vivienne took his face in her hands. "I told you your people would protect us."

"I will never doubt them again."

It took a few hours for Samuel to explain to the police what had happened with Murdock, the document he'd signed to save Vivienne, and the fight in his house, but in the end, Murdock was arrested, charged with a list of crimes longer than Potter's shopping list.

When he went to bed with Vivienne after the chaos had finished and the dining room was tidy again, he wrapped his arms around her and waited for her to fall asleep before drifting off.

No nightmare bothered him.

forty-two

Sipping her morning tea, Vivienne skimmed the articles on the front page of *The Times*.

A few days had passed since Dr. Tucker's arrest, and news about him kept filling the front pages of every newspaper. He'd been charged with attempted murder, and fraud. Good news and the addition of Potter's delicious chocolate biscuits were the perfect combination for a great day.

Samuel's lion eyes seemed bigger and full of light. The shadow that had darkened his face in the past weeks was gone.

She stroked his knuckles. "Are you sorry you had to renounce knowing your parents' names?"

"To have Murdock arrested? No. Besides, he's a confidence man. He was probably lying to save himself, and I wouldn't have any chance to verify the information was correct until later. But I was tempted for a moment."

Mrs. Foster entered the sunroom. The household was still in a chaotic state with Bernard cooking breakfast, Potter sleeping more than usual, exhausted after his brave deed, Richard needing a few days of calm to pull himself together, and William neglecting his footman's duties because...

"Lady and Lord Huntington are here," Mrs. Foster said, a nervous note in her voice.

Vivienne tensed a little. "Show them in." She rose when her parents entered, and they couldn't look more different from one another.

Father's smile reached his eyes, wrinkling his skin. He radiated sheer happiness. Mother was as pale as usual, in her black gown, with her shoulders hunched.

"The world is a better since that thug was arrested." Father squeezed Vivienne and Samuel in a fierce hug. "Justice."

"Mother?" Vivienne offered a chair to her mother, who refused.

Mother cleared her throat. "Superintendent Johnson visited us days ago. He told us about Dr. Tucker, and I read every article about him I could find. I went to see him in prison."

"You didn't." Vivienne gasped.

Mother swallowed a few times. "I needed to hear his version and ask him why he'd lied to you, and the conversation was eye-opening. I know he pointed a gun at you." She shivered. "I believed he was someone I could trust, that he sympathised with my pain..."

Mother's sorrow was palpable.

"He deceived many people," Vivienne said.

"Let me finish." Mother took a deep breath. "Instead of protecting you, I put you in harm's way. You, your father, and Samuel tried to warn me, but I didn't listen. I was blinded by my grief, lost. I must apologise and thank you for having..." She paused, pressing her lips.

"Take a deep breath," Vivienne said.

Mother took out the silver box from her pocket. "Will you keep this for me? I think it'll be good for me to live without it for a while."

Vivienne's eyes stung with tears. "Of course."

"It was a decision that cost a lot to your mother," Father said.

"And we both agreed she will wear something different than mourning from now on."

"I missed your wedding." Mother sobbed. "And I feel soiled by having been so close to that thug."

Samuel signed, "That's his legacy."

Father called Mrs. Foster. "Summon the captain, please."

Vivienne tensed a few minutes later when Captain Jackson entered the room.

"If you want to complain about the bacon being too cooked, it wasn't me." He skidded to a stop when he saw Mother. "What the h—"

Father gave Mother a nod.

"What is this?" the captain asked.

Mother took a slow step towards him. "Captain Jackson, I must apologise for having treated you like a criminal. I realised my dear Adele's death wasn't your fault, and I thank you for having saved my Vivienne's life."

The captain stiffened. "Your words ruined my life, professionally and personally."

"I'm aware of that," Mother said in a low tone. "I regret what I did."

Vivienne was sure what she would do in the captain's place. He'd lost his reputation because of Mother's hatred towards him.

"I hope you'll forgive me one day." Mother hunched her shoulders, defeated and frail.

A complete range of emotions crossed Captain Jackson's face. His facial muscles contracted and relaxed before he gave Mother a shallow bow. "I'm for putting the past behind and start over," he said. "That's what every single person in this house has done. Me included. I don't see why you shouldn't have the same opportunity. But I will tell you it'll take me some time before I forgive and forget."

"Fair's fair," Mother said. "I'll need time to learn to forgive myself, too."

Father held her hand without saying anything.

Vivienne thought the captain was generous and honest. Her mother had a lot for them to forgive. He'd expressed everyone's sentiment.

She put the silver box in a special place on the mantel. Not only was Mother finally free from her cage, but so was Adele.

AFTER LUNCH, Samuel headed to the police station with Vivienne and Captain Jackson, and none of them talked much, each of them lost in their own thoughts. But it was a sweet silence, filled with happiness and hope, as the captain would say.

After a few more silent minutes, the captain said, "You know... the night we risked our lives has made me think."

"About what?" Samuel asked.

"Life, death, friendship, love." Captain Jackson scratched his chin. "I want to court Alice."

Vivienne laughed and patted his hand. "Finally. It won't be easy, but I think she cares about you."

"She is so fierce and brave," Captain Jackson said. "I like that about her, and I'm prepared to woo her."

When the carriage stopped at the police station, William opened the door and pulled down the steps.

"Sir, I have something to tell you," William said before Samuel could enter the station.

"Yes?"

William cleared his throat. "I thank you for your generosity and for having given me the opportunity to work for you. But I want to be a policeman. I won't steal anymore, I promise. But I talked with a few officers, and they told me I could join a special investigative unit where my skills would be useful."

Samuel squeezed his shoulder. "It's your life and your path. I'm sure you'll be a great officer."

William beamed. "You'll be proud of me."

"We already are." Vivienne patted the footman's shoulder.

They entered the station together, and a little shot of tension rushed down his neck as an officer led them to the cells.

"Thank you for coming," the officer said, going down the stairs. "Dr. Tucker was quite insistent."

He could imagine.

Holding Vivienne's hand, Samuel walked over to Murdock, who was locked up behind the bars in a damp grey cell.

Murdock straightened and put down the book he was reading. "You came. I didn't expect that."

Samuel signed, and Vivienne spoke for him. "What do you want?"

"Have you thought about my proposal?"

"We don't want anything from you. I used to be afraid of you, but you're only a pathetic, little man." Vivienne's voice quivered when she said that, translating from Samuel's sign language.

"I'll tell you everything if you help me get out of here," Murdock said. "This is your last chance to know everything. I'm the only one who knows where to find your parents."

"Is this why you dragged us here?" Vivienne asked.

Murdock smirked. "What's more important than family?"

"Goodbye, Murdock." Samuel turned his back to the man who had abused him. Although he also felt he'd turned his back on his family.

They walked back upstairs, ignoring Murdock's shouted pleas.

Vivienne rested her head on Samuel's shoulder. "I'm so proud of you, husband of mine."

Samuel had seen many people with odd or extraordinary skills during his years with the circus. But Lady Huntington's ability to keep an eye on twenty...maybe twenty-three children all at once was something he'd never thought possible.

Hell, he wasn't even sure how many children were scattered around the garden, running, playing, and yelling. Every time he counted them, he found someone new. Vivienne's brothers and sisters were visiting their parents and had brought all their children, he laughed, and maybe even their neighbours' children.

It wasn't the first complete reunion of the family in years, but he and Vivienne had been so busy travelling around the Mediterranean Sea, he hadn't had many opportunities to meet her brothers and sisters and their families.

One of the children—John, James?—did cartwheels across the garden.

"Did you see that, Grandmama?" the child asked enthusiastically.

Lady Huntington laughed, her green gown complementing her fair complexion. "That was wonderful, Liam."

Liam? He signed slowly because his mother-in-law had

recently learnt sign language. "Is that Liam? I thought it was John."

"No, darling." She touched his arm. "We have two children named John, actually. The eldest John is twelve. He's Eleanor's son. The other one we call Johnny, and he's ten and Albert's son. This one is Liam, Charlotte and Oliver's son."

Who the hell were Charlotte and Oliver? He scrubbed the back of his neck.

"Charlotte is my niece," Lady Huntington said.

Oh, right.

Lady Huntington laughed again as Liam performed another cartwheel. He'd never realised how similar the countess's laughter was to Vivienne's. Watching Lady Huntington laughing and smiling, her face rosy and full, was a pleasure after the years she'd spent grieving.

Vivienne walked over to them, smiling. Her body had flourished fully in the past year, and no trace of her ordeal had remained in her beautiful soul and body.

"We need to go, darling."

"Come tomorrow." Lady Huntington kissed Vivienne's cheek. "The children are organising a play for us."

There were so many of them they could set up an entire production plus the audience.

"We will," he signed.

They hugged and kissed countless children on their way out; some of them had hands sticky with obscure substances.

Lord Huntington surveyed the small army of children with a proud smile.

"I'll see you tomorrow, Father." Vivienne hugged him.

Lord Huntington hugged Samuel. "Thank you for being here. There's nothing I love more than my house filled with children and grandchildren."

Yes, Samuel too would love to have such a big family.

As he climbed into the carriage, he paused to look at the oak tree under Vivienne's window. It'd grown to its former glory, its leafy branches thick and strong with life.

When he arrived home, Captain Jackson waved an envelope in front of Vivienne. "We must talk."

"About what?" Samuel signed.

"I'll tell you later." Vivienne kissed him on the lips before following the captain to the sitting room.

Samuel retired to his study, but he couldn't focus on reading as constant chatter came from the corridor.

Murdock's conviction had triggered a series of formal complaints from people who had been swindled by him to finance his non-existent clinic.

Samuel wanted to do everything to help those in need. But he'd underestimated the amount of work required.

Some people were as deceitful as Murdock and filed formal complaints in the hope of receiving compensation for a wrong they'd never suffered. While Samuel had set up a fund to compensate true victims, determining who was lying was a chore. He'd hired a group of people to take care of that, but he liked to be involved in every decision.

"Sir, I'm coming." Potter entered the study. "Mrs. Foster told me you wanted to talk to me about next week's dinner." He offered Samuel his palm.

Samuel used his index finger to write his answer on Potter's palm. The type of sign language he used with Potter was different from the one he used with others, but Potter had learnt quickly to recognise the words.

"Excellent choice, sir." Potter nodded. "Nothing better to celebrate your anniversary than the same cake I baked one year ago for your wedding."

"Thank you," he signed on the cook's palm again.

"Sir." Potter bowed and guided by one of the ropes, left the study.

Samuel tried to focus, ignoring the voices. Silence dropped quickly, which was suspicious.

He raised his gaze from the papers and tilted his head.

Since the captain was engaged to Dobkins, arguments and loud voices had become common, but not between Vivienne and the captain.

He drummed his fingers, wondering if he should intervene.

They were arguing and talking over each other, and he could grasp only a few words.

"...a big surprise," Vivienne said.

"No, we straight-up tell him everything," Captain Jackson rebuked.

He rose from his chair and walked out of the study, only to bump into Captain Jackson.

"What's going on?" he asked.

"I think this requires tact," Vivienne said, at the same time as Captain Jackson said, "Let's get it over with as soon as possible."

Then they started talking together, accusing each other of being a coward, and he didn't understand anything.

He waved his arms to get their attention. "Tell me."

"We have—" Captain Jackson started, but Vivienne swatted his shoulder.

"He's my husband. I'll tell him." She brushed a curl of hair from her face. "We didn't tell you anything because we didn't want to give you false hopes, but we hired an entire team of investigators to search for your family." She handed him an envelope. "They found something. We didn't read the letter."

Samuel hesitated before taking the envelope.

"Hurry up, mate." Captain Jackson urged him. "I want to know."

He opened it slowly and unfolded the letter. He skimmed over the greetings from the chief investigator to what he'd found.

Mr. Samuel Lyon's real name is...

Sean. His real name was Sean McEvoy. His parents, Matilda

and Harry, died of influenza when he was three years old. But his sister, Brigid, and his brother, Arthur, were alive and living in Edinburgh. They were both married with children.

"Well?" Vivienne prompted. "Good news?"

"My brother and sister are alive. I have siblings, and I am an uncle!" He signed so quickly the letter fell from his hand.

"What did you say?" Vivienne asked. "You were too fast."

Captain Jackson picked up the letter. "He has a sister and a brother in Edinburgh. His name is Sean!"

Cheers erupted, and even though he couldn't produce any sounds, he opened his mouth and shouted his happiness anyway.

"What are we waiting for?" Vivienne threw her arms around him and kissed him. "We're going to Scotland to meet your family."

about me

Love stories have always captured my imagination. What's better than two people falling in love with each other? I write steamy romance, usually with a paranormal twist in an historical setting. Add a touch of suspense and mystery and a pinch of darkness. I love stories with  strong, sexy heroes and mischievous heroines who pull no punches.

I live in the City of Sails, New Zealand, drinking tea (coffee gives me anxiety) and devouring books.

Join my newsletter for exclusive content and the chance to receive an ARC copy of my books. Just copy and paste this link into your browser:

Barbara's Newsletter: https://bit.ly/39yZ4Lw

also by barbara russell

If you want historical romance:

<u>Victorian Outcasts</u>

If you love steamy paranormal romance set in Victorian London, my Royal Occult Bureau series is for you:

<u>The Royal Occult Bureau Series</u>

Are you into shape-shifter romance? Check out my da Vinci's Beasts series, set in WW2:

<u>da Vinci's Beasts Series</u>

For more Victorian paranormal romance with witches and sexy warriors, see the Knights of the White Blade series:

<u>The White Order Series</u>